BY CHARLES BU

Flower, Fist and Bestial Wail (1960)
Longshot Pomes for Broke Players (1962)
Run with the Hunted (1962)
It Catches My Heart in Its Hands (1963)
Crucifix in a Deathhand (1965)
Cold Dogs in the Courtyard (1965)
Confessions of a Man Insane Enough to Live with Beasts (1965)
All the Assholes in the World and Mine (1966)
At Terror Street and Agony Way (1968)
Poems Written Before Jumping out of an 8 Story Window (1968)
Notes of a Dirty Old Man (1969)
The Days Run Away Like Wild Horses Over the Hills (1969)
Fire Station (1970)
Post Office (1971)
Mockingbird Wish Me Luck (1972)
Erections, Ejaculations, Exhibitions and General Tales of Ordinary Madness
     (1972)
South of No North (1973)
Burning in Water, Drowning in Flame: Selected Poems 1955–1973 (1974)
Factotum (1975)
Love Is a Dog from Hell: Poems 1974–1977 (1977)
Women (1978)
Play the Piano Drunk / Like a Percussion Instrument / Until the Fingers Begin
     to Bleed a Bit (1979)
Dangling in the Tournefortia (1981)
Ham on Rye (1982)
Bring Me Your Love (1983)
Hot Water Music (1983)
There's No Business (1984)
War All the Time: Poems 1981–1984 (1984)
You Get So Alone at Times That It Just Makes Sense (1986)
The Movie: "Barfly" (1987)
The Roominghouse Madrigals: Early Selected Poems 1946–1966 (1988)
Hollywood (1989)
Septuagenarian Stew: Stories & Poems (1990)
The Last Night of the Earth Poems (1992)
Run with the Hunted: A Charles Bukowski Reader (1993)
Screams from the Balcony: Selected Letters 1960–1970 (1993)
Pulp (1994)
Shakespeare Never Did This (augmented edition) (1995)
Living on Luck: Selected Letters 1960s–1970s, Volume 2 (1995)
Betting on the Muse: Poems & Stories (1996)
Bone Palace Ballet: New Poems (1997)
The Captain Is Out to Lunch and the Sailors Have Taken Over the Ship
     (1998)
Reach for the Sun: Selected Letters 1978–1994 (1999)
What Matters Most Is How Well You Walk Through the Fire (1999)

Charles Bukowski
12-31-63

CHARLES BUKOWSKI

LIVING ON LUCK

SELECTED LETTERS 1960s–1970s
VOLUME 2

EDITED BY
SEAMUS COONEY

An Imprint of HarperCollinsPublishers

THE LIBRARY OF CONGRESS HAS CATALOGED VOLUME 1 AS FOLLOWS:

Bukowski, Charles, 1920–
    Screams from the balcony: selected letters, 1960–1970 / Charles
Bukowski ; edited by Seamus Cooney
    p.   cm.
    Includes index.
    ISBN 0-87685-915-5 (cloth). — ISBN 0-87685-914-7 (pbk.)
    1. Bukowski, Charles—Correspondence. 2. Poets, American—20th
century—Correspondence. I Cooney, Seamus. II. Title.
PS3552.U4Z48   1993
811'.54—dc20   93-36411
[B]   CIP

VOLUME 2
Bukowski, Charles, 1920–1994
    Living on luck: selected letters, 1960s–1970s (Volume 2) / Charles
Bukowski ; edited by Seamus Cooney
    p.   cm.
    Includes index.
    ISBN 0-87685-981-3 (pbk. : alk. paper) — ISBN 0-87685-982-1
(cloth trade : alk. paper)
    1995

Second Printing

EDITOR'S NOTE

This second volume of Bukowski's letters begins, like volume 1, in the 1960s, thanks to the recovery of additional interesting letters from that decade. As that decade ends, Bukowski is liberated from the drudgery of his post office job and embarks with some trepidation on his career as a professional writer, encouraged by a small regular stipend from his publisher John Martin, who undertook to pay him $100 a month to enable him to write full-time. Throughout the 1970s, as royalties begin to overtake the stipend and he gradually gains confidence that he will be able not merely to survive but to prosper in this new career, the letters return again and again with wonder to his sense of how lucky he is to enjoy being able to live by writing. By the end of the decade, he's the owner of a comfortable house and a new BMW. His worries now are how to protect his fruit trees from frost, how to lower his tax liability, and how to deal with Hollywood directors and stars.

As in volume 1, the letters have been selected and transcribed from photocopies furnished by libraries and individuals. Bukowski's correspondence was astonishingly voluminous, and only selections are given from most letters. Editorial omissions are indicated by asterisks in square brackets, thus: [***]. Ellipses in the original letters are indicated by three dots. Bukowski often typed in CAPITALS for emphasis or for titles. Here, book titles are printed in *italics*, poem titles in quotes, and emphatic capitals in SMALL CAPS.

Dates are regularized and sometimes supplied from postmarks or guessed at from other evidence. A few spelling errors have been silently corrected. Salutations and signatures are for the most part omitted, except for a few examples that give the characteristic flavor. Some attempt is made to preserve Bukowski's layout, which at times includes multiple margins, but a printed book cannot reproduce such effects unaltered. As in the previous volume, a few letters have been printed verbatim

5

to give the flavor of a completely unedited letter.

References to *Hank* in the editorial matter are to Neeli Cherkovsky's biography of Bukowski, published by Random House in 1991.

Acknowledgments

The editor and publisher thank the following institutions for supplying copies of some of the letters in this volume:

> University of Arizona, Special Collections
> Brown University, Providence, John Hay Library
> The University of California, Los Angeles, Special
>   Collections
> The University of California, Santa Barbara, Special
>   Collections
> Centenary College, Samuel Peters Research Library,
>   Shreveport, Louisiana
> The State University of New York at Buffalo, Poetry/
>   Rare Book Collection
> The University of Southern California, Rare Books
>   Collection
> Temple University Library, Special Collections

A section of photographs follows page 138.

LIVING ON LUCK

Selected Letters 1960s–1970s

Volume 2

• 1 9 6 1 •

[To John William Corrington]
January 17, 1961

Hello Mr. Corrington:

Well, it helps sometimes to receive a letter such as yours. This makes two. A young man out of San Francisco wrote me that someday they would write books about me, if that would be any help. Well, I'm not looking for help, or praise either, and I'm not trying to play tough. But I had a game I used to play with myself, a game called *Desert Island* and while I was laying around in jail or art class or walking toward the ten dollar window at the track, I'd ask myself, Bukowski, if you were on a desert island by yourself, never to be found, except by the birds and the maggots, would you take a stick and scratch words in the sand? I had to say "no," and for a while this solved a lot of things and let me go ahead and do a lot of things I didn't want to do, and it got me away from the typewriter and it put me in the charity ward of the county hospital, the blood charging out of my ears and my mouth and my ass, and they waited for me to die but nothing happened. And when I got out I asked myself again, Bukowski, if you were on a desert island and etc.; and do you know, I guess it was because the blood had left my brain or something, I said, YES, yes, I would. I would take a stick and I would scratch words in the sand. Well, this solved a lot of things because it allowed me to go ahead and do the things, all the things I didn't want to do, and it let me have the typewriter too; and since they told me another drink would kill me, I now hold it down to 2 gallons of beer a day.

9

But writing, of course, like marriage or snowfall or automobile tires, does not always last. You can go to bed on Wednesday night being a writer and wake up on Thursday morning being something else altogether. Or you can go to bed on Wednesday night being a plumber and wake up on Thursday morning being a writer. This is the best kind of writer.

...Most of them die, of course, because they try too hard; or, on the other hand, they get famous, and everything they write is published and they don't have to try at all. Death works a lot of avenues, and although you say you like my stuff, I want to let you know that if it turns to rot, it was not because I tried too hard or too little but because I either ran out of beer or blood. [* * *]

For what it's worth, I can afford to wait: I have my stick and I have my sand.

The mention of Frost below alludes to his reciting of his poem "The Gift Outright" ("The land was ours before we were the land's. / ... (The deed of gift was many deeds of war)...") at the inauguration of President John F. Kennedy on January 20, 1961.

[To John William Corrington]
[ca. February 1,] 1961

I am listening to "Belly up to the bar, boys!" and I took the ponies for $150 today, so what the hell, Cor, I will answer, tho this letter-writing is not my meat, except to maybe gently laugh at the cliffs coming down. And it has to end sometimes, even though it has just begun. I'd rather you were the one who finally didn't answer. And I'd never kick a man out because he was drunk, although I've kicked out a few women for it, and the "wives-to-pinch," they are gone, mental cruelty, they say; at least the last one, the editoress of *Harlequin* said that, and I said, ok. *my* mind was cruel to *yours*...

I think it is perfectly ok to write short short stories and think they're poems, mostly because short stories *waste* so many words. So we violate the so-called poem form with the non-false short story word and we violate the story form by saying a lot in the

10

little time of the poem form. We may be in between by borrowing from each BUT BECAUSE WE CANNOT ANSWER A PRECONCEIVED FORMULA OF EITHER STORY OR POEM, does this mean we are necessarily wrong? When Picasso stuck pinches of cardboard and extensions of space upon the flat surface of his paper

did we accuse him of
being a sculptor
or an architect?

A man's either an artist or a flat tire and what he does need not answer to anything, I'd say, except the energy of his creation.

I'd say that a lot of abstract poetry lets a man off the hook with a can of polish. Now being subtle (which might be another word for "original") and being abstract is the difference between *knowing* and saying it in a different way and *not* knowing and saying it as if you sounded like you might *possibly* know. This is what most poetry classes are for: the teaching of the application of the polish, the rubbing out of dirty doubt between writer and reader as to any flaws between the understanding of what a poem *ought* to be.

Culture and knowledge are too often taken as things that please or do not disturb or say it in a way that sounds kindly. It's time to end this bullshit. I am thinking now of Frost slavering over his poems, blind, the old rabbit hair in his eyes, everybody smiling kindly, and Frost grateful, saying some lie, part of it: "... the deed of gift was the deed of many wars"... An abstract way of saying something kind about something that was not kind at all.

Christ, I don't call for cranks or misanthropes or people who knock knock knock because their spleen has a burr in it or because their grandmother once fucked the iceman, but let's try to use just a little bit of sense. And I don't expect too much; but when a blind blubbering poet in his white years is USED ... I don't know by WHAT OR WHO ... himself, they, something ... it ills me even to drink a glass of water and I guess that makes me the greatest crank of all time. [* * *]

11

Robert Vaughan, whose essay in Trace *Bukowski responds to below, edited a short-lived magazine called* Element, *published in Glendora, California.*

[To John William Corrington]
February 14, 1961

[* * *] Now, Bill, since we are discussing poetry and what makes it or doesn't make it, and I think it *is* important to attempt to figure out just what we are or aren't doing, and along this line I have written a letter to James Boyar May of *Trace* regarding an article that appeared in the Jan-Mar 1961 edition. And since Mr. May probably will not publish this I would like to repeat the letter here, because, in a manner, it falls in with our discussion ...Well, it goes like this:

Dear Mr. May:

In regards to Robert Vaughan's "Essay on the Recent History of Immortality," I really don't know *where* to begin. I rather imagine Robert V. as an intellectual and serious person (I know that he edits a magazine), and that his morals are proper and his study of the poem is more complete, certainly, than mine. And it's just here where the difficulty begins. If anybody has ever been forced to attend a poetry class or made the mistake of attending a poetry party, one is made to realize what is "proper" in poetic and artistic approach, and if I may use a discarded term...I don't give a SHIT about either. Mr. Vaughan and the class professors make much of the fact that PROSE IS CREEPING INTO POETRY! God damn it, here we work with our IMAGES and some guy comes along and says ... all that matters is a red wheelbarrow in the back yard, gathering rain. These are not the exact words but I don't have time to look up my Williams. It *was* Williams, wasn't it? Oh well ... Anyhow, the prose statement in a poem seems to bother the editors ("This is excellent, but it is *not* a poem!") and it seems to bother the Vaughans and the professors. But *I* say, why not? What the hell's *wrong* with a 6 or 7 or 37 line long prose statement that is broken into the readable advantage and clearness of the poem-form? As long as it says what it must and says it as well or better than the

12

mould and sound that says THIS IS A POEM, SO LISTEN TO ME. What's wrong with a 7 line short story or a 37 line novel which is placed within the poem-form, if this form makes it read better than it would if chunked together as a regular sentence or paragraph of regular English prose? Must we always DEFINE AND CLASSIFY what is done? Can't, for God's sake, can't ART be ART without a program and numbers?

There is NOTHING "basically immoral about a poetry that does not attempt to communicate emotions or dredge up from the reader's subconscious a prior experience." In fact, I would be tempted to say that a poetry that DOES ATTEMPT to do this is ... Christ, I don't like to use the word "immoral," just let me say that this type of poetry ("that attempts") is apt to be confused and repetitive and dull, except to the school of holy rollers who have LEARNED THE RULES and yap and holler when they see the face of their god in the mirror. I know that much poetry is a hand-holding of the lonely at heart. But hell, there are clubs for these people, dances, and bashful kisses upon the terrace. Great poetry sharpens its swords for larger game.

"If the creator does not have, for his firm foothold, a moral attitude or ethical approach—" etc. Let me say that there are no firm footholds in creation. Ask Van Gogh who blew his brains out among the blackbirds with a borrowed shotgun beneath the hot sun that moved the hand that moved the color. Although Van believed in God there wasn't any APPROACH here except the approach of the unknown, THE PROSE PAINT OF HIS COLORS that made Gauguin and Pissaro and other post-impressionists, great as they were, laugh at him because they painted down through the learned rule, the POEM within the line—if I may stretch a point to lay bare these similarities. And when Tolstoy found God his lines went limp, and Turgenev on his deathbed grieved for him because although Tolstoy had given up his land and his coppers for God, he had also given up something else. And although Dostoevski ended up on believing in Christ, he took the long road to get there, a most interesting and perhaps unwholesome road over roulette tables, raping a small child, standing before a wall waiting for the rifles to fire, he found that "adversity is the main-spring of self-realism," he found his Christ, but what a most *interesting* Christ, a self-made Christ, and I bow to him.

13

Now I realize that in the (and within the) word "Morals" Mr. Vaughan does not specifically mean religion, but more the religion of thinking and writing in the way that we should. Morals transferred down to 1961 mean a way of thinking and acting that is acceptable upon a fund of realistic and humane reaction to what has happened and what will probably happen. But actually, although the Robert Vaughans mean well, and I have nothing but respect for them, they clutter the way of forwardness. Give me men of *apparent* evil, for they are the forerunners of a future good—much of what was *evil* at 5:30 p.m. yesterday is something else today.

I think sometimes of the great symphonies that we have accepted today that were hissed at and walked out upon when first heard.

"Writing poems is difficult: sweating out the coming of the correct image, the precise phrase, the turn of a thought..."

Writing poems is not difficult; living them is. Let's be realistic: every time you say "good morning" to somebody and you do not mean "good morning," you are that much less alive. And when you write a poem within the accepted poem-form, making it *sound* like a poem because a poem is a poem is a poem, you are saying "good morning" in that poem, and well, your morals are straight and you have not said SHIT, but wouldn't it be wonderful if you could... instead of sweating out the correct image, the precise phrase, the turn of a thought... simply sit down and write the god damned thing, throwing on the color and sound, shaking us alive with the force, the blackbirds, the wheat fields, the ear in the hand of the whore, sun, sun, sun, SUN!; let's make poetry the way we make love; let's make poetry and leave the laws and the rules and the morals to the churches and the politicians; let's make poetry the way we tilt the head back for the good liquor; let a drunken bum make his flame, and some day, Robert, I'll think of you, pretty and difficult, measuring vowels and adverbs, making rules instead of poetry.

Well, that's the letter, more or less, Cor, although I've changed and added a few words in transposing. I thought, though, that you might want to hear it. Poetry can be such a depressing thing, such a dead thing. How they want to run the

14

chains around us! Why? I really don't understand. It seems as if they are trying to make it ... well, like learning to weld or be an engineer. Always this is *right* and this is *wrong*, meanwhile not getting to the core at all. [* * *]

[To John William Corrington]
February 23, 1961

This is a short one. I am on a tear, ill and shaky; no complaints, I guess it's something I must burn out of my system, and if I make it, I make it. I don't want to short-circuit you but your last letter shed more light than a powerhouse. That sentence makes me sick. You see how easy it is to roll off a log and just *say* something? I hate to do you a disservice with an ill description ... I only repeat, I can barely see out of the front of my eyes this morning.

There was another one who wrote me for a while. But about what? New listings of magazines, about how he met an editor on the street. This guy lives with editors, sleeps with them, goes to the parties, snudges [sic] his nose up all the blind spots—and in a manner, for him, it pays off. He makes a lot of pages and his poems are full of words like STAR SEA NIGHT DEATH LOVE WOUND and you name the rest. What his name is doesn't matter and you can multiply him by the hairs of grass that look so sickly up at me from my 3rd floor rented window. I had to sock him down in a poem to stop him from nibbling the eternal edge of my guts. [* * *]

Cummings, yes, sometimes. His weakness is that he has devised a form that is easy to fall into. What I mean is that he can say almost anything or nothing and run it through his form and he has a lot of people believing it. This is Cummings, they say, the way they say, this is a Van Gogh, and all critical faculties fall lax because they have been pre-sold. People are pretty hard to sell, but once they believe, they believe and you cannot make them say no with a hammer. That's not good. Cummings must be made to produce every time he sits down, and not merely sign his name. *For Whom the Bell Tolls* is one of the poorest novels ever written but nobody knows it because Hem wrote it. Nobody knows but another writer who is close enough to smell it.

Nobody knows that a smaller work like *To Have and Have Not* was really art. And I don't like the word "art." How they sound on words and drivel on them and drive us away from them. I had a wife once who divorced me because more in essence than reality I would never say I loved her. How could I say this without dragging in Hollywood and my next door neighbor and patriotism and the barber's cough and the cat's ass?

Really, Bill, I am sick this morning. Must stop. [* * *]

[To John William Corrington]
March 1, 1961

[* * *] The problem is, Corr, that as we work toward a purer, looser, more holy warmth of expression and creation, the critics are going to have to work a little harder to find out whether it's water or piss in the holy grail, and even then they might end up wrong. You know the old comic strip joke about the painting hung upside down or etc., well, there's a lot of practical truth in this. But pure creation will always have its own answer finally, and it will neither be a set of disciplines or undisciplines, it will simply be. [* * *]

[To John William Corrington]
April 12, 1961

[* * *] There are some men who can create with a perception of what they are doing and what is happening not only to them but to those around them. I am not one of those. Sometimes the poem wans on me, everything wans on me. The sense of excitement, of explosion is gone. I have been sent a couple of free journals by editors these last few days and reading through them I am disturbed by the fact that we are all writing pretty much alike. It could well be one man's voice under 36 different names. I do not care for this at all. I had long ago given up hope of being an extraordinary poet, and most of the time I do not think of myself

16

as a poet at all; but when I do think of it, at least I would like to think I have failed with a more or less individual voice, but it seems as if we have pared everything down to a ghastly likeness. Whether this is caused by a simplification of language, a cutting out of extremes, a sidewalk grammar I don't know. You can look at the new buildings going up and the old buildings going down. Everything is now a straight line and a square corner. Ornament is gone. It is a reaction. Falsity *can* breed in ornamentation. But falsity can also breed in the flat voice. Steiner, I believe the name is, says in this quarterly *Kenyon Review* that we are drifting toward mathematics and away from the word, and to this I must agree. By the way, I know that the *Kenyon Review* is supposed to be our enemy... but the articles are, in most cases, sound, and I would almost say, poetic and vibrant; the poetry, of course, remains almost unbelievably flat and lifeless. It seems that forever in the university circles we are allowed truth in the article or the discussion, but when it comes down to the old brass tracks [*sic*] of actual creation we are supposed to take it easy and look the other way. [* * *]

In the following, Bukowski defends his earlier favorable mention (in a letter not included here) of an article by Harry Hooton, an Australian poet, in a recent issue of Trace.

[To John William Corrington]
April 26, 1961

[* * *] Hooton, of course, overstates his case. Why must they be such holy-rollers about everything? Your enemy or the devil might turn out to be a pretty good guy if you could learn his language and drink beer with him and pinch his wife when he goes to the bathroom. He has Yeats "sneering." Hooton beats a loud drum. Yeats could have told him, "The best lack all conviction, while the worst are full of passionate intensity." This is most certainly a "message"... but without preaching; or from the same poem:

"...what rough beast, its hour come round at last,
Slouches toward Bethlehem to be born?"
Yeats died in 1939. [* * *]

Eliot, of course, began well, then got fancy with the *Four Quartets*, took on Catholicism and Criticism, was listened to by everybody, and paled off because he sold too many things at once and was not essentially a fighter or strong enough to stand firm. And yet Eliot did leave us something, perhaps a clearer flowing diction, and if Hooton says he voted with Yeats, that should make him (T.S.) pretty strong. About Stevens, I don't know. The Kenyon school, of course. Stevens tries very hard to be bright by saying nothing in a manner that would seem to imply something if only *you* were intelligent enough to understand, but, of course, since you aren't, you should be god damned glad to god damn read the shape of the words anyhow. Tate is another dry as dust faker who has had no more than one or two toothaches of the soul...and although Hooton did not mention Tate, and it is getting out of bounds to do so, I get out of bounds anyhow. I would never like Tate if I drank beer with him for 40 years or I pinched his wife's autographed copy of Wallace Stevens.

To hell with Hooton.

Give me Conrad Aiken, Robinson Jeffers, Ezra Pound and Yeats. [* * *]

[To John William Corrington]
June 8, 1961

Just got out of jail, I must see judge Friday, 1 p.m. [* * *] I will be 41 in August and I don't know whether the courage is gone or what, but the sight of jails that once meant nothing to me now sickens me to the roots. I don't like people messing with me and closing doors on me and throwing me on the floor with a bunch of other silverfish. A common drunk rap, of course, calls for no shame, just, of course, as murder calls for no shame if you murder the right one, *Crime and Punishment* be damned. The worst is, this might cause me to lose my job and I have no training of any sort and the job as a job means nothing, of course, only to keep me breathing and eating in order to write a poem. My old girl friend, who was with me, has a knot on her hard Irish head that would have killed the less hardy; believe we were walking down the street and she kept falling and I kept trying to catch her when the fuzz netted us both in their wily civic net. Her landlady finally bailed us out and I guess the reason is that I have been giving her the flirt on the side, kissing her behind the ear and filling it with idle banter. If I were the writer of *The Hostage* they would have greeted me with a brass band but since I was Charles Bukowski, they threw me in and I sat there and a fat Mexican gave me 2 cigarettes and advice. "Don't worry," he said, "it doesn't matter. Since you are with the Feds you probably will be out in 4 hours." I hadn't finished my 2nd cigarette when my name was called, I shoved some cash upon a trusty with slow typewriter fingers and the release was speeded up. Outside I met Irish and hardluck Bob who I'd seen at the track earlier that day. I gave him 7 one dollar bills, tipped the cabby a buck and we sailed across the silken 5 a.m. skies that had no bars and no locks. I gave Frenchy a 50 buck bill (bail money), a kiss behind the ear, and there went my profits from the track. But you were right when you said you somehow had the idea that I was destroying myself or trying to go goofy, but maybe my soul is tough as an Irish head or maybe my luck will hold.

[To John William Corrington]
November 17, 1961

[* * *] I am soft. Deer I cannot do in. I was riding with this gal in the car and it was Sunday and I was looking for a liquor store and we saw this sign, CHICKEN, and she said, oh, let's get a chicken, we'll have a nice roast chicken, and I said sure, and I drove up to the place and they had chicken all right, only it was standing up and it had white feathers, 60 or 70 strong had white feathers and when I walked in a couple of them shit and one of them winked at me and I just stood there and the guy said, yes, a nice chicken, no?... and I turned around and walked out and the gal said, where's the chicken and I said, hell, they all looked scrawny, you can't tell what you're getting with all the feathers,

19

and she said, that's easy, you just pick em up and feel em with your fingers, and check the eye, get a clear-eyed chicken. Chickens are just like people, if the eye is not clear he is malfunctioning.

How do you kill 'em? I asked.

My father used to whirl em, WHIRR, ZIP!!

Let's have a banana sandwich, I said.

I remember the slaughterhouse down where the streetcar turns, and the floors were greasy with blood, green floors, blood has a special smell that will not leave and there is nothing harder to remove than a blood stain, blood is life, and death came on minute after minute but unlike the docs and interns and nurses at the L. A. County General Hospital I could not get used to it, and I did not have a car then and I would get on the streetcar and people would smell the blood on me and look, look, and then go home and eat a porterhouse.

I am not building a case for the vegetarians who might be too soft for the formula we were conceived in and have to work out of; I will eat meat, only I don't want to see it happen, not anymore, not once more, I don't want to hear the sound. When life changes to death in that very small instant it is an explosion against the mind that can never be rebuilt.

No deershoots, kid, I might really go wacky tying roping the thing across the hood. Guys like Hem would think me queer.

Although, I don't know how we got on this. There is a funny story. It was told to me by this person who used to go to group therapy sessions to try to help himself. Played some instrument in symphony orchestra but right now, like me, not doing much, just hanging on. Well, he went to this guy's house. The guy said, come on, I'll show you something. I've got 2 chickens. You save money. you get 'em when they're young and grow 'em. I wonder how you kill em? he asked my friend. Well, this guy didn't know how to kill 'em. He got a hammer and he let them out in the yard and he tried to kill both of them at once. It was a mess. The chickens would not die. He kept hitting them with the hammer. The noise, you know, the blood, one eye hanging out on a long string, a beak all twisted back into the head and the thing going on, running, and the other one just standing there, the hammer coming down on the head and slipping off and the thing just standing there waiting. Finally, my friend, out of mercy, he did not help but he got excited and started giving instructions and finally the job was done, and then the guy took the 2 chickens and threw them in the garbage. His girl friend left him and never spoke to him again and she never spoke to the one who gave the instruction either. [* * *]

[To John William Corrington]
November 26, 1961

[* * *] Yes, killing a chicken with a hammer is imbecile, although I doubt this person was sadistic, simply not a clear thinker, the way the story was told to me. [* * *]

And don't think that when I walk into a butcher shop that I don't know. A voice always says to me, "They have done it for you." It costs me in several ways, but I don't think becoming a week-end huntsman would spring me clear. Old lady Hemingway said she felt or liked to feel "chic" when she made the kill. I don't think much of old lady Hemingway, she read too many of the old man's books. No more than we have. But believed them. But as I said in one of my poems now floating around, it seems sport to knock Hemingway now, so I will lay off for a while. [* * *]

[To John William Corrington]
December [?3], 1961

the hem can be over-evaluated like anything else, and while he understood the mathematics of life and cut it fine, bravado and hardfire, there was essentially some music missing, and what he cut out in his figuring as unnecessary is what turned the shotgun in on him. He wrote well early and then got burned in the Spanish war thing. Won't these fuckers ever learn that politics is the biggest whore, the biggest hole any fine man can fall into? Hem built an image and had to write up to the image. It's all right to be tough cob but it doesn't wear well when you get into your fifties. It's better then to have some soft culture, something like the organ works of Bach, some Vivaldi, something going for you that may have a knife-edge but still a screen for softness to enter. You are still young, though a very wise young, and Hem is good to you like your 7½′ barrel with 20% more reach n' yr 6 shots in 5 inch square at 50 to 60 feet firing rapid clip. There is beauty in this, I can see beauty in this, and I can also see that you are nobody to mess with if you get pissed. I hope I don't sound like an old man preaching. I've gone the route. You should've seen my fight with Tommy McGillan in a Philadelphia alley in 1948. They're still talking that one and they wouldn't serve me for 3 days because I busted their hero. Faulkner? Faulkner is a cutie, he left jabs, jabs, jabs, and an occasional hook. But who am I, shit, to say? I have never written a novel, don't feel like writing a novel, although if I live to be fifty I will try one. I made myself this promise once sitting in a bar. I figured then that I would never live to be fifty so it was a soft promise and I was not too worried about it. I still may not have much to worry about, ah so many parts burned out and missing, including good fat portions of the mind, but mainly there is some singing left, the gut is soft and the sun comes down.

[* * *] Of course we all fail and it doesn't take a Faulkner to say it, it would be short-peckered wisdom indeed if we thought we could pull the curtain on God and expose his kisser ... or the small pile of bleached bones. All we can do is work against the tide as best we may. I think that's why the horses interest me: the beauty of loss, the working against the irresistible mathematics of death. You can piss on death and forget it until it finds you. Most people do this. That is why they cry at funerals. [* * *]

●

• 1 9 6 2 •

[To John William Corrington]
January 12, 1962

yr damned intelligent well written letters are backing me off
into some back closet fulla mops and old *Esquire*s but I carry on
because, as I once decided, coming out of a St. Louis basement
where I was getting 55 cents an hour for packing ladies' dresses
into boxes for shipment and the fat little Jew smiled his yellow-
face smile because I was in his cage and he had a 12 room house
and a wife more beautiful than I cd even have in my dreams
                    I decided that I was losing
                    not the money part
                    fuck that
but if I may be corny—the soul part that I was packing away in
boxes with the ladies' dresses—and since I was losing this, wt
could I do besides start a ladies' dress shop myself—which even
if I could wd be very obnoxious—I decided
                    that since I was losing
                    I COULD EITHER GIVE UP AND LOSE IT ALL
                    OR LOSE ALMOST EVERYTHING
                    BUT SAVE
                        SAVE THE LITTLE BIT THAT WAS LEFT.

this does not sound like much; it does not seem like much, but
that night walking to my room between the frozen trees of a St.
Louis night, it seemed very right, it was my savior grown and
walking beside me, a tiny flame. It made sense then and it still

does now. You say you never care much for losers, but it's all I've known, from celling with proud swindlers to shooting crap under a swinging light in Albuquerque (or was it El Paso?) as a member of a railroad section gang. Well, I don't like winners. Winners get fat and careless and write things like *The Old Man and the Sea* which is printed in *Life* magazine for a public which was long ago gaffed by the formula, and while it is typical of little men like myself to bitch and scratch at the great dead, I will still have my say. Hemingway wanted to save man by giving him a sense of honor through action. The trouble with his action is that it was A STAND AGAINST SOMETHING: an army, a bull, a dog with horns, a country, a fish, the sea, the moon, the rich, the poor, anything that countered movement toward some *seeming* need for victory. Shit on that. That is child's play. We need knock nothing down. It's time we begin picking up. saving what is left. what is worth saving. so when we clean our shotguns we only clean our shotguns. I do not have the master's talent but I can see a lot of fool in him, which does not make me better, but sometimes in packing in the dresses the mind did say, will say, no one must fool me now because there is so very little left; but how did I get on this? does not sound too good. it is a kind of preaching. I forgot to laugh. dead in a bed I will laugh, or in a gutter I will laugh, or red on a mutual ticket in a cool Arcadia wind where my great dead uncle raped a lady he had picked up on his dandy motorcycle. ah, my family, all maniacs, and now all gone. just one. the end of a bad line. a tiny flame. [* * *]

> three niggers smiling could not reproduce
> the tumult of that kiss

I don't know why, but that's a very good line. it's a shame you have to lose it. it reminds me of a room full of electricity and heat when it's very cold outside and you sit and listen to the clock tick. of course, Jon [Webb]'s got to protect himself. for all we know, the mag's his only income. by doing the work himself, enough dollars to carry on. This is a bad time. People are frightened of doing any wrong. A formula has been set up and everything has been pushed inside of this formula. I don't know if this is the right way of doing things at all. I must agree with some that fucking wd eventually clear up the whole mess. I have 3 black mamas chasing me now. One with long black hair she winds over her ears in shell shapes n wata big can tits wowwowwow, only my

24

bloody ass says no, and I run out to the race track with my new system (60 bucks profit today) and come back here and read your good letter. The main trouble with the black race is that they wanna be white; outside of that and hot weather, they are ok with me. but back to the poem, opening lines: 3 niggers smiling ...the trouble with the word "nigger" is that it is very poetic. negro is soft and round and says nothing. It is as it looks. I had the same trouble with the poem "On a Night You Don't Sleep" (see *Flower, Fist and Bestial Wail* if you have the beast around) and I had to go with nigger because that is what he *was* when I saw him through the doorway with the salt water in my eyes and this Barbara Fry walking along mumbling nonsense by my side. I thought, if I put "negro" then I am a coward, I am doing something because I am told to do something and not because I want to, and that's about where we stand on the racial question now. The racial question is too large for me. [* * *]

[To John William Corrington]
January 22, 1962

I am unable to write. The woman I have known for so long has been critically ill since Saturday and died 2 hours ago.
This is going to be the longest night of them all.

[To John William Corrington]
January 28, 1962

I am somewhat over the thing now, alive, that is, something gone, that is, but the language of the thing is bad, I cannot get through, writing has nothing to do with it, and it is better to leave it alone if it will leave me alone. In the week gone I have done things that are not in the classic normal mourning, but she will know that they were necessary.

A letter from Sherman. Jeffers died. Couple of nights back I thought, well, maybe I go see the kid, I feel better. It's a hundred miles round trip to San Berdo, hadn't slept or eaten for 5 or 6 days. The kid's split with the wife again. Found him out back someplace on "I" st. He had his book of poems propped on the mantle, *So Many Rooms*. The typewriter was going when I knocked on the door. Went to liquor store where he tried to tap me when I opened my wallet but I wasn't in the mood. Went back and sat there a couple of hours while he read me his poems.

Met a high yellow negress at racetrack next day and she wound up riding me at her apartment, bobbing, bobbing, bobbing, and I said beautiful, my dear, beautiful, and grabbed her can, but it wasn't any good—I guess the old woman was watching me from heaven and she shut off my water, and the negress rolled off and I finally fell asleep.

Went over to Winski's and we made the rounds—A turkish joint upstairs next to the *Daily Racing Form*, people sitting on the floor, women dancing alone; then a dull American place, then a strip joint, and all the time Winski talking sex sex eyow sex sex sex sex—I'd like to chew on her gold panties all night etc., and there was my old woman down underneath, the grass already knitting the cuts of earth, the worms making their move, the son already half way back to Texas in his god damned Mercedes Benz after a quicky cut-rate funeral, and so passes a bad taste, and along with it the only real woman and real friend I could ever stand.

I don't think that following up one death with another one is the answer. If I am wrong I am real wrong but once the razor goes through or the other leg swings out the window it's too late daddieo...Any other profound statements of this nature will have to wait another letter.

Right now, a quiet beer. This quietness. And giving her the real homage. Jane Cooney Baker. deceased. but never gone.

[To John William Corrington]
May [?15], 1962

[* * *] the jon jazz bit not for me. I prefer the symphony—Shostakovitch 5th, Symphony in D by Franck, Stravinsky, the better parts of Mahler, etc., but don't care for the symphony

crowd. Stiff phoney crows, all this marble hall exaltation, this church-like holiness. They ought to play this stuff in the juke-boxes of beerhalls, bars. Think of trying to hold the price-line with a whore while listening to Beethoven. This would be life out of the stems of flowers. [* * *]

[To John William Corrington]
May 27, 1962

I received your letter in which you mentioned your father's cancer, and that you feel more than lowly is understood. It is our own deaths that will be easiest to take; it is the other deaths, the coming of them, that we cannot bear. I have tried, in these cases, to apply history, the history of death, the fact of death; I have tried to think of Napoleon gone, Hitler, the bird, the cat, the movie star, the hero, the murderer, names of things, of things that once were ... but it did not help. The mind cannot overcome the instinct. The mind is only a recent development; the instinct was there long before. When love burns to the ground do not be ashamed of your grief, or even your madness or bitterness.

My mother died of cancer. I took her the most beautiful rosary I could buy on Christmas Eve but when I arrived the door was locked. I was standing there twisting the knob when a nurse walked up and said, "She just died." My old man died while try-ing to drink a glass of water. The water kept running and run-ning and they heard it and when they came in he was dead on the kitchen floor. With Jane I stood there wiping away her guts as they ran out of her mouth. Death is eternally everywhere, I need not tell you that. The ways are hard whether they are God's ways or simply ways. To say that I understand the machinery of it or accept it would be a lie, or to say anything to help you at this moment would also be a lie. You know as much as I.

I am lucky. For me, there is nothing else left to die, outside of C. Bukowski. They will find me through the sense of smell. By then, I will be stiff enough to slide down the stairs like a board.

I can see some landlady going through my stuff with one of her old biddy friends. "Say what's all them magazines under the table? I never seen such funny-looking magazines..." And then everything into some bag for the Salvation Army. Farewell, C.B.

One of my last friends, a dishwasher, set himself on fire or anyhow somebody set him on fire and he walked up the steps, drunk, a black monster of himself, flakes of walking ashes, and he got to his room (the only home he knew) and fell on his rented bed and died. Farewell friend.

We go on with our little poems and we wait.

One god damned hell of a situation.

[To John William Corrington]
June [?25], 1962

[* * *] How are you going to lecture on the novel? How do you do it? Are you going to read them *Finnegans Wake*? Are you going to tell them that Faulkner's novels are slick as onionskins and that you can fall right off the page because most of the time he is writing about *nothing* and he throws in all these pages of italics to show you *something* is going on, but really, nothing is going on at all, and because you really at first believe this and don't want to, you finally figure that something profound is going on, else why all the pages this way? And so it is better to believe it is profound because they tell you it is than be the first to stick your neck out. Faulkner will never take the shotgun because he is too clever to let you believe that he has failed. Steinbeck was very good at one time when he had ideals but his ideals trailed off and he flattened out. I think Sartre's 2 or 3 books around the war in France are some of the best writing I have seen done. Where these Frenchmen get drunk on wine in the church; the battle in the tower, from the tower, all the many things I have forgotten but that stick in me like threads of a good happening. I don't do much reading anymore. I don't read anymore. Maybe the *Racing Form*. The time comes to end reading. The time comes reading makes you sick. This is where some music and drink and love come in. Music and drink, anyhow.

[* * *] Answering yr bit. I was a Catholic. As a kid. Just got past the catechism bit. We had to memorize it. We were on the front porch, Frank Sullivan and I. "God has bodily eyes." And Frank put his fists to his eyes: "You mean like this? Like *milk*

bottles?" And we laughed and then we got scared. At 13, 14, 15, I stopped going and there wasn't much my mother could do and the old man didn't care. I don't like to hit on the subject because it is a puzzler. Jane was C. Slept with rosary under pillow. Well, hell. [* * *]

[To John William Corrington]
October 8, 1962

[* * *] Yes, the giants are gone and it makes it a little tougher when you stare down at the white paper. Before the death of the giants you used to think, well, they don't expect anything from me anyhow. Now there is this hole and the hole must be filled and we don't know how it will be done or who will do it. But writing is entirely different now. I mean we are raw again. We are beginning again. And it is good this way. Facing the raw. This is what the thing was meant to be. Only it's no longer Left Bank Paris or Carmel or Taos, it is all of us; and some of us, a few of us, will come through. This will be done through force, energy, magic, belief, and a way of living. But it may be, perhaps, that the age of giants is over. This is hard to believe. I'd rather not believe it. [* * *]

[To John William Corrington]
October [?9], 1962

[* * *] It might amuse you to know that "Home from a Room Below the Plains" was written out of an experience I had when I was a mailman one time. Terrible hangover, stupor. I had some letters for this church. Was new on route. Couldn't find mailbox. Wandered into church and down some steps. Dark. I saw a switch on the wall, one of those handle things by a black box. All the lights in the church came on and probably some of the candles too. And there was the priest's cassock and stuff laid out on the table. Very holy looking. I threw the switch back off

and wandered around some more. Found a can and took a crap. And almost took a shower. All this time I have this mail sack, dragging it around. Finally came out of there and found the mailbox in the parish house next door. It was one god damned odd experience of many odd experiences and it came out as a poem some years later. So you see, you cannot always tell what a man is writing about, but if you put it down as true as it seems to you, they are apt to take it anyhow. [* * *]

[To John William Corrington]
October 10, 1962

[* * *] you mentioned something in your letter that has been rattling in the dry leaves of my brain—which is, the death-thing which is due me & the fact of your letters being there, which should be seen—someday—by somebody, some people, some something besides myself. And if I go at 1623 or wherever I am, chances are they will simply hustle everything out of here and burn it in order to make room for the next drunken roomer. My only living relatives, an aunt and uncle, have disowned me and I do not leave their address around and since their name is different than mine, they will not be bothered finding a hole for a dead body they detest. This brings us to the letters, and I want to get them out of here before something happens. I was thinking of mailing them to Cuscaden, but somehow, I don't know, something warns me not to. I think I will mail them back to you —if this will not keep you from hanging more sheets in your typer directed to 1623. So, soon you will get a package or 2, and I will be able to die in peace, as they say, will be able to die without picture-aftershadows of pokers and flames punching your good letters to pieces. This is all pretty dark, but it has been hanging over me. Look for them back then. I am going over them again Sunday, and then back to Baton Rouge. I wish I could be yr Boswell but my age, my heath, my drinking, all against me. [* * *]

Yes, you are right. They are putting a lot of light on me right now, and it is the test. There is little doubt that obscurity and aloneness and failure are the agents and angels of the good Art,

30

and I am being tested here, even, in this 1623 place: there are bangs on the door where formerly there were almost none, but just as before, I don't like to answer. Only now they intend to call me "snob" where before they called me "nuts." What they call matters little. I like to think I have been cleaved enough to come through. I should stop writing for 10 more years like I did the other time, but I don't have these kinds of tens left anymore. [* * *]

[To John William Corrington]
October 28, 1962

[* * *] Well, I had a quote from Pascal written on a piece of paper which I was going to write down here. But now I have lost the little piece of paper which is not as bad as losing a good piece of ass but what I mean is that you would understand the quote but not need it. [* * *] Anyhow, to put the Pascal into my own words—: Only things done in quietude secure and holy, without direct aim at fame or applause, are worth more than the applesauce shit of a turkey.

[To John William Corrington]
November [?15], 1962

WE KEEP GETTING BACK at this argument about the novel. It is like being married. There is this thing that is always hanging there, and, BANG!, you've always got an argument about the same thing.

You keep telling me that (in essence) a great writer makes a great novel and we don't want to knock the thing because so many people fail with it. BUT I WILL TRY ONCE MORE. god damn. What I am saying is that this is not the TIME for the novel. Now, I don't want to bring in the bomb. It's there. But let's forget most of about the bomb. Yet it is this and it is something else. It is in the air. IT IS NOW WRONG somehow to write a novel. Don't

31

ask for proof. Don't ask for reason. I am, let's say, an old wham-my woman in a tar shack killing chickens and drinking their blood or whatever and sticking the feathers in my ears. I only sense that this ass-time 1962 is simply not the time. DON'T SHORT-CHANGE ME. I KNOW THAT ART TAKES PRECEDENCE. I know that a lion can be gorging a good man's balls and that he can go right ahead while he's still living and paint that madonna or whatever is bothering him with ice cream and taffy. This is not the point. The point is that this is not the time. For the novel. Do not ask me how I know this or why or how. I cannot tell you.

bill bailey, won't you please come home?

If you can swing the thing with ROMAN BOOKS for our letters for $150 or $300 or for 50 cents, go ahead, swing. It has been a hard year. I am backed down to a hard-caked dirt. We've got plenty of time (maybe) to write more letters but the time for sell-ing may be too late. Or maybe too soon. Then I don't know if you are kidding or not. [* * *]

I am glad Nixon got pole-axed here in Calif. That man's face has been bothering me for a long time. It is a face of power. It is a face that attempts to say one thing in order to get by and yet it means something else altogether, and if you are one of the boys you know what it means and you put your hand under the table-cloth and you got it made and fuck the rest. I'm glad he's going back to lawyer. That's where he belongs. Pal with the judge, and fooling his clients. If he ever comes into a place to eat where I am washing dishes, I will take his dishes and cups and saucers and break them with quiet languor and then have a gentle pull from the wine bottle. [* * *]

Jim Roman, a dealer in modern first editions, operated from Fort Lauderdale. He was to publish Corrington's The Anatomy of Love *in 1964.*

[To John William Corrington]
November [?24], 1962

Well, your letters are enclosed in case you want to swing with Fort Lauderdale or however it's spelled. Maybe a publisher might pick them up in this way. They are no less than great. There must be something about the letter-form that allows a man to become looser and freer. Perhaps in the poem we pack too much on-stage stuff.

I'm not sure all of them are here—the introductory ones aren't. How was I to know? Anyhow, good stuff, you are wide of soul and lay down a pliable law.

I hope you write me some more. Viva Villa!

[*In holograph with the preceding*:]

I return herewith the letters of yours I could find. Maybe some day one of us gets famous and some fool wd pay $ for these, and since you and I did not do them for $, the laugh's all on the swine and the readers. Even if they don't ever "make it" anywhere they have made it

here

with me.

Guys like Roman go bugs over this stuff, mainly because he's trying to beat lit. history before it happens—which is intriguing but dangerous. I would pretty much bet that Corso, Ginsberg, etc. will not be around after they are gone awhile. When you go up fast, you usually come down that way. I think it is the pleasurable simple workman (not Bukowski) who will hold his ground. But who gives a damn???

we are here now
(for what we know is a short time).
and here are your letters

                    gracious godly friend
                    kid,
        they are good, very,
                    and your praise
                    and sticking stilts
                    under an old man
                    when hardly anyone wuz,
        this was a nice gift,
        and as I sit here tonight
        mailing these letters back to you,
        let me say
                    that
        they were not
        will not be
        can never have been
                    wasted.

---

*Corrington was to publish one of the first critical articles on
Bukowski in* Northwest Review, *1963.*

[To John William Corrington]
November 29, 1962

[* * *] If you are going to article me, all right, but I don't
know what the poems mean, so maybe I better find out. And
then, for all your work, tend to ignore it. What I mean is this.
When I write the poem it is only fingers on typewriter, something
smacking down. It is that moment then, the walls, the weather of
that day, the toothache, the hangover, what I ate, the face I
passed, maybe a night 20 years ago on a park bench, an itch on
the neck, whatever, and you get a poem—maybe. I don't know
much what you can say about these poems. "Old Man, Dead in a
Room" is my future, "The Tragedy of the Leaves" is my past,
and "The Priest and the Matador" is a dawdling in between. But
I'd rather have it in your hands than anybody I know. You jab

well, carry a good right, are younger than Archie for sure, and you can't be bought for a tankjob. [* * *]

[To John William Corrington]
December 13, 1962

Dear South ribbon talking pure word:

Yes, it is terrible, this essence of spotlight. You carve a thing in a cobweb room maybe when you are not feeling so good and feeling a little crazy, spitting flecks of blood out through a broken tooth where somebody hammered you when you were too drunk to see it coming or too drunk to care... you carve a thing and then somebody sees it and runs down the hall with it and shows it to the other roomers. You are running behind him, you need a shave and a fresh pair of socks and 2 or 3 operations to get the tigers out from inside of you. And he is hollering, holding this thing you've done up in the air, he is hollering, "Hey! *Hey*! Looka this thing *Smitty* did! Who'da thunk Smitty'd do a THING like *this*? Jesus, jesus, looky, LOOKY!"

And, South, as you know, then, 9 times outa ten, no, more than that... you're fucked. That night some old well preserved gal will tap on your door and give you the thing she has been saving for some ivory god. Little girls will slip notes under your door at night. The milkman will show you some thing he has carved out of wax on cold nights. The worshipers will sob and tremble for the hairs from your razor. You're fucked. You sit down to scratch things on another brick with a can opener... and what is it? hmm... must be something wrong with the brick? Or maybe the opener's dull?... Now, let's see... HOW DID I DO THAT OTHER ONE? They SURE liked that OTHER ONE. Let's see... I think I was thinking of birds with their feet frozen to phone wires in Texas, awakening in the morning, stuck there, slicing God's air with wings, stuck, stuck, and then tired sick falling upside down, and frozen in the cold air that way... the end of a lunatic life. Yeah, *that's* what I was thinking... and then I put in the eyes... and the nose... and... And then there's a knock and a man with prince nez, princ nez?, he wants to know the color of the house you

35

were born in. And then behind him stands the old gal with the thing for ivory gods again. And then...

Let me say that the spotlight Jon puts on me I accept with honor from the German blood that unpollutes the Polack in me; I cannot deny this: I still play with the old words: honor, truth. That I am pretty well pulled to pieces by the spiders of the world does not affect me, I hope it does not god damn effect [sic] me, in this sense. Anyhow, I still like to play with bluebirds and old dreams among the toy cannon. I go my way, antiquated and ruined. [* * *]

[To John William Corrington]
December 24, 1962

[* * *] Don't keep urging me to leave the City of the Angels, this beautiful fucking place where Saints jack off in the sky. I am beholden. Look, kid, I don't got no trade, savvy? Here maybe there are a couple of race tracks I got the smell of, and I know where the rescue missions are located, and it only gets cold at night, and there are a couple of places where maybe they will let me sleep on the floor or drop me a dollar from a hardshell hand. I traveled until I was almost cuckoo, from 19 to 28. I saw it. Sometimes I weighed 200 pounds, other times, 128. I saw that there was nothing. I saw the South like a gourd of light, with dryslab faces and poverty, history running like shit from the walls and everybody burning to poke you down. You, Willie, are a good kind of South, but there's another kind of South too, and you know it. But no better or worse than New York or Chi or Philly. But to go running off through the same scene would be like taking a dose of salts after a good bowel movement. Here in L.A. they leave you alone. You lay dead in a room for 5 or 6 days and it's not until you begin to stink or fail to pay your rent that they come in and drag you out. This has advantages if you are not heavy in love with the roving tribes. Here I've just got phantoms and a dirty floor from my own feet. Peace, cousin. [* * *]

...On the poems about Jane, I *kept* copies, sent them out somewhere....As to the poems I put *in* the letters, that is what they are for, the letters, and I do not save these poems or intend them for publication. If I can't spare a couple off the elbow, then what the hell's the use?

No, Jane doesn't leave. Some deaths won't. They are imbedded, fingered in the brain forever. And the life comes back, scores of life like an old movie. I've wanted to write this story but it's too big for me. I am weak and let it go. [* * *]

●

•1963•

[To John William Corrington]
February 19, 1963

[* * *] It seemed to me the man in Camus' *Stranger* showed more courage than the Hemingway man because his courage was a courage of acceptance rather than defiance. With Hem victory or at least a good defeat seemed reasonable. With Camus—this did not matter. Or so I gather, having heard a few chapters over the radio (*The Stranger*). I could not be this type of Camus because I could not accept everything in order to dismiss it, or ignore it, or play at rot. Somewhere between Hem and Camus I stand, or sit this morning, sick, pale, white, old. Tomorrow it might be better. [* * *]

[To Jon and Louise Webb]
May [?20], 1963

I am so in love with the book you are doing. this keeps the keenly biting down somewhat and I go on, but very much afraid I am hypo of some sort and only decency of—of what?? effrontery? is in destroying myself, and I keep drinking and looking out of windows, flowers, grass, people down there … grass people down there … ah, ha, I can still laugh, and you people are so good, god damn it, my madness, I am so unkind, this is the book, my love, yours, but I look ahead, and if I am there, here, anywhere, I have a title for another book, be there another book, another me, another anything: LEAP OUT OF ANY WINDOW. Really my love grows sadder, my life grows realer, too real, I can hardly beat it like cherries blooming in a fucking glass of scotch, within the gall of scotch...things crawling growing inside my sick-gut mind, the whole world waving   waving

                    hello and goodbye
                    and I've been so rotten
there's so little left to do. you either bleed to death in small drops
or you go out like a snarling tambourine, why not, car doors slam
across my living
                my way
                        and their way
                                tangle like angry panthers
                                in a cave
and they know the way
   they know the way

        And,
                yes
                        of course I've been drunk
                        u might have guessed

missed work missed work
god damn them
and so a job I hate prob. gone
and I can do nothing
have no trade
            but maybe luck
                        luck
                            image
                                flat floating fish
                                stunned and pecked to death
                                getting by
                                in a lost mirage.

Please do not take this letter too seriously or bother making phone calls because all our dimes are thin, thin, thin, like slivers in our final coffin poking our eyes alive, g.d. g.d., this is the

ending of the birdsong, this is the coconut eaten, this is slime
upon the walls, this is a flat tire, this is dirty laundry, this is
everything eaten from its insides out and its outsides in, this is a
bad morning,
this is a bad day, this is gas stations under moonlight, this is
the lousy screw with his precious freedom walk outside the bars,
    these
are the bars filled with the lonely hemorrhoids of life, this is the
world waiting upon the mailman and the bomb, this is a cat
crucified by a dog, this a man cruxed by a woman or the other
    way around,
this is a worm crawling an apple under a temperature of 69
    degrees, this
is all is Christ dangling from nails   dangling dangling
this is the horse that did not quite qinuto quatro win
this is the whore that did not quite love
this is the city that did not burn down to new empire
this is the rodent staring with the square blue eyes
these are madmen's tears
like the lava of a fish crying for greater things,
these are tootsie rolls and buns,
these are things that smash me dead
like blank faces
like envelopes
like buns
like mercenary women
like countries that proclaim justice
because they are strong enough to say what they want
to seem to believe;
…like that last kiss and that first kiss,
like the hands that once loved you
resting upon coffin-bottoms while oranges still round young
and full to the shape of the sun,
and these things you know,
please cry with me,
please be weak,
please do not become knowing
or fancy as that man
who takes the bull to hell
like a spider working a fly,
oh Hemingway was a liar,

I do not call this Art
and I do not call this Life,
for all your fancy jurists and all your fancy ways
and all your fancy gods—
I cannot see, I cannot see,
and I grow tired
the larvae crawl the eyes of my soul,
the bricks fall,
Stalingrad again, or Greece
or Berlin
or the fingers of myself
working out toward a god
or a leaf or a sound or a symbol
or a meaning.

I am not wise enough
and this is a terrible thing;
it is so easy to become wise enough
that I cannot do it,
I cannot see it
I cannot be it.

It is a becoming thing
and becoming things fit me
like loose shelves and [? saucers]
in an earthquake.

ah jesus
I talk too much
I mouth words like a mimic
I roll and stroll
and beat my silly bloody breasts
and miss the point
miss the point.

ah, god damn, sweet soldiers,
sweet whores, sweet friends,
the point is in
and down
and working,
can't you see

that???
like a gaunt and noble
and giant cock
working forever
reaming the original guts of life
out of you?
Pan, Pan, I am so sad,
and where does the working go?
where's the Peace?
where's the victory?

oh, god damn it, I know:
we are tried
again and again
and that's our sustenance:
working finely with these master
teeth,
but I grow sick of Henry Miller
and the balustrades,
I'm tired of D.H. riding the thighs of his
eternal and saving cow,
and when Hemingway met an enemy without a flag
he surrendered
which is not bad at all
but he should have known earlier
or he would not have fucked around with so
much stuff,
but still a great man
whatever great means
or I would not be talking about him
in this round dull and sickening morning,
now now now
where are we at? ha?
what's it mean?
I'm not the first to toss this grain
of salt,
but really am more vicious and desperate and
wanting
perhaps
than many of the rest,
and that is why you read this

and that is why this screen in front of my face
is all that separates me
from the sweet black pavement that looks for its own
freedom.
You think I bluff?
Of course.
so long... as long
(you are the pretty grammarian)
as I remain alive I bluff.
your criticism is justified
but your life
is not? not.
period.
definite statements
are generally
like love:
they turn out
badly. Of course,
you know that real love
like real life
only comes along in the shape
of a body
every 2 or 3 centuries.
I know. You think it is
Christ or Joan of Arc
or something obvious.
I do not think that way at all
and that is why we do not get
along.
But the real Christ or the fucking real
man is the man
who does not cuckold to the Arts,
a man who does not suck the nearest breast,
is a man who paints the walls of his life
kindly
and nobody
ever knows,
and this is the man of men
the walls of walls
and Hells Heruculius [sic] Jericho does not bring them
down,

only the sweet substances of his hands and his walk
and his life
like a bumblebee in the flower of a bull's death
sings these sweet songs to us,
o go away
go away
everything
the swaying of the planets
the muscles on a freak
the flat floating sorrow of a punk pudding
my insides screaming for the love of violins
such a giant drunk falling falling
across the face of this world
oh sweet cream and peaches
oh sweet love and hate
oh sweet dynasties of burning,
oh walnuts and tits
haunches and dogs,
oh simple moon
voices   lips   eyelashes
destroy me
I beg you
I beg you
destroy me forever
because my eyes have grown too large
my wisdom like a beautiful peacock
that can only separate pebbles from corn,
yes, yes, that is so,
do not laugh,
or what the hell
laugh
yes do laugh ...
I am so serious
like a god damned kid with a yoyo,
and I too dislike serious
people—
when you're serious about life and death
you not only become a bore,
but serious enough ...
you destroy yourself.

this is not what I mean.
what I mean is
what are we going to do this afternoon
while sitting around
eating apples and
destroying hangovers
and preparing for
future hangovers?

all that I can see is the
bird-like and drifting
Savannah of sunlight,
my harmless
so far
arms and hands and
veins,
and darling
sweet love of life
and child and blossom
do not think I am cruel
because I am afraid,
and now
spreading across my mind
they ring a god damned gong
across the afternoon
why? why?
as I am drunk again
as I understand nothing
as the sink is stopped and as the flowers
poke holes in my eyes
as love runs like a rat down the drain
and I become myself
ugly
real
vicious
standing with the worst armies
in the worst time
in the worst land
in the worst minute
or the worst light
slashing through this screen

taking me taking me
goodbye forever oh friend of my love.

[To John William Corrington]
August 28, 1963

[* * *] Well, they marched for freedom on the capital today. That's nice. I prefer a black and WHITE freedom. Someday they are going to find out you can't get a job whether you are black or white. And when you vote—either way, either man can be bad. And they are going to find out that water tastes the same, but then you can't blame a man for wanting small things. They want to go into any church; I don't want to go into a church. They want to vote; I don't want to vote. They want to live where the white man lives; I don't care where I live. They want equal rights, which means the rights I've got, and these rights are so small, so insignificant in the living of everyday life that I spit on them. There are rights that are talked about and then there are things that happen. A man will never make it through the machinery of the State. A man must make it through his own bones and mind and his own laws. Great men don't wait on the State. They ignore it or make their own to suit their passions. So the thing in Washington today, the Freedom March, while seeming a lot in essence, in spirit and etc., the forwarding of Man, wow, it is hardly all that at all, and it rolls along in its quiet slime drowning itself as it inspects itself. [* * *]

[To John William Corrington]
September 3, 1963

[* * *] I wait mainly on your next novel, the Civil War is all right, and you prob. wanted to write it with your South hand, but must guess (since you ain't talking) that most of the rewrite was to make it stop looking like the South won the war. And yet, even now, the way the Feds have to play with the city cops it looks like

47

the South wasn't played with too much. I really don't know what the war *was* fought for; I mean, I've read the history books and I still don't know. A lot of wars, I think, are fought mostly over SPEECHES AND PROCLAMATIONS and then after everything is over, the whole works returns to the same hard bubble. Yeah, I know. This is pretty simple thinking. [* * *]

[To John William Corrington]
October 18, 1963

[* * *] I may have to move from here. Only reason I have stayed here so long is that I am forced to live in apartments or rooms, and all these years here there hasn't been anybody with a loud T.V. Now there is. The guy downstairs died of a heart attack and somebody else moved in there. This somebody blares the T.V. up through my floorboards. I don't have a T.V. and I don't mind other people having them—as long as I don't have to listen. I can listen to lovers' quarrels and/or beatings without distaste but these quiz contests, news broadcasts and COMEDY? that stinks up through my floorboards is like getting slapped across the soul (?) with a dirty floormop. The masses give me trouble not because they are basically stupid but because they push their stupidity into my life. People are always talking about vague things like "freedoms" or newspaper things like "civil rights," and this all sounds good and makes them think they are saying something. This wordage is putty without shape. The most needed thing is THE FREEDOM AND RIGHT OF PRIVACY FROM OTHER PEOPLE'S SOUNDS OF LIFE. It is difficult for a poor man to attain this. Neeli Cherry of *Black Cat Review* asked me to write something about "Civil Rights," but I knew what he wanted. What other people call civil rights, I don't even want. Nobody really has any rights anyhow, not even the rich; you save what you can and try not to be fooled too often. There's a law for them and a law for me and if my law is broken too often, I am dead. I didn't write the article for Cherry on c. rights. Somebody else will give him what he wants. Sure.

I have been visiting people lately, which is only mostly to explore that they are not there mostly and to see if I can sit still and listen to TALK. Hit Jack Hirschman's for burned steak and scotch, and next night went to—rather a week later—Orlane Mahak's big picture window that overlooks the sickening Sunset Strip, had Brazilian chicken and rice, but brought a woman along who liked to TALK and so she talked and I sat there mostly which saved me. I talk quite stupidly, you see; I cannot get the thought out of my mind into proper order to be made into sound for the air. In fact, I don't want to. I am like a child hiding what he thinks is a hell of a hell of a hell of a jewel in my back pocket, and I don't want to show it to anybody. If I do, it will be in the proper temple. But after one visit people don't bother me anymore and I don't bother them. That's the sweet part, daddy. When I walk out the door the first thing the good people do is look at each other and say, "Jesus, was THAT Charles Bukowski?" If I knew how to talk I'd sell all the old streetcar tracks in this town to the Black Muslims.

[* * *] Somebody at one of these places, I think Mahak's, asked me: "What do you do? How do you write, create?" You don't, I told them. You don't try. That's very important: *not* to try, either for Cadillacs, creation or immortality. You wait, and if nothing happens, you wait some more. It's like a bug high on the wall. You wait for it to come to you. When it gets close enough you reach out, slap out and kill it. Or if you like its looks you make a pet out of it.

Then this woman who likes to TALK jumped in: "You can't make RULES! That's all right for YOU to say 'don't try' but you can't make a rule like that for everybody. It's like saying—"

"O.K.," I said, "I quit."

I've heard all these things centuries ago and I still hear them, the same old sayings and terms, things like... well, they like the word CULTURE and they like the word MIDDLE-CLASS and when they put them together like MIDDLE-CLASS CULTURE, this really sounds like something and it makes them feel good but it doesn't mean anything, it is like CIVIL RIGHTS or FREEDOM, words long ago washed way away and left meaningless by abuse and overuse. [* * *]

President Kennedy was assassinated on November 22nd.
"The book" is It Catches My Heart in Its Hands, *published by the Webbs' Loujon Press with a foreword by Corrington.*

[To John William Corrington]
November 27, 1963

I have been putting off writing thinking maybe the book would come and it did come—the day after Kennedy was assassinated, and now I have the book on my right side and the beer on my left and I am king prince lightning Ruth in '28, Nap at the top, Hitler in Paris [* * *]

Your foreword is more honor, and quite prophetic: "the marksman will not be long in coming." I don't look into myself to see why certain wheels turn; I feel this is dangerous. First, if you get to know what you are doing you are apt to keep doing it, or second you might become so self-conscious you end up sounding like an old Rudy Vallee recording. Both are bad. [* * *]

[To John William Corrington]
December 7, 1963

[* * *] Somebody told me tonight when I said that the real men work in fish factories, somebody told me that men that work in fish factories are too tired to write, I told this person that English teachers are too *untired* to write, she told me, or started to, this broad, she started to tell me about the agonies of an English teacher, but having known English teachers, having looked upon their faces, and having worked in slaughter houses, cake factories, railroad gangs, madmen, I told her not to tell me about the agonies of an English teacher ... correcting essays, planning midterms, grading by the albatross scale, and writing *poetry* in between all this agony of deciding whether they are homosexual or whether Clayborn who teaches Advanced E. 2 is a punk [* * *]

You aske' me what I think a tha Kennedy. I don't think

50

anything of the K. Down where I work they have a black sign under his picture: MARTYRED. Do you really think so? Harvard? A fine piece of ass that starved herself to keep a figure that would kill babies. Do you think a man is martyred because he follows the open downhill path? Is it really HELL to be born with more money than you can ever spend? Is it hell to never think about where the rent is coming from? Is it HELL TO HAVE SOMEBODY ELSE PUT A BULLET INTO YOUR HEAD INSTEAD OF YOURSELF PUTTING THE BULLET THERE? Where does hell come from and how do you spell it? Do only the top-figure people suffer? How many dead were buried on the same day K. was buried? Who bull-like bleeds from a sword? Hell, ace, who gets cut when they are shaving? Kennedy followed the wigwam in. He *could have* turned the presidency down. I WOULD HAVE. Oswald was a fink, true. He read too many books and lived too little. He was never in love with the sunlight or watching a cat walk across the rug. Kennedy was, a little. Ruby, he never saw anything. And now, being alive now, I think of Lincoln, he got it too, but I keep thinking, for all the turning he caused, could we not through the years of not-knowing, of awayness, [have] over-evaluated this man? Huh? What ya think, Willie? Maybe I only got beer running out of my oyster ears. [* * *]

Willie, you prick, I am drunk, but this instance of burning, these dry ash tears rolling down my fat arms and belly, I thank you for the good foreword, and only hope you are partly right; I remember once talking to the old man over the phone when he told me he was going to put my photo on cover of *Outsider* #3, and I asked him, "How do you know that this isn't going to give me the fat head?" And he answered, "That's the chance I've got to take." Which was very kind. Anything I hate, it's a sense of false humility. Saying such things as, "Oh, I really don't *deserve* this." But almost worse, is feeling that you do deserve it. I hope that my evenings, nights, mad-drunk in drunken alleys, g.d. jails, hospitals, I hope I remember these things, I hope I remember the broken-winged bird in the cat's mouth, I hope I remember the rifle poking out of a 5th story window, I hope that I remember what I should remember, I hope I do not ever become a Will Rogers plying humanity through his simple and lovely face that the only thing to do is to love humanity because it is the only thing to do, win big the big love, I am lifting another beer and hoping I remain the same and grow the same as whatever seed was planted within me from a hateful father and an indifferent mother. See here, you Freudianists, get out your notebooks, and you have the ANSWER. Well, I've read Freud too. He had enough sex but not enough climaxes; his brain was too far above and, at the same time, too far below his belt. Love, which I hardly know and am very afraid of, Freud never considered. I am not speaking Christianity which is shit also. I am speaking shit commonsense living wherein we, you and I and she and Oswald-ex, are all involved in. Thanks for good foreword. And when I am dead, bad enough, worse enough, when I am living somebody will tear the mind of my chicken limbs apart for burning, and they will be right, we are all wrong forever, there is an unanswered question, some face burning in the night, and for a time I thought too it was Marxism we needed or Plato or a rereading of Shakespeare or the alls of anything, ugg pal, it appears Willie we are all irrevocably lost forever and like Tom Wolfe, Mencken, Ruby, we do we do the best we can.

•

•1964•

[To John William Corrington]
March 6, 1964

I divined that you had turned on me out of some mysterious nature inherent in x-English teachers, all of whom I trust very little, I g.d. being crabbed by nature and busted by a heft of drizzly and ignoble Southern California sunsets, I felt that when you did not respond to my last letter ... Then too, some English mailman may have stuck the letter into a snow bank. Anyhow, you louse, I am still alive and I feel that my head is no fatter than usual in spite of articles on one Bukowski in *Northwest Review*, *Descant*, *Americas* the, and *Polish American Studies*. The latter written by the Rev. Joe Swastek, Librarian of Alumni Memorial Library, SS. Cyril & Methodius Seminary, St. Mary's College, St. Mary's Preparatory, Orchard Lake, Michigan. I got a letter from him this morning wondering if I had done much beside the poems and drawings in the *Epos* number. He wants to fuck up the library with it, which is very nice, I think. I'll send him on to various. [* * *]

Bukowski was now living with Frances Smith, who was pregnant with their daughter Marina.

[To John William Corrington]
April 2, 1964

[* * *] Well, I have got me a pregnant woman and I thought she was too old and that I was too old, and I can't understand it [* * *]

I sit here now with pains above the stomach and wonder what's left, what a man can do when he's been slugged by the years and the bad jobs and the bad job now and maybe nothing later, I mean when you walk out, when you can't go through that door anymore to look at the impossible faces, the tiny continual hell of doing an idiotic boring searing task at a rate almost beyond bodily endurance, and, getting paid very little, very. Sometimes they forget what they are doing; sometimes they even go insane and take pride in what they are doing, or in what they are not doing. I wrote a poem about this called "The Workers." I don't know if I got it down right, I think I might have; anyway, I felt g.d. better for 5 or 10 minutes after I wrote it. [* * *]

Corrington's novel, And Wait for the Night, *was published by Putnam's, New York.*

[To John William Corrington]
May 1, 1964

[* * *] I got your book for which, you know, thanks surely, and your book sits on the shelf on top of *Twenty Poems of Cesar Vallejo*, which is pretty good, I guess, and alongside another book, Gray's *Elegy*, which was bought in a used bookstore for 49 cents and is inscribed in very faint pencil: "Miss Mollie Zahrnde. Elkader, Iowa, Dec. 9, 1903." Copyright 1893, by Estes and Lauriat.

The paths of glory lead but to the grave.

[* * *]

Corrington's The Anatomy of Love and Other Poems *was published by Roman Books, Fort Lauderdale.*

[To John William Corrington]
May [?8], 1964

o my I got *Anatomy* from Roman and

this is it. You are writing better and better and better, what the hell are you trying to do? push us all down on skid-row? You've got a kind of a classical style that talks human language here, and believe me it makes me feel good to tell you how good you are, baby. There is not a fag line in the whole book. You'd look good in the ring, bull or square, I'd say you'd take the ears and tail home in your pocket & the other man's gotta fall; you'd look good reading Hans Christian Anderson; you'd look good painting a flagpole for a children's Maypole dance ... U iz now what the criticizers kall—a major poet of impact. You are there. Willie, I keep reading the book and it's a good thing like a good fuck all over again, but more, of course. [* * *]

[To John William Corrington]
May 16, 1964

[* * *] Listen, baby, not to hurt, I know it is so hard to do—like fighting a bull, and *I* am not even *doing* it; but to say, I liked novel very good but felt middle section dragged a bit. I've got to say, on the other hand, that *Anatomy of Love* is a major work of poetry and/or art and that I am proud to receive a letter occasionally from you from England, Texas and/or Louisiana and/or

in Hell where u undoubtedly are occasionally. No man could write that well from a continual heaven. [* * *]

Veryl Blatt (later Veryl Rosenbaum) is the author of The Way It Was *(Torrance, Calif., Hors Commerce Press, 1964) and other books.*

[To Veryl Blatt]
October 11, 1964

[* * *] Yes, the world's a cat's ass, a real driveling disgust, and the sweetest thing *is* getting away from them, their sounds, their decayed unlaughing laughter & faces as brutal and ugly and impossible as any matter you can dream up,...and the eyes, the eyes, no eyes at all. I can well understand men who run into caves and *stay* there. I don't have the guts or the know-how. I walk through their streets, lighting cigarettes and getting drunk and buying their newspapers. but nothing anywhere really. Going to sleep is getting to be the finest thing, and death itself, aside from physical pain, will not be so hard. Well, this is a lot of loose talk for a Sunday but I have to go into a cement building full of 4,000 people and work tonight when I'd rather suck on beer, smoke a cigar and listen to Stravinsky. When is the world going to be arranged for the people to do as they wish to do? [* * *]

[To Jon and Louise Webb]
November 19, 1964

[* * *] after dinner—our Frances has picked up and gone into the other room. These broads mash me. table talk. I asked what they would do to a man who said (to the authorities) that he was a coward, that he thought war might possibly kill him and that he didn't want to die. He would not state that it was against

56

his morals or his religion. Just that he didn't want the thing to kill him. Frances said that they would probably consider him an idiot. maybe I resented this because this was the very inference I made to the psychiatrist without saying the words when I faced this situation. And then I told her that if a man were really a coward he would have lied about his reasons anyhow, giving religion or morals as an excuse. Then I added that honest men were not truly cowards. F. then said that that was not so, that we all had fears. I said she was picking at words, distorting what I had meant for the sake of argument. Then F.: "Well, if Charles Bukowski says it's so, then it's so. Isn't *that* it?" I said, "You and I have had done with each other for tonight. I don't know whose fault it is, yours or mine, but something's wrong here." Then she went into the other room.

most of the time I attempt to avoid this type of talk and/or yak because I am not interested. I know that her groups become heated and gabble, DISCUSS, they simply love to DISCUSS, and F. is trained in this ping-pong type of thing. Actually most of these people have just lived on the edge of living and so they are full of a bilious sort of stale and clotted energy which they must expel as a sort of poison. I am too tired to argue. It doesn't matter. Let them win; I just don't want to hear it. I didn't even want to hear it in Junior High school, these little mouths with papers in their palms, saying, DEFINE that! ah well, we go on. but no wonder I layed drunk in the alleys, no wonder I lived with the whores.

"If Charles Bukowski says it's so, then it must be so."

Maybe she's got something there. But it is the first time she has attacked me through my name—meaning that since I have gotten a lot of poems published that this has distorted my ego or made me a bad judge of any meaning. It is possible, of course, yet I am unhappy with her technique. Also little comments on my playing the horses and drinking but as I see it I was doing this when she met me and if it weren't for the child I would not be with her now. I have lived with many many women and it all ends up the same: they want to shave you down to a wooden dummy to do their bidding, and, after all, I'm CHARLES BUKOWSKI!!!!

so to hell with it. [* * *]

[To Veryl Blatt]
November 23, 1964

[* * *] the baby is like a shiny apple, except the eyes, loops of
eyes extracting signs from the air, and look, there it sits knitted in
all that skin, a child, a girl, and outside—the bucktooth world,
ah, myself sucking on a cigar and wonder, wondering.

there are too many ways to drown even if you don't want to
drown.

it is terrible
staring down at a red and white
checkerboard oilcloth and
wondering.

The "2 books" are It Catches My Heart in Its Hands *and*
Crucifix in a Deathhand, *which would be published in mid-
1965. Ed Blair was a New Orleans poet, collector, and patron
of the Loujon Press.*

[To Jon and Louise Webb]
December 25, 1964

[* * *] That the *N.Y. Times* has put us with the big pub-
lishers and *The Collected Poems* of D. H. Lawrence etc. for rec.
Xmas reading is fine—we 3 small tough beer-drinkers, sidewalk
painters, criers in the dark. Hell, we put one over, didn't we?
And you're right: the fat head is for the rest; we'll just go about
our business.

You two people are almost myths now, almost literary his-
tory and you're still alive. The love of my luck was falling into
your hands for these 2 books. No other poet of this century or
any other has been so blessed.

Blair speaks of the envy of the others. Let them god damn
envy! Those Black Mountain School snobs, let them smell their
own turds! The Kenyon boys, let them write their celluloid
senseless inoffensive poems; the Corringtons—let them write
their novels of incest and beetle love and honor and refuse to

answer their mail; and all the others: let them go to hell too.

I am for the small man who has not forgotten, for the man who loves his beer and his women and his sunlight but who is not quite wise enough (ever) to know where next month's rent is coming from. [* * *]

●

• 1 9 6 5 •

Cherkovsky's Hank *(pp. 145-149) reports that Bukowski finally met Corrington during his sojourn in New Orleans with the Webbs in March 1965. The meeting was not a success and left Bukowski with "disdain" for his former correspondent, who had now turned to the novel as being more important than poetry.*

[To John William Corrington]
March 1, 1965

I wrote 2 some year back and no response so I gave it up thinking that the England thing and the novel and James Joyce had you by the balls. However, I will soon be 45 and don't care to argue about it. I always answer my mail, tho', whether it's a whore from East Kansas City or Dr. Spock. [* * *]

The girl-child is Marina Louisa Bukowski and I am a sucker for it. Very large mouth and eyes and when that mouth opens and spreads into the big grin laugh, all sunflowers and sun, and I break in half, she has me. [* * *]

The book Veryl Blatt had written about is Crucifix in a
Death Hand, *published by Loujon Press.*

[To Veryl Blatt]
May 27, 1965

my thanks the good letter on the book. now that the book is
over it seems a very strange thing, an almost non-happening,
except now I am glad I went down there and saw those 2 people
put it together out of matchsticks and starvation and (as you
said) love. they battled rats, roaches, hurricanes and my drunken
presence. I did manage to sign 3100 pages, some of them with
message and/or drawing, but outside of that I was in the way. this
book was a little harder than *It Catches* in that I had to write
directly into a waiting press. that's good and it's not good. I
mean, it's like coming up with the bases loaded all the time. yet I
imagine any poet in America, in the world, would have been
most glad of the chance. my luck all came late and there is only
so much they can do to me now with these two books behind me.
I'm glad you're keeping the 2 books, your kids, your typer and
yourself. it is difficult for people like you and I to live out the day,
and I too have been through the bloody divorce thing, and christ
I can't figure it all—the breaking up, the looking again, the not-
looking again. If I could only sleep for ten years but maybe by
then the Chinese will have called our hotshot bluffs. if I do not
hold the trend of thought here—been to track all day, worked an
hour in pits, said to hell with it and came in. played with Marina
[* * *]

---

*Veryl Blatt, together with her husband Jean Rosenbaum, was
planning to gather and edit a collection of Bukowski's letters.*

[To Veryl Blatt]
November 9, 1965

[* * *] It's too bad Corrington and Webb won't let go of
their letters—the bulk of everything is here—but I felt from the

beginning that Corrington would hold out. he has changed very much in the last 2 years—ever since getting his doctorate and writing his first novel. He has stepped up out and away from me. I got worried about him near the end when he said, "I am going to use your letters to help send my son through college." Through college for what? *we* are trying to live now. It's strange how cold things can become and how, basically, so many poets are like real-estators, holders of stock, investors … C. has plenty of money; he ought to loosen his grip; he won't. the fact is, that I was writing to the wrong man. [* * *]

[To Veryl Blatt]

l.a. of course
thanksgiving
o lord you are so good to me you
Fucker!
[November 25,] 1965

veryl, you lovely baby of blue-eyed hurrah:
    I have written Blaz for o.k. on intro and of course we'll get it. the most crazy thing on these letters, almost all of them drunken, is that most of the people have kept them. I don't write so many letters anymore and maybe that means that I am dying, and that's the way it works. but the letters where [*sic*] a BLAM! a typewriter somewhere, an electric light, something to drink … who needs more? anyhow, even I am curious as to what I pumped out into the vacant air. [* * *]
    so listen, this Linda West c/o KRMG radio, I may have her other address, I think I do, but sure there is time, I am weary and drunk now and out of cigars and smoking these chickenshit little g.d. female cancer cigarettes. But Linda West only laughs anyhow, I doubt she saved anything. she read *It Catches* and here came this letter, so far as I can remember it:

    "Dear Mr. Bukowski:
       I have read *It Catches My Heart In Its Hands* and hear you have a new book out. I will gladly review your new book over the air here. I have always liked your poetry. I

63

imagine the kind of man you are and I also enclose a few poems of my own that I thought you might be interested in.

(then more drivel talk)
(then)

I often wonder about you. are you tall and slim with burning eyes? or are you short and fat with a waddle and a slur out of the side of your mouth? are you cruel? do you live in a Villa? is your maidservant more o more beautiful than a cloud?"

and I answered her, as well as I can remember, only probably answered her better:

"Dear Linda West:
I am short and fat and oversexed and I live alone except with a female dog. I think that your poems are very beautiful and I can't see why anybody doesn't publish them. I am cruel by nature, almost vicious, although not quite. I don't have any education but I love to fuck fuck fuck, especially young girls who work at radio stations. I even like to fuck old girls who work at radio stations, who work anywhere and who would be willing to submit to my laying upon my ass and writing while they did whatever they had to keep their souls and more, importantly, my soul, alibe, and if not alive, alibe.

yours,
        buk

look Veryl, that sheep may safely graze I better cut it off (ow, I mean, this letter)

_____

●

64

•1966•

[To Jon and Louise Webb]
March 21, 1966

[* * *] doorbell just rang and here was a little boy in the dark ... "Sir, I am working in competition with 5 other boys..." He has some magazines and newspapers there. I tell him as gently as possible that I cannot buy anything. god, they get to them EARLY!!! what? competition. a discouraging word. when I write a poem I don't think about shit competition. but christ I guess I am in competition with Ezra and Shake and Jeffers or, if not that, then with Judson Crews, Carl Larsen and Peter Orlovsky. yet, I am a hundred times more unhappy to see this kid this way, begging his papers under the lamplight. [* * *]

[To Veryl Blatt]
April 2, 1966

[* * *] listen, I know that the book of letters a long way away but if it ever happens, run what you wish. only there is something I'd wish to strike out in reference to Sheri Martinelli. I don't know if I did, but I might have mentioned her in other letters as "Pound's x-whore." she's a fine woman but don't think she'd understand. In a sense, I am a romantic; I mean when I call a woman a whore, I mean, in *my* language, a woman who loves *one*

65

man and *one* man only and I use the term in fondness to depict faithfulness, and there is no derogatory intent involved. I know that this turns around the standard concept, but damn standard concepts. I also use "whore" to mean "death" which is also, in a sense, "love" to me. so you see, I am mixed-up. yeah. anyhow this is all I would want struck from the letters [* * *]

Joseph Conte was the editor of a racing journal called American Turf Monthly.

[To Joseph Conte]
Late April, 1966

sure if you can ram the #6 poem through, I'll take a year's subscription, I'm hooked on the horses but rather mathematically, playing with odds and systems, experiments. I've found that the further away you can get from a racing form the better chance you have. one system is based ENTIRELY UPON INDEX NUMBERS and shows continuous profit. the other is based entirely UPON THE ODDS LISTED IN THE RACING FORM AND THE ODDS ON THE TRACK PROGRAM. both systems work, in short, because they *reverse to an extreme* everything the public does or wants. the only problem is getting up your guts to play the things. [* * *]

[To Joseph Conte]
June 12, 1966

[* * *] got July issue and #6 poem, looks fine, and think it will fit some of your readers. but the horse-poems just don't come anymore—just the madness of the crowd, that whole body of many-legged, headed, cocked and cunted, wailing and greedy and angry animal. also suicidal. a hell of a gang. and the insiders shove it to them and collect—deliberate 5 pound overweights, first time starters, fillies against colts, bandages, bleeders, class

jumps, the works. they jam it to them like bayonets and take away the money. whatever the crowd has learned changes and no longer becomes true—first they ruin the price and 2nd they are manipulated against. enough lecture. [* * *]

your magazine can help the stabbers, although it can't help me, I like to read it, sometimes to reverse the information and play the opposite, or ingrain it in my thought cells. I'm not knocking your mag; it's a way of making a living, and I like the photos—there is something in the photos working on me—not a method of play, but a fucking art process. I have made a painting of horse and jock, a bit obscure and heavy with color, perhaps comic, oil pastel, and maybe some day I get the bigheart or drunk or find something to mail it in and I mail it on to you. then, maybe not. I don't like to make tasks.

[* * *] tell Torregian I said to go to hell. I don't think he has read over 4 or 5 of my poems. If he thinks I am "pragmatic and social conscious," tell him to read my article in *Earth* 2: "In Defense of a Certain Type of Poetry, a Certain Type of Life, a Certain Type of Blood-filled Creature Who Will Someday Die." I do think that what he means in his criticism is:

one: first, he hasn't been published enough; which is not a crime but which sometimes puts the blinkers on the open mind.
two: I write too clearly, therefore there must be something the matter with me:

a: not sensitive
b: not poetic
c: not there.

this is age-old fallacy stuff and I can't be bothered with it.

[To Joseph Conte]
June 27, 1966

o o o o, listen, the poem by Lottie Adler is not for me, a rhymer and "Life is Beautiful" type of thing. you'd be surprised how many of these I get in the mail—mostly from women. I guess it's the mother-instinct, wanting to save the no-good boy from the bottle, the jail, the alley, madness. also much of this comes from reading Keats, Shelley, a kind of wilted and *nice* romanticism, but they don't even need this. just the thought of what poetry *should* be, what they think it is, out of a movie or out of a highschool English course. the whole thing's basic and I don't mean to pick. the poem is lousy. the only way this woman can save me is to throw me some *pussy* and she isn't going to do that. tell her to read the *Artaud Anthology*, $3, c/o City Lights Books, 261 Columbus Ave., San Francisco, Calif. or at least send for my review of the book picked up and reprinted by Ferlinghetti out of local liberal rag. Artaud wrote the *iron* line, like reaming fire through cement. he's been dead since March 4th, 1948, so Lottie won't have to send him a poem.

Artaud one of the few writers I look up to. Artaud, Dostoevski, Celine...read Celine, Joe, this guy was laughing while they were killing him. *The Stranger* by Camus. there simply hasn't been a hell of a lot of good writing done—too much talking around corners, too much airy bullshit, too many lies. [* * *]

[To Joseph Conte]
July 18, 1966

ow, you ask an opinion and I cannot give you one because I would not want to be responsible for putting you into a jail cell or an army, either one. in a sense you are asking me whether it is better to eat hot shit or cold. your decision will have to be yours. in world war II (see *Confessions of a Man Insane Enough to Live with Beasts*) I lucked on through or insaned on through, one leg in jail, one arm out, ass in between, but whether I knew what I was doing subconsciously or whether I was all jacked-off in the head I'll never know, but it was probably a little bit of each. but for all I went through there is not much that I can say to help you. [* * *]

talk with your girl friend or close friends. most men figure that the easy way out is to go and hope that they don't have to kill anybody or be killed or mangled, but it doesn't always work this way. once they get hold of you they point you about the way they wish to. and a jail cell can seem pretty final; you would have to battle both the screws and your own mates in another type of power play. like I say, it's yours. my sympathy, but god damn if I can tell you anything.

[To Joseph Conte]
Early October, 1966

[* * *] I can't write any system articles, Joe. I wouldn't tip my hand on the good ones that I know. I know, I know, I am working for a living at an impossible job. if I know so much about the horses what am I doing cleaning the shithouse? I don't know, Joe, I don't know. maybe the Anita meet will get me over. I have developed what I think of as my 4-ply play; in other words, there are sometimes 4 bets in a race, but usually 3 fall on one horse and one on the other, or it goes 2 and 2. I'd like to think I've got the whole thing in a box and I think maybe I have: the horse the stable is shooting with; and the *logical* overlooked overlay, and my overlay may read 8 on a morning line of 8, or even 9/2 on a morning line of 5, because I use my own rating not the trackman's. I also have a weirdy called my overlay-underlay, plus one other juicer. the morning line fools most people and it's meant to; it is deliberately jacked out of line to draw the money in from players who take the line as God. sounds like madness, I know, but almost everything is, so why can't I join the crowd? [* * *]

[To Joseph Conte]

Hey Conte!
Oct. 20, 1966

Fairly drunk.

3 fairly good days—$70 average—trotters & pacers, maybe luck, but fairly new-old insight. Fairly, fairly.

Kid, I consider myself a pretty good fucking horseplayer (poetry is like taking a shit)—horses are the Empire (like fucking) (see Frued's pupil) (but nothing that *simple*) Fruedy's are too obvious, much too much college mother-boys & unlived.

It seems like anything anybody *else* does that you *don't* do—then *that's* caused because you wore shoes a size too small and you wanted to fuck your mother. Right?

Actually, the so-called most well-balanced individual usually ends up in some useless & dry position such as President of the United States of America and ends up fucking (up) a lot of mothers & everybody else too.

The pyschiatrist (spell?) is the high-paid fuzz that makes up (lies) excuses for individuals who cannot understand a decadent & horrible & useless society (govt.) & a dec. & whore & useless life. He is paid to call these people crazy (insane) (physchotic—spell?) instead of the life & the way surrounding them.

The pyschiatrist is the pretty-boy liar of a stabilized hell.

As you must guess, I am drunk—but mean what I say.

Then too—the poet as preacher is a dishonest & copious extension of his normal function—see Pound, Ginsberg, so forth.

God damn...where am I? can you read this???

Answering your question—the newspaper bought by the largest % (percentage) of horseplayers entering local tracks (Santa A.) (Hollywood) (Del Mar) (Los Alomitos) (Pomona) is not an L.A. paper but The Independent (published in Pasadena). This is the one that "moves", the horse-addicts suck them up. The _whole_ front page is covered with horserace bullshit information, so much so that one of their handicappers are squeezed over onto another page. The larger metro LA. papers (Times & Examiner) merely blow up the print on their one or 2

70

handicapers in an attempt to cover the page. In fact, the largest circ paper (the L.A. Times) does not even _bother_ to reset type in order to blank out SCRATCHES!! except in the case of harness races where scratches are by *rule* not *morning* scratches but *overnight*, prob. before midnight???

The Independent advt. rates are undoubt. much lower, babe. So don't say old Buk never done your rag any good, what? But would prefer you check with some other horse in this area to make sure I am not bullshitting you. And so, Aunt Jeriamiah fucked a burning duck.

By the way, most of the articles in your mag *sound* good but are basically unsound as is most horse-info—

like most bologna—

    A) horse must have had race within 14 days
    B) 2 year old and maiden races are bad plays
    C) handicap races are bad plays

and on & on.

The people who own & run horses take advantage of public information & education on horses to invert all possibilities for their own profit.

Furthermore, overlay & underlay winners are caused by 2 concepts:

    A) public misconceptions, greed & fear.
    B) the track handicapers's *deliberate* distortion of the line
    in order to confuse & bring in the most possible betting
    $$.

Hang in, kid,

Buk

William Hageman of Pasadena was the editor of The Willie,
published from 1967 by Manic Press, San Francisco.

[To William Hageman]
November [?25], 1966

[* * *] when I said there were only 4 or 5 poets in the world
who could put down a line or 2, I meant 4 or 5 poets who could
DO ME ANY GOOD. the rest of them flatten my spirit, it's like swal-
lowing sad sawdust, like being tricked again and again. the only
way we are ever going to move the world a notch is through PURE
ART, and baby, not much of it seems to be around, and I include
myself. the best thing about mimeo is that it takes the pressure
more and more away from THOU MUST SUCCEED IN ORDER TO PAY
THE PRINTER. and it usually eliminated 8 or 10 hands in the pot,
all printing their own stuff.

●

• 1 9 6 7 •

*William Wantling contributed to many of the same little mag-
azines as Bukowski and had a book published by Douglas
Blazek's Ole Press. An ex-convict who had spent five years in
San Quentin, he took an interest in matters such as capital
punishment and penal reform (see Hank, p. 164).*

[To William Wantling]
oily Febru 1967

[* * *] saw headline in paper: CONGRESS VOWS FIGHT ON
CRIME. and I almost sat down and wrote a mother essay, 8 or 9
pages on what crime IS and what it APPEARS to be, how our whole
social structure houses and pardons and builds laws for everyday
sanctioned robbery and crime against each other, whereas a
direct and HONEST CRIME is punished by police, judges, juries.
the difference says our society is this: you can take a lot and give
a little, but you can't take everything and give nothing. this is the
essential difference between Capitalism and the Gun, and the
reason why all judges, juries, cops are finks. the dope bit is all the
same—it isn't the dope that matters to them; it's how you get it,
who hands it to you. if it's in the doctor's handwriting it's all
right, he is supposed to know whether you need dope or not,
that's why he is so well-paid. but who knows better than I DO
WHETHER I NEED DOPE OR NOT? who knows whether I need
oranges or eggs or sex or sleep or dope? I do. Who knows whether
I am sick or not? the doctor? who is more IMPORTANT? why is

73

everything twisted backwards? but you know all this. [* * *]

well, now I need sleep, if I can only SLEEP! little girl slept with me last night and pissed all over me as usual. but she is a sweet box of candy. she is joy. I look at her and light goes all through me. I am soft, man, soft, and I don't mind a bit. to feel some kind of love after the jars and holes they've had me in, it's the neatest of miracles. [* * *]

Corrington's novel, The Upper Hand, *was published by Putnam's in 1967. The parody letter is "A Letter from Chuck Buck" by Felix Pollak in* The Smith, *no 7 (15 October 1966), pp. 40-47.*

[To John William Corrington]
February 11, 1967

so you've done a moderne novel? May? good. now Putnams. you get around. slip me a free one, book I mean. I've got a whole bookcase full of free books, mostly poetry. I take much pride in my free books, most of them being vury good because the people wanted me to read them and felt I would see some light within the pages, and it works, easy like. [* * *]

I'll mail you the *Smith*. your name is mentioned in there. it is a parody of me, or whatever you call it. they pretend they have intercepted one of my letters. I write letters. by the way, I have never submitted anything to Ed Sanders. I wonder where they get that stuff? it doesn't matter; I think you might even call it a fun-piece except the satire is the sharp exaggeration bit, you know, and believe he detests my style and my guts—which is going to happen to all of us at one time, and it is part of the rocks in the shoes. [* * *]

as to the poetry writing, I am writing very good again after a kind of 2 years slump. which lasted from about Oct. 64 to Oct. 66. I do not mean that my poems were not being published, I mean that I did not care for them. now they come out full of butter and steel and my fingers hit the keys and it is easy. but my health shot. [* * *]

74

[To John William Corrington]
February 22, 1967

[* * *] I am not so worried about whether I am writing any good or not; I know I write a valley of bad stuff. but what gets me is that nobody is coming on that I can believe in or look up to. it's hell not to have a hero. it gets harder and harder not to have a hero. somebody to blow out the fire, knock out the goof, give you the word. my heroes are dead and the replacements seem very shoddy indeed. what can I do with Mailer, what can I do with Lowell? what can I do with anybody I can name? the thing is, when you first start the big boys have already been there a while. you look around. well, names. Dos Passos. Hemingway. Frost. Pound. Cummings. so forth. so forth. Jeffers. so forth. so you look round and let them go. they've been there. maybe you don't really like them but they are old boys in a picture book on the coffee table and it's kind of sad and kind of interesting. LeRoi Jones, Andy Warhol, D. DiPrima, Ray Bremser, you gotta be kidding! where's the big wooly guy with the diamond eyes and the cement lines? let me the HELL OUTA HERE! [* * *]

Bukowski's "Notes of a Dirty Old Man" column in Open City *(July 14–20, 1967) gave a sardonic account of his trip to Tucson. In it, Jon Webb is transparently disguised as "the great editor."*

[To John William Corrington]
November [?15], 1967

thanks for return of *The Smith*. being attacked by men of no talent is only a bit enjoyable for me, to me. also somebody, a gash, attacks me in what she conceives to be my poetic style in the latest issue of what? what? oh, *The Sixties*. they seem to be worried green shit about me, and that's all right. I don't worry about 'em.

yes, it's sad about Jon Webb and me, kid. he gave me two great books and was publishing and pushing me when hardly anybody else was. I can't forget these things. but I did write the column in *Open City*, but I hardly think it's a hate-column or unjust or dirty; I just told a story of a few things that happened on some very hot Tucson days. column enclosed, and if you think I am a fink or disloyal, well, shit, then it can't be helped. Tucson was hell, kid, I stayed at Univ. of Ariz. cottage and it was between 100 and 110 degrees every day, and I was the only one who could drink, except Lou's old father, and I quaffed a few with him. but it was a rough trip. Jon kept trying to get me into an argument about the hippies. and I stayed out. he wanted me to write something attacking the hippies and I didn't quite feel like doing it. I am neither pro or anti-hip. I just watch. I mean, like I am neither pro or anti-milkman or pro or anti-tree, and I am not even sure about the war. the black-white war, the Vietnam war or any other war. then they wanted to play cards. so we played cards for hours, for dimes, and they seemed to enjoy it. I'd win the money most of the time and give it back. they have this gambling bug. which is their business but I am not bitten this way except with horses. so they keep running off to Vegas. where Lou plays the slot machines—the biggest percentage gyp evoked against the gambler, the worst play you can make. they told me that the ladies get a free pair of stockings for each FOUR jackpots they hit. they told me that Lou had won either 14 or 16 pair of stockings the last time they went, and Lou doesn't use stockings. their business, but I view it as a type of madness, especially when they are crying broke most of the time. naturally I didn't put this crap in the column and I only tell it to you because I consider you a friend and figure I can talk straight with you, and want you to get the FEELING of what occurred while I was down there. ah, plus I looked at old Jon a bit oddly for couple of days—he'd dyed that beautiful double wisp of white hair RED. god. and all day long it was, "Lou, have I taken my pill yet?" and there'd be a long discussion on whether Jon had taken his pill, and then Lou had this bad lung thing and couldn't breathe and that was sad, but she still snuck her smokes. and some kids came by and they both ran in back and I had to talk to the kids. I showed them some of the books and I showed them the press. very nice young kids, clean, quiet. they left. then Lou hollered out, "Jon, you can come out, they're gone now!" and out came Jon, with quivering and quavering voice saying to me, "WHAT'D YOU SHOW THE *PRESS* FOR?" I didn't answer him. I didn't know what to answer. dirty gossip? Jon *is* hard to get along with, kid. he's always got the sword out, slashing at something. then he'd try to bait me on the hippies again. and it was hot and Lou couldn't breathe and then the cards came out; none of this in column, and no man's perfect, not me, not you, not Jon, and this ain't news, kid, I get attacked plenty myself—the other day a poem-letter knocking my life and ways in local underground paper. it wasn't even a good poem. but back to Jon and Lou, they are bookmakers supreme and good people too, but sometimes I write and I wrote this column which I enclose. I sent the column to a reporter of the Tucson paper who interviewed (bigshot) me, and told him not to give the column to Jon until he felt that Lou was feeling better, but I did want Jon to see it; I don't like to hide or sneak punch. evidently he eventually saw it because when I wrote him he didn't answer and so I knew. Jon is a very sensitive cat, not a sloppy hardened beerhead like me, but I guess he figured it as a kind of disloyalty, just like people figured I was being disloyal to you when I attacked one of your books of poetry. but it isn't disloyalty; I would be the first to come up with blackjack and snub-nosed automatic to blast a hole in some human wall or inhuman wall if you were in a jam and needed to get on through. there's still some German in me. which means loyalty, honor, all those old-fashioned words, and I half expected both you and Jon to understand this, but sometimes maybe I don't think or figure too good. well, enough of all that. [* * *]

so here I am, 47 years old, hanging from the same old rotting limb, Jon pissed, you half-pissed, and my little 3 year old daughter more beautiful than ever, a perfectly formed body jumping with life, gold-red hair, she loves me. and the other way around. if we were both standing at the edge of a cliff and somebody said, "o.k., one of you will have to jump." I wouldn't hesitate—I'd push her right off. no, kidding now, man, *I* would go. and I've never been that way before. but I have some of that feeling for you and Jon, even tho I don't show it too much, and now the old gang is fucked up and torn to shit. which shows you what a dangerous instrument the typewriter is. [* * *]

jesus, what a gloomy letter! but I am badly hungover and all horrors magnified, I guess. so now that I've cheered up your day I'll let you go. [* * *]

DeLoach was editor of Intrepid *(Buffalo). See vol. 1, p 296.*

[To Allen DeLoach]
Late November, 1967

[* * *] I've been writing so long and failing so long that there is hardly anything anybody can do to my balls now. I was always a very slow starter, and even in my early twenties, laying around drunk and jobless in N.Y., Atlanta, Philly, New Orleans, Miami, St. Louis, San Fran, I always had the thought: "Bukowski, if you can ONLY LIVE TO BE FIFTY, you will be there." I am 47, and I *might* make it. with me, it is this strange thing filling up inside of me, day by day, year by year, I can feel it happening through all the women and drunks and fails and sleepless nights and suicide days, I feel this FILLING THING working down inside of me. deaht, of course, I meant to say DEATH but doesn't it spell nice "deaht"—deaht is always there, but the filling thing functions on merrily and without any help from me. I've got some kind of LUNCH stewing up inside and it's nice to have, I mean while walking down the street or shitting or fucking or breaking your leg, it's there. how sweet can the gods get when and while they are ripping you to pieces? [* * *]

●

• 1 9 6 8 •

[To John William Corrington]
January 3, 1968

ah, balls. listen, everybody writes me, "why haven't you answered my letter?" [* * *] listen, I have this large blue coffee can on the shelf and it is full of unanswered letters. this neither means that I like or dislike the people who have written them; it means that I am drunk or playing horses or sick or non-electric, can't do, you know. no snob, just no time; I'd like to be a snob but I'd rather have the time. here, let me show you—I reach into this can and I pull out these and find that I OWE letters of response to: one: Jack Micheline (c/o Cohen); a Steven Osterlund—who wrote last August asking where he could get holden a some of my pukes; a Willie who calls himself the "manic"; an x-horse magazine editor called Conte who is now in Augusta (postmark says Sept. 25); a Douglas Blazek; a William Stetson (his postmark, Aug. 22, unanswered); a Bassett at the William Morris Agency—1350 Ave. of the Americas—postmark, June 12, '67; a Larouche of Albuquerque; a William Wantling; a Marcus Verily Grapes who writes very drippy letters; a Jim Roman (his dated 6-26-67); a Heinrich Fett of Andernach, Germany, 547 Andernach, Privat Str 1, my 79 year old uncle who says "I don't understand why you haven't written. Are you well?"; an A. W. Purdy, 137 Waverley St., Apt. 3, Ottawa, Canada (his mark: Oct. 11); an Ann Menenbroker of Sacramento, who I ask to please RELENT but the letters arrive, one two three a week; my x-wife, one Barbara Hayakawa of Aniak, Alaska; one Scott Reed of

Edwards, Mississippi; a Hale Chatfield of Hiram, Ohio; one Stuart McCarrell of Chi (his mark: March 19, 1967); one Dan Georgakas, a most interesting and violent anarchist; one H. Norse of 23 St. Marks Crescent, London; a Boatright; a DeLoach; a Charles Potts, Listade Ciereaex or something, L, no Jalisco, Mexico; a Richmond, Steve, of Santa Monica, Calif; a Bob Peters, dept. of English; a Fox, dept. of English; a Winski, writer of lurid sex tales; a Sherman, writer of lurid sex tales; a John and Susan Cornillion who promise to visit "this summer, if we may"; a Ben Tibbs, who always sends me a dollar for Christmas; and more and more, Christ, there are others that I have simply thrown into a big closet box and have closed the door on forever, I simply throw my dirty sox on top of them. shit, meaning what?

I guess that each of these people does not realize that there are other people writing me, and sending their little signed books of poetry. all right, I'm not Henry Miller. I've not made it as one writing. I work the post office. my ass is bloody. I went to the track today and lost $100. what do I have to do with anything? I can't keep up, I can't keep up with all these people. me, I write Jon Webb but he doesn't answer. well, that's dirty laundry and a kind of joke but I guess you know I am hurting, drinking beer, and it's vaudeville, good show, not snot. I think you read. I really think that you do; otherwise I wouldn't fuck with you, or visa versa—as the Spaniards yoused to say. oh yes, I like your IBM. send me one in the mail, right away. I want my little girl to know what they look like because I will be punching one, I mean she will be punching one all day for some greasy pinching slob because I don't have money enough to send her to college let alone buy her pretty candies and ribbons, tho she is beautiful without, they will prb. kill that. like the sparrow is on the eye of god and he better start cleaning out HIS bunghole.

back to letter-writing. belles lettres. yah. and your, our same old argument about Faulkner and tons of falcon stream of conci. dirty-boy italics. ah, let's not get on THAT again. oh boy. only, I mean, I just CAN'T answer all these damn letters, and I'm not even famous or even decently bearable to the sky, I mean I can walk down any street and bow wow, nobody will even sperm-like separate me from the pebbles, which is good, I am lucky to live and flow into the tons of open areas waiting, see, you know; so, I mean, I still can't answer ALL THESE LETTERS BECAUSE IF I DID I

WOULD DIE BECAUSE SO MUCH CLAIMS A MAN, FINALLY, IN ONE WAY OR ANOTHER THAT HE HAS TO MAKE CHOICES. if he makes the wrong choices he is dead before his time—war, women, horses, friends, literature, whiskey, the way he points his head when he sleeps ...

(I owe a letter to Carl Weissner) (a good boy, a good German boy. a shepherd.)

so, with the letters, feel good. I eliminate or they eliminate me. I must answer: William Corrington, Douglas Blazek, Harold Norse, Carl W., Jack Micheline. the others may be good boys, and so was *Guys and Dolls* a good musical, so is *Marat/Sade*—the Nuts, also good.

but. of course, I am pissed. you inferred, as they say, in your last, that I could dish it out but could not take it. mother, I have been taking it for a long long time. in the factories. from the whores, from the goslin bosses. from godly goldy lox. from Amos and Andy, the 3 Stooges, Bob Hope, Santa Claus. all the shits. I have for a long time held still for a literature and a culture that pretended to be life and talk about life but I will no longer do that. [* * *]

I mean, babe, I *have* been taking it. and so have you. and when these college profs rip my doorbell, I do not hate them. they bring me whiskey. they've heard some tale. and they have a class in the morning. so they sit and listen to me talk and wonder where it comes from, where the hell the wonderful SECRET IS IT MUST BE SOMEWHERE, EH? *they* look so much better, talk too much better, have more, feel fucking ass more, —how come their words don't come out ... o.k.???? me, *I* can't tell them. only maybe they got too much butter in their ass, maybe they aren't old enough or burned enough or the ass comes too easy or looks too good and when the nails come up through the shoes you don't beat them down with a hammer, you buy 3 new pair.

looking down, if I may, it seems that hardness kills, the tough boys kill each other, I have seldom seen a living man in a factory, and looking up, it seems, if I may, that softness kills, I have seldom seen a living man teaching a class in English Lit. I. and so when they come around and bring me whisky and I get drunk and cuss them, there are later little letters in the mail that they still love me and understand me. this is their training and not their passion. in a sense, it *is* their passion, like ham and eggs for Sunday breakfast, but it is NOT their blood-passion, and the sooner they learn their blood-passion, the sooner they are going to have trouble where they work, and the less they will need me. who am an old man, drinking beer. [* * *]

books? *Terror Street* holding up because I've got to do this tape and 34 more drawings. could have done the whole bastard thing while I was losing $100 to the horses. but it's not always like that. sometimes I win. one meet I won $3,000 and took off 3 months and slept in different motels along the coast between L.A. and Mexico, while still keeping my apartment (with shack-job) and fucking every whore and some non-whores in between, feeling good, looking at the ocean while drunk in the moonlight, lifting the bastard coronet of that bottle, knowing that it would *never* be that good again. like that, I mean, now, maybe it's even better, there's the little girl, Marina, walking through it all, but I am sure she wouldn't have been a shit to either of us (me and her) if she hadn't appeared through the spectrum of the other. like that.—I mean, I have fairly-well worked-out a kind of battle palsma [?plan] to face, death, you know, take it good like that, easy, rather like I do now, only she, Marina, has brought me a kind of holiness, a kind of teaching and I do not laugh as much or hate as much, the other people, she tells me that they are something other than I think, and I accept *some* of this. we have long talks in the dark, before sleep, this 3 years old girl and I, and since her picture is clear, unlearned, unburned, but clear, still, I pick up, I back up, and I don't *use* her—she simply fills me. Or, so I think.

all I need now is 60 days in jail or 10 years, and my whole thought processes will be realigned. everything happens for the best and the worst. like when Marina was first born, the line popped into my head, "she will probably be fucked by a sailor who never read Walter De La Mare." that was then. now, I think, so what? what could be more beautiful? only that, if she wants a sexual fulfillment, let it be hers, and let it be as near the man she likes as is holy possible. the problem of the poor being that they just usually submit; the problem of the rich being that they never know what they are loved for. [* * *]

[To Jon and Louise Webb]
March 18, 1968

[* * *] and, I'm having problems with the Penguin royalty dept. god damn. first the guy writes and says you must fill out enclosed forms before we can begin to process your check. he doesn't *enclose* the forms. a few weeks go by and I write him, "you didn't enclose the forms." he sends the forms. 2 months go by. I finally get myself to fill the god damned things out. go to a notary public. all that shit. drop letter with forms into mail. the other day I got another letter from royalty dept. "sorry, but we sent improper forms. would you mind filling out the enclosed forms?" now I sit around and look at them. if I fill *them* out, it works like this: I mail them to the Dept. of Internal Revenue U.S.A. there are 2 copies. then the Dept. of Internal Revenue is supposed to mail one of the copies to the United Kingdom Income Tax dept. and then I don't know *what* they do. inform Penguin that I am in the clear or something? it looks like a process that will take months or a year. I don't suppose this would bother anybody but me. I can imagine a guy like Corrington blithely filling out the forms with hardly a thought, and even feeling good about it. [* * *]

[To William Hageman]
June 21, 1968

[* * *] write-up on Ginsberg meeting Pound in current *Evergreen*. Ginsberg comes on poetic and phoney. Pound talks straight English without the lacy bullshit. Pound I think has found out he had *style* but the content was educational, a kind of structural flow that took care of itself, sounding well but not ever really ever *saying*. too much of anything. that's what always pleased the college boys—the whole thing was a very stylish yawn—which takes some *doing*, don't get me wrong. Pound was worthy. but I think he knows now that he was just making a good pudding instead of hellfire. esp. now that everybody is bullshitting him on how great he is; a kind of ass-kissing before a death that must be very near. for us, too, maybe. but he's older, surely. [* * *]

83

by the way, certain things I don't like—that is, the new boys coming up and thinking that they are changing the language. I've been watching this since 1932: "&" instead of "and." "laffing" instead of "laughing." I don't even want to go into it. it becomes boring. not that it might be wrong, only that the boys hu r duing it thinks its sompin gnew ... not their fault that they are not as old as me and the woodwork. (by the way, when you see an "&" in one of my poems it is put there by some damned editor.) [* * *]

The third correspondent mentioned below was Douglas Blazek, who later did in fact return Bukowski's many letters to him (see Volume 1). Corrington apparently never did so.

[To John William Corrington]
October 15, 1968

well, how to begin? I wrote you a lot of letters one time and NOW I want them back. now, wait wait. a certain Univ. is offering me quite a bit for my little mags, notebooks, paintings, books and *letters* that I have written to others. a lot hinges on the latter. the letters. there would be enough money for me to take a year or two off and simply write instead of dying on that post office stool where I have been for ELEVEN YEARS. often nights down there I've felt like I'm actually going CRAZY. or I get these dizzy spells where I hold to the case as everything spins. the old soul is simply saying, no, no, no, no more please! I do need more time to write [* * *] I need the letters to get free, break into the open and get some downfield blocking. I'm 48; I've played the tough drunk who spits blood out of the side of his mouth long enough. I need a little breather. o.k.

yeah, o.k. so I have written these various poets, 2 or 3, so far that I have written letters to. one, no answer. the second just sent me back a kind of literary essay, badly written, with no mention of my request for letters. the 3rd just sent me a kind of juvenile bit about how he rather kept those letters under his soul's pillow and how they saved his life when he had to put in those 6 tough years at the foundry. he just *can't* part with them now! oh, no no

84

no, ask me ANYTHING but that! his wife now works while he pounds out reams of poetry that is getting duller and duller.

so, it all works out. I've said for 3 decades that the poets were shits and they keep proving me right. and if I *ever* write any fucking memoirs I'm going to name names and shits. it's about time we bombed the stinkers out of their closets. anyhow, there are 3 or 4 more to write to, one or two women, say 6 more all told. if I get completely shut out I don't ever want to hear the word POET in the same room I am sitting in. I have explained to all these people, will explain, have written a couple again who didn't seem to hear well the first time—I've explained exactly what this will *mean* to me. these fuckers write about LIFE but it's all shuck. that's why some of them write so badly. they'd rather kill life than live it—mine or theirs.

so, Willie, for Christ's sake mail me the letters, set me free. I remember returning all yours upon request one time when I lived at 1623 N. Mariposa. lining the things up on the rug and trying to get them in order of date before sticking them in the envelope. I'm not playing angel, Willie, but when you asked for your letters back it never *occurred* to me to say "no." it wouldn't make sense. that's just the way my head works. I hope yours works the same way. [* * *]

well, man, curve ball or straight?

[To John William Corrington]
November [?28], 1968

all right, I am a shit and of the breed, but at least you had class enough to say you'd send the letters, so fine, it means a lot, a break, I've got this collector-editor working with the univ. library, and he's a good boy, I mean he knows how to *talk* to these librarians, I *don't*, so I leave it in his hands, and he's doing the whole thing without fee, the guy simply likes me, but of course it means giving up many things I have: tapes, paintings, notebooks, magazines, books, typescripts—really cleaning out the closet, and I'll prob. feel better after everything's gone—like a bad woman you think you needed, ya know. so, *do* send the letters. it's fine of you, and will prob. help me get a year or so off from the grind, and much going on now, I need the TIME— [* * *]

p.s.—oh yes, also, if you could send your own letters back, the ones you wrote to me, *that* would help too. think of it, man, it's almost like being dead—the scholars pawing over us, and it wasn't so long ago that I was running errands from the corner bar stool for sandwiches and newspapers. don't return this letter. it's for the bathroom wall. yours. and listen, thanks again for all.

●

•1969•

Hugh Fox, then teaching at Loyola University, Los Angeles, wrote Charles Bukowski: A Critical and Bibliographical Study *(Los Angeles: Abyss Publications, 1969), a mimeographed book on his work. Gerard Dombrowski was editor of* Abyss.

[To Gerard Dombrowski]
January 3, 1969

[* * *] Well, you asked me about the Fox book on me. You want it straight? It was dull, straight, academic and uncourageous. It was textbook frogs hopping their dull lilypad hops. Dull; I said it twice; I'll say it thrice: dull, dull, dull. THE POEM-MESSAGE or FORCE was completely overlooked in the mama-taught thing of this belongs here and that belongs there—: this is this school, and that is that school. Fuck that. I used to g.d. have to fight the bullies all the way home from grammar school to college, and they used to follow me, mocking me, daring me, but there was always more than one, and I was one, and they knew I had something packed in me somewhere. They hated it; still do.

Very well mum, you printed the Fox book on me. In a sense, it was congratulatory, but as a man who has lived in the worst circumstances of life, often not eating and not caring to; often wanting to eat and not being able to; often living for a month behind pulled shades and eating green potatoes and listening to the works of Bach and the footsteps of my landlady—knowing that almost everything was impossible and sickening—getting drunk on rotgut wine; being drunk at 12 noon and laying in alleys behind bars hoping trucks would run the life out of my body; being poked in the back with sticks by small black children as I lay senseless like some dying piece of meat; while working the factories, the slaughterhouses of the world, while being kicked off the back-end of tomato-picking trucks by those who sensed that I did not belong there; while traveling with the railroad track gangs from New Orleans to Sacramento and having to fight them one-on-fifty; while living in a scorpion-filled paper shack in Atlanta, while all the things I could go on and on with—do you REALLY THINK that I could accept the soft-Fox fucking dissertation on when I was an Existentialist or a Burroughs or an immortalist or a whatever??? I have your book around the corner, and I'm sure almost that he called me none of these—but what I mean is—he pasted his chickenshit labels all over me. This poem is this. This poem is that.

How the hell can Fox know what a poem is? He is/was taught what a poem was/is.

I am a poem.

There is no way out.

I doubt that I can match Dr. Fox's degrees. But his poems begin to sound more and more like mine. But there's a catch—ability plus experience can never match a shadow, and that's what Fox is—a SHADOW of Buk. It just ain't gonna work, no matter how hard he works. Or they. All the Bukowski copyists. Every time I get a free copy of a little in the mails, I open it and it all sounds like Bukowski—very bad Bukowski.

That's their problem.

But I do hope that some other bellowing, water-mouthed prick comes along to take the heat off of me so that I may/can go about and do what I have to do. [* * *]

[To Marina Bukowski]
September 16, 1969

Hello Marina, little one:

Every time you phone me, it is so very good to hear your voice. You have the most beautiful voice in the world. Thanks very much for phoning me. I always feel good for days and days after you talk to me. And I feel that I will see you again some day and that keeps me going. Sometimes when I get sick I think about you and it makes me well again. PLEASE BE VERY CAREFUL WHEN YOU CROSS ANY STREET. LOOK *BOTH* WAYS. I think about you all the time and love you more than the sky or the mountains or the ocean or anybody or anything. Please stay well and happy and don't worry about me.

all my love, little one,
Hank.

●

• 1 9 7 0 •

Carl Weissner, editor of a German little magazine, became Bukowski's German translator and literary agent, as well as regular correspondent and friend.

[To Carl Weissner]
January 20, 1970

[* * *] I am out of the god damned post office and I am playing typewriter-boy and painter. If I fall flat it is my own fault—the child support, the rent, the utilities still come due, and I do love the child, would hate to lose her. 12 years on the job, and then to finally quit it, cold, half a century old. The first ten days I damn near went outa my skull—didn't know what to do with my hands, my feet, my mind. I almost cracked. And after a series of drunks at wild parties and alone, I ended up in bed deathly sick, shivering, depressed all the way to hell and almost to the kitchen butcher knife. I sweated it, staring at the ceiling, unable to sleep—shades down, I stared at the ceiling while being an inch from bottom. At the same time, the bathroom and kitchen sinks clogged up, and I vomited, trembling, into the toilet and it rained outside, and then some people came by with guitars and threw all the wine bottles, beer bottles, whiskey bottles in the trash, dumped the garbage. They made me laugh, they made me get off that stinking gloom bed. And I went out into the rain with them. Nothing to eat for 3 or 4 days—my stomach raw. And I ended up drunk again...

Now I seem to have pulled together (I hope), and it seems to be going easier as each day goes by. I suppose it was a transition from the 12 year thing, and when you look at it, maybe ten days shot going from one to the other isn't too bad, what? Christ, I even give poetry readings now. [* * *]

See Charles Olson Reading at Berkeley, *a transcript of the reading discussed here, made by Zoe Brown and published by Coyote, San Francisco, 1966.*

[To Carl Weissner]
February 16, 1970

[* * *] Yes, I saw the transcript of the Olson reading in Berkeley. Frankly, man, it was sickening. He was begging to the audience, sitting in their laps like a baby. And his poems are so straight-laced. He broke out of his laces and slobbered all over everybody. He even begged people who were leaving to come back. Then a woman told him they had to close the auditorium at midnight, and he begged for a few minutes more, and then went on longer and longer. Something wrong with a man like that, sucking at the cunt of an audience. Thank god, I hate to read [* * *].

What the hell you doing reading the *Nola Express*? Lively little rag, though, courage, but young young. The govt. will finally bust them in half. All these undergrounds have this suicide complex. I think they really want to get spanked by papa instead of replacing him. I could be wrong. But sometimes they swing those roundhouse glory rights, and miss, when the steady left jab might take the whole fight. [* * *]

Dr. Renate Matthaei was editor for Verlag Kiepenheuer &
Witsch, in Köln. The fake Henry Miller blurb invented by
Weissner for the German edition of Notes of a Dirty Old
Man *and that Bukowski finds "quite accurate" reads as fol-*
lows: "Each line in Bukowski is infected by the terror of the
American nightmare. He articulates the fears & agonies of
that vast minority in the no-man's-land between inhuman
brutalisation and helpless despair."
The novel Post Office *was eventually published in Febru-*
ary 1971.

[To Carl Weissner]
February 23, 1970

[* * *] glad you got hold of Dr. Matthaei, and I would prefer
you to translate *Post Office*, of course. [* * *] The money thing
does become important when writing is your only income and
you want to go on writing without diluting your style or missing
too many meals. Also, the beer bill rises when you sit by the
typer near the window and things begin to move in toward you
from out there.

I want to thank you for some of your suggestions—you've
been a *great* moral support. In looking over the contracts in the
drawer I see I've signed quite a few. There is that tangled word
horror where I sold away movie rights to these guys for $50 while
I was drunk. I think I told you about that. 2 year option. I've got
to sweat another year and 5 months. That's on *Notes*. [* * *]

I think you'll like *Post Office*, maybe even better than *Notes*.
There's plenty of sex in there for laughs and enough horror and
madness to float the typescript to you across the Atlantic. I try to
photograph rather than preach. [* * *]

I'm not too happy with the fake H[enry] M[iller] quote, and
I would not tell Martin about it or he'd flip—maybe. But if you
think it will make a difference in selling 2,000 or 5,000, go
ahead. It's best that we survive. By the way, I like the blurb *itself*.
Quite accurate. So what the hell, go ahead. [* * *]

[To John Martin]
February 23, 1970

I answered Weissner but I enclose his letter so you'll get some idea of the German scene. I told him to go ahead with the Henry Miller blurb but not to tell you or you'd flip, and now here I am sending you the letter. So you must pretend not to read the H.M. blurb part. These Germans may save my ass yet. I do trust Weissner because he lays everything in the open, and is one of the better writers in Germany, and I think can do a better job of translating than anybody. Also met him personally, you know.

Now you lay off the beer, keep your feet on the ground, Sparrow. Remember what ol' Franky D. said: "We have nothing to fear but fear itself."

Neeli Cherkovski, then known as Neeli Cherry, was a poet and editor of Black Cat Review. *He later was to write Bukowski's biography,* Hank.

[To Neeli Cherry]
[ca. April 12, 1970]

I figured they'd run you out of Germany fast enough. But you're living without working and that is an acceptable state. I sit here by the window, drinking coffee and rolling cigarettes and watching the long-legged nurses stroll home. They check their mailboxes and quickly lock themselves into their plastic cubicles. Let them; they shit, have monthlies, fart, scream. There's a new movement here now—The Women's Liberation Movement—there are a lot of clever lesbians in it and some man-haters, and they have certain piteous points—like their breasts, but damn if I don't think the ladies have rather ruled the cock-and-ball set right along. But they claim they are not represented with dignity—not enough female doctors, so forth, and then some guy says, there aren't enough female garbage collectors, and then it goes around and around. Everybody everywhere is screaming for dignity and representation but their minds and souls are mud and shit, and how can you give dignity to shit? Guy over here other day said, "I think everybody who writes should have a guaranteed income." Why just everybody who writes? I'd like to see most writers put into those ovens you were looking at. guaranteed. [* * *]

[To Carl Weissner]
April 14, 1970

great, my friend. I'm glad one of the Melzers finally stirred into action. [* * *]

sorry all this bitching and money talk shit, Carl. but it is part of the stew. but I felt all along that whether I got the advance from Meltzer or not would be the thing that made me or broke me. it's just one of those things, Carl. once I get rolling here, learn how to better operate the ship, I feel I might go on, in spite of all. now that Meltzer is coming through the scene changes to one of hope. I mean hope of survival. there should be a way to get hold of my health, and the writing is coming along like a stampede—no dizzy spells there—wrote 35 *new* poems in the last 2 weeks. as good or better than any I have written. have also started a second novel, *The Horseplayer*. I am writing it in a more leisurely fashion than *Post Office*, which was quick-paced because I wanted it to be—because I didn't want to preach, only tell. first 2 chapters on the *Horseplayer* all right; in fact, the first chapter is a classic. I even had to laugh myself. I may never finish the H.P. or I might. Not pressing it.

sometimes I get in here, writing, writing, lounging, in trance-state; a couple of days go by and I realize that I haven't even been outside, and there I go—fresh air! sunshine! walking down the sidewalk, and then, friend, that first human face ... [* * *]

The Days Run Away Like Wild Horses Over the Hills *was published on December 30, 1969.*

[To John Martin]
[? March–April 1970]

[* * *] I slipped off again, a week or so ago, but it was not nearly the agony trip that mid-January launch-out was. And each time I come back down, I am stronger again. These 2 good paintings today are an indication that the old Bukowski is coming back. Sardonic, easy—fucked-up but basically steering the wreckage. You won't be able to laugh at me over the phone any more as my voice quavers. Hitler is back. Thank God and the angels and the collected works of Turgenev!

The nurses are coming in now and I look at their legs and their asses and I love them. I am back at the old window. [* * *]

Yes, the Cal State thing. Felt shitty reading. I don't like it. It is just a survival sort of thing that must be done. But the guy who set it up said he had never heard such a good crowd reaction since ... anybody. Well good, so I was lucky. And I did have the Sparrow brochures which I walked around handing out laughing, saying, "Buy this, mothers..." If you have any ads left, ship me another bundle. Giving a small reading up at a rich dentist's place, booze and broads, lambs turning on spits in the fire, all that shit. But I will keep them off my soul, which is mine and mine only, next Sunday, but if you have any ads I will jam it to them. I am worried that you might have published too many copies of *Days* and I want to help you hustle them off. Right on, right on ... Hey, I see where they called out the National Guard to protect my archives at the Un. of Santa B[arbara]. Good stout lads all!

[To John Martin]
[? April 1970]

meant to get these off yesterday, but 2 young guys by, and so there went a whole afternoon. they didn't like Henry Miller, they didn't like Pound, they liked Celine. then one of them handed me one of his things. I didn't like it.

so I'm coming in late with the work, but everything has its meaning. with these 2, I learned, mainly, there isn't any competition. one of them claimed you had to have connections to get

96

published. I said that 2 things helped—talent and talent, the connections would take care of themselves. when I was young and it came back I threw it away. everybody thinks they are a genius; that's why they aren't.

when they left, after drinking my beer, or as they left, I said, "I have Henry Miller's address if you want to drop by there."

"that's an insult," they said.

with these young guys it's always a pleasure to cut down the giants but the best way to cut them down is with your own work and I don't mean the work of your jaws. if Henry Miller had walked into the room, they would have shit and fawned all over him. the only reason they come to me is that I am the Image of the Loser, the Man who doesn't care, the Man who didn't quite make it, the man who will drink a beer with a bum. what they don't realize is that I *do* care, would like to do my work, and have the kindness or the cowardice not to cuss them and send them on their way. unfortunately, people like something in me, they can't let it go. I will simply have to work around it all and still do my work. my old theory while working ten to 12 hour nights and days in the factories and in the post office has always been, save what you can, don't give in. the theory stands now; whether my work holds up depends upon what is left of me.

and so that's kind of a bitch but that's o.k. because I know when I am bitching I am all right. [* * *]

[To Neeli Cherry]
May 10, 1970

little here. I am hanging on. just came off 2 weeks at the track, got way ahead, then gave it all back. I've made up my mind that I don't know anything about horses.

action in U.S.: student strikes at universities. Nix moved into Cambodia. National Guard fired on students at Kent State. wounded many, killed 4. then at Univ. of New Mexico, where I'm supposed to read this Friday night, the National Guard bayonetted ten. Prob. later in month I'm going to read at 2 colleges in Washington. I'm not like you. I hate to read. but no money coming in right now. the bank account is sagging. [* * *]

nurse pushing an old woman by in a wheelchair. it's sad, sad. I'll never get that old, something will kill me first. or maybe I'll bury you, spit on your grave from my head of white hair, rotten Andernach teeth grinning in the sun, rolling a cigarette and farting.

before the horse bit, wrote 50 new poems in 3 weeks, most of them quite good, maybe not from your viewpoint but from mine. and that's the one I go by. now I'll be in all the littles again just when they thought they had buried me. Blazek's gonna shit. there goes the old woman again. I'm running out of magazines to send to. even *Evergreen* took a poem; also lucked into *Stony-brook*—Creeley-land—with quite a number. there's little doubt that getting out of the post office has given me more time and energy. it's good, though it's hard sometimes facing my own mind 24 hours on 24. a job keeps you from thinking. [* * *]

p.s.—Martin going to publish novel. the Germans also want it. 3 companies interested. so I'm going to get up typescripts for each and take the highest bidder. I feel like Hemingway. gotta get a shotgun. [* * *]

[To John Martin]
[May 10, 1970]

sad letter. the system fell apart and I gave them their damned money back. worse was all the time wasted. well, that's out of my system anyhow. now back to playing the literary game. [* * *]

I can't agree with you on the dictionary idea for the novel [*Post Office*], but if you insist, we'll go ahead. keep writing down words. I think though that most of the terms are obvious, even to an outsider. but I'm glad enough that you are probably going to do the novel, so I'll compromise if nec. I do think the dictionary has a cheapening and commercial effect, however. Think it over a while. [* * *]

Lafayette Young had sent Bukowski a small gift of money. Niki is his daughter. Carson McCullers (b. 1917) was not *the daughter of Kay Boyle (b. 1903), whose story, "Rest Cure," was first published in* The First Lover *and Other Stories (New York, 1933).*

[To Lafayette Young]
May [?], 1970

I just read stuff, very little of it at that, only what goes for me, and so I am not an educated man in many senses. Did I *understand* you properly—via *Harper's Bazaar*, Nov. 1943, that Carson [McCullers] *was* the daughter of Kay Boyle? Too friggin' much, if true. Kay was a beautiful woman. Her style was way ahead of her time. I used to see many of her short stories in *Story*, where I was first published, 1944, just before my mad ten year drunk that almost took me out. Wasn't it Kay B. who wrote that short story, "Rest Cure," about the death of D. H. Lawrence? It would be very miraculous if Carson were actually the daughter, I mean had been, of Kay Boyle. Anyhow, I remember "Rest Cure," and if Kay Boyle didn't write it, she should have. As per her novels, they were not as tight as the stories. And comparisons are hell and unkind, but I'm afraid Carson outwrote mama. I'm afraid Carson McCullers just about outwrote everybody. I used to read Carson McCullers in bed in cheap rooms while I was starving and drinking wine and it was holy—my skin shivered and crawled and I didn't cry because I was too proud of her to cry.

Don't worry about alcoholism; it keeps us from committing suicide.

As per Niki and her "The Lost Generation," I hope she got it right. Those were interesting people, Gerty and Hem and Fitz and the gang. That gas station mechanic who called it the Lost Generation, though, was either an utter Romantic or he had nothing to compare it with. There can't be any generation more LOST than our present one—being born into a war-after-war era, the Atomic Age, the Pollution Age, the Computer Age, all in one. They should be LOST, they know. There has never been another generation as knowing and as brave. They don't even call themselves lost. rather, they say, hell, let's straighten it out. Stay in there Niki. [* * *]

99

Black Sparrow Press had published Dorbin's A Bibliography of Charles Bukowski *in 1969. A videotape of the Bellevue reading mentioned below was published by Black Sparrow in 1988.*

[To Sanford Dorbin]

A Monday in June? yeh. 1970

Sandy fu Chris' sake:

[* * *] Took the train down to UNM and read there. drank there several days and threw off a drunken half-fuck. then back, and a plane up to Washington where I read at West. Wash. State College that night, got drunk, insulted the profs. got real sick drunk and was awakened in an upstairs bedroom at 8:30 the next morning and told we had a long ride to Bellevue for a reading at 11:30 a.m. good God Jesus. I kissed the prof's wife goodbye and we got in the car. stopped for refills. meanwhile, no eating. as approached college started heaving out the window. no time to stop. heaved right up into the parking lot where I staggered out and into the building and started reading, dead sick, and the bastards put me on video tape, and I got a few drinks down as I was reading and managed to bring it off. away to this cabin and more drinking and more drinking at the airport—I missed my plane while sitting in the bar over an hour early—finally got in only to find a certain lady wanted to see me and I stayed with her 2 nights, or she stayed with me, I mean, and more drinking, no eating—food, that is—and I finally put *her* on a plane, and then back and trouble getting straight, coming down, and it's easy for me to see why it killed Dylan Thomas, but I think if it ever happens again, I'll go a little easier. The readings came at a good time, a money-lag time. the sex mags, everybody, hollering "tight money." Even Norse lost 2 sponsors he's had for years—tight money, they say, and the market. so, it's a shitty time and the hustle is on. so understand, I am hanging to the branch; not with a rope, a thread ... whatever, that means....

on articles, well, yes, there's my name and somebody's done some work, but you know if I took the things seriously I would no longer know who I was—well, I don't anyhow—but I think you know what I mean. I mean if I were to comment on certain aspects of the article I'd feel as if I were talking about my cockhairs, my snot, my eyeballs, my brain, my heart, my gut, and I don't know anything about them. they operate me. I suppose I am not very clear today. I've been hav[ing] a 2 or 3 week battle with 12 or 14 Islanders who live in rotating shifts in the court in the center. we park on the front lawn. the landlord has lost control of this place, except to collect rent. the bastards keep blocking me in in hope to make me give up parking there so they can move in another one of their 6 or 7 cars. I am a bit outnumbered and they go to all means to block my car so I can't get out, even to parking across the front of me by using the apartment house driveway next door. I go crazy over shit like that. I've mailed in for a 9 inch switchblade. this morning I got them out of bed and made them move a car that had me blocked. I came back and got blocked again by another car. mad. I stop them one by one as they walk by the door. "Hey, buddy, got a minute? I wanna have a little talk with you. What's wrong with you guys? Now, I'm not a hard guy to get along with. But why in the fuck???..."

there's always some god damned thing. no women. or having a woman and having a lot of shit trouble with her. or hangover. or parking. or toothache. or money slipping away, or just the general stupidity and viciousness of the human race. I think I'm going to have to move the hell out of here. I can't fight them all.
[* * *]

[To Neeli Cherry]
June 4, 1970

drinking beer, waiting for Marina to come over.

fridge shot. things getting tough. Knight-Adam hollering backlog. Out in *Evergreen* for a week now but no check from them. read within 2 weeks at Univ. of New Mexico, West. Wash. State College and Bellevue Community College. 660 total, no 600, but no travel expenses, and drinks, airflight, drinks, taxi, drinks in the airport, buying drinks for parties, almost lost on the deal. got laid a few times by sweet young things, tho. long drunken sweaty fucks. now back, still trying to get sober. bankroll diminishing. it looked so good for a while. I might have known. if you ever come back, look for me on skid row. this time you won't have to drive me down there. [* * *]

I can't beat the horses any more. I must stay away. I wish I were back in the post office. at least they dulled my mind and tired my body. now everything comes at me with knives out, there's no rest, no relenting. it's balls away. I'm on the cross.

In fact, I'm tired of writing. what's the use?

[To Neeli Cherry]
June [?18], 1970

fighting a battle with 14 Islanders who have suddenly possessed a court in the center. have sent in 3 bucks for a 9 inch stiletto. I may go but before I do, they will know that I have been here. And I'm not talking about poetry.

yes, I've had 2 or 3 good young fucks lately—the poetry con, you know—but now that it's over I hardly feel any different. it just doesn't work, and the strange idea has crossed my mind that a man may be able to exist quite nicely without sex at all. I like the color of their dresses, the way they walk, handle their buttocks, but I wonder if all the rest is needed? the sweating, the farts, the agony, the come, the declarations? the dirty sheets, the stink and the closeness?

the most beautiful woman is the one who walks past your window and then she is gone. [* * *]

ate at Norm's the other day, sirloin special dinner $1.35. found a seat at the counter, at the end, fine, nobody in the next seat, then just after I ordered here came this fag in and he sat next to me, ordered a coffee and he made that coffee last all through my meal. then he kept looking at me. I thought, next time he looks at me, I'm going to straighten him good. he looked again and I turned to look back, I was going to say, "What the fuck you looking at?", but when I turned he looked straight ahead, quickly. then he jumped up and left. but I was finished eating. the mother had ruined my meal. [* * *]

[To John Martin]
June 22, 1970

[* * *] the boys are bad-mouthing you for publishing Forrest. one phoned and said he was on KPFK, unbelievably bad, and Cynthia fawned all over him. I said, "oh yes, is that so?" somehow these poets seem to think that I am supposed to defend Black Sparrow, and I feel like doing so since you have done and are doing some good things for me. but, basically, you have a right to publish anybody you want to. I think of something John Thomas told me one night, "No matter what you do, a certain number of people are going to dislike it, others will like it, and the vast majority will not give a damn one way or the other." Once you understand this, the snipers will not make so much difference. [* * *]

Gerald Locklin had published Sunset Beach, *a book of poems from Hors Commerce Press, Torrance, California, in 1967. He has since published many further volumes.*

[To Gerald Locklin]
July 4, 1970

Hello G. Locklin:
    yes, I was a bit pissed on your non-arrival [for a reading at The Bridge], having built you to the mob. I don't often step out to recommend a poet, but had seen your stuff in *Wormwood* and recognized a new tick and flare, a decent originality. for my money, which ain't much, but anyhow, for my money there are only 4 poets around doing it now—you, Ron Koertge, Bix Blaufus and, er, Bukowski. there may be others—I hope there are—but I haven't seen their work. and I get sent many magazines full of listless and stupid pages. so I'm glad you're there, anyhow, even if you get your dates mixed up. I have a prejudice against teachers, but if the work is strong enough, fuck it. Bix is going to teach somewhere in Oregon in a few months, and he's as real as catshit.
    [* * *]

103

[To Carl Weissner]
July 5, 1970

[* * *] all in all, I seem to be surviving; of course, your getting Meltzer to come through was a big spiritual boost, the shot I needed and I sat down and rapped out 3 or 4 dirty stories, immortal, and some other shit. there's energy coming from somewhere because, for the time being, the days and the nights are mine, and if I fuck them up it's not nearly so bad as somebody else fucking them up for me with a time clock, you know.

this is a shitcan letter, it's so hot, fan on my ass, but it's not all bad, even got laid a few times lately. the ladies come by and knock on the door, and that's rather nice you know? even when I strike out I get a few grabs.

like I say, this is a shitcan letter but wanted you to know I think about you, you've done some good things for me, Carl, and all I do for you is holler and moan my troubles. so this is basically to let you know it's not all that bad. there's always PANIC especially when I hit the streets and look around or go into a barbershop or a supermarket. but that has always been there. I've learned more to live with my panic like a man sometimes learns to live with a bad woman. of course, now and then it gets too much, it can't be helped and one simply drinks until the pleasure of unconsciousness. you learn how to do that too.

so, it's o.k., the war is forever. [* * *]

[To Lafayette Young]
July 12, 1970

[* * *] you know, I almost go mad sometimes, like this year, total days fucked away and torn up. but all and all, it is better than it has been. I've gotten more writing done this year than any 3 years previous. it has to happen without a job in the way. now I get in the way, but it's realler, I can't blame any boss any wife any job any kid for ripping me up. I am the enemy, and it's good for laughs—sometimes. and the luck is good. like last night I was going to write myself a kind of grade b quicky short story for one of the underground papers that pays me 20 bucks a story. they

are good people, so I don't try to write them shit. let's admit it, my grade b stuff is not too bad. so I rolled a cigarette and brought out the beer and turned on the radio to some symphony music and said, well, it'll take about an hour, I'll take it easy, enjoy it and get it in the mail. so what the hell happens? halfway through I see that I've got a grade a story and that makes the rest of the writing better too. so the undergrounds will have to wait— it's off to *Evergreen* or one of the sex mags and Bukowski is lucky again. It's called "All That Pussy." so all I need is beer and smokes and half a swing and I'm a writer. [* * *]

[To Neeli Cherry]
July 12, 1970

[* * *] so feel good picking your apples even if they are fucking up your head; at least you don't have to worry about foreclosure, all that shit. even I seem to be surviving, although there was a frightening dip in reserves a while back, it made me dig in, write a half dozen immortal short stories and a hundred new poems, almost all of them quite good. get me near the cross I SCREaM LITERARY. now Sunday, drinking beer, rolling smokes, sitting in this dirty place, barefooted, gut hanging out, watching the dead Sunday people walk by. I even eat at Norm's now and then when I am too lazy to cook, get that dollar thirty-five special and watch the waitresses' asses joggle about in their sweaty panties and the cook sweating and dazed and trapped over all that hot tin. found best to go in about 3 p.m. I feel like a millionaire. I don't drive but walk down and walk back, slowly in the sun, feeling like a jr. league Hemingway, spitting shreds of tobacco out of my mouth from that first cigarette, and watching the people rush about here and there in panic. [* * *]

[To Carl Weissner]
July 23, 1970

[* * *] read at Long Beach State College at noon yesterday, sober, with the sweat running down the arms. hard money. $50. they don't pay a man a damn until he leaves the state. also threw a young guy off my front porch a couple of nights ago. he was standing there pissing, a huge swath of curved piss right into the bush out there, and I get very tired of guys pissing on my porch—women never piss out there—so I picked the guy up and hurled him over the bush and into the night. he didn't return. [* * *]

yes, Martin has me worried. I'd prefer *Post Office* in its original raw form. of course I was a little bit out of my head when I wrote it, but it wasn't sloppy or lazy writing; it was written as it fucking well came out, and that meant turds and blood and the rest of the wash. I'm told that parts of it are in the present tense and parts in the past. that's all right with me. I know most of the rules of grammar but I'm not interested. he has inferred that he doesn't want to detract from my style, so there we are on the merry-go-round. he's a nice guy but he does treat me too much like an idiot. he admits I'm his best seller but at the same time he'd rather I wrote more safe shit. what the hell. well, maybe I worry too much. I'll go along with the single tense, but I feel the rest must stay. we'll see. I get depressed writing about it. [* * *]

[To Carl Weissner]
August 8, 1970

[* * *] The novel will be issued in the Fall, says Martin of Black Sparrow, which prob. means Winter, if I know publishers. Martin has done some good things for me and one thing he is worried about is that the Germans might get hot pants and bring out *Post Office* in Germany before it gets out here in America. He wants to be first. So I said, "O.k., we'll simply tell them that the novel can't be released in Germany until it is released here. O.k.?" When I talk like that it gives me a feeling of immense

power, as if I were some 1970 Hemingway instead of an old fuck who is trying to keep off of skid row. [* * *]

[To Carl Weissner]
August 20, 1970

[* * *] these people are on me again for the sound of my typewriter and I'm a little pissed tonight—not at you, old buddy. they make all kinds of shitty noises but a typewriter is verboten. was drunk one night and cussed them back—"Yeah! You and your fucking dogs! Calling your dogs all the damned time! MICHELE! HERE MICHELE! Why don't YOU shut up all *that* shit noise!" I'd been drinking about a week, trying to forget my 50th birthday.

when I go out on the street Michele barks at me. "Chew his leg off," they tell the dog. I ignore that. bastards own the high-rise next door and are afraid the sound of typer will disturb their dear tenants. I dress in old clothes, need shave, red-eyed and hungover. they dislike me and my sounds and my looks very much. they like to see a man vanish at 6:30 a.m. then come back in in the evening, eat, flip on the tv. they have hours of leisure but all they do is sit on their steps and walk their dogs around and collect rents. I don't know what they are waiting for, what they want and I don't care. they want me. that's one place I would like to see burn. those people are completely dehumanized by their jobs and their walls. this society is unbelievable; they all do the same things, talk the same way, share the same hours, *look* alike (MY GAWD!), like and dislike the same things ... never seen drunk in the streets, or in anything but freshly-laundered clothes. and they *don't like* my typewriter! what precious rum dum shit! what snail slime! what framed turds they are! they may have bellybuttons, elbows, assholes and all that ... but they're completely DOWN THE RIVER, out of it, useless, worse than useless, not as good as a dead sparrow ... may their asses rot on burning spiral points in hell FOREVER!!! fuck. [* * *]

[To John Martin]
August 25, 1970

hope you'll keep filing my stuff for me—I'll put you on salary some day—yeh. I have a rough first draft which I sometimes keep and which I sometimes lose, and also many poems sent out are never heard from again. so it's for the good of the Cause. my Cause.

I miss the horses—they kept my juices stirring and also put a little money in my pocket. Del Mar is just too far to drive without auto insurance. Garden Grove, where Marina is, is far enough. I just don't want a bunch of litigation on my neck for a freeway crash. that's not my idea of living. [* * *]

haven't heard from Weissner yet—wrote him at his Spanish address. I hear he's busy translating Warhol's "a". maybe I should have mentioned something about Carl's (that's Weissner) novel. his publisher sent it to me. I didn't. it's one of those cut-up Burroughs things and I've always been bored by those things, I can't help it. the publisher asked me to review it but I couldn't review it and be honest without hurting Carl's feelings. so there's always some shit. [* * *]

[To Carl Weissner]
August 31, 1970

[* * *] sitting here with a busted mouth after a week's drunk. really feel freaked-out, sick, pitiful. the blues, the depressive fits. I even wept, soundlessly. it's so much trouble just going on and a man gets tired of being brave.

anyhow, your letter cheered me. you have a way of saying kind things without bullshitting, and then your stuff is funny too, you know. anyhow anyhow I must guess that you are as desperate as I, only you take it better. fucking recession over here—god damned crap asses just don't want to let go of the buck. they *sit* on manuscripts now and when they finally accept them they delay payment until eternity. I'm speaking of the short story field. [* * *] so anyhow, this old rat's not dead yet. and the poems and stories keep popping out of my ears. this year I must have written 150 new poems, a novel and maybe 30 short stories. now all this stuff is not excellent but some of it is—sometimes I think I am just fucking away everything but the typer keeps doing it. and it comes out easy. tons and tons of shit. my machinegun sure—tattattattat a tattutuetutuetattutattu… [* * *]

[To Neeli Cherry]
September 1, 1970

[* * *] I may have to go to Greece and beg in the streets. recession here, everybody hanging to the buck. mags that used to pay right off don't anymore. one outfit has owed me $175 for 3 months. now they owe me 175 for a later acceptance. I can't live on OWE. all the other mags just sit on manuscripts for months—*Evergreen*, all of them. It's a real tight frightening situation. [* * *] lately people have been telling me I'm famous. a shit hell of a lot that does—the money's slipping away and I'm on the skids. I'm still hustling the poetry circuit—around here—for pennies. even read at a coffee house in Venice—$55. christ, I'm sweating raw pure blood. [* * *] my novel, *Post Office*, will be out in Nov. hope I get an advance. Black Sparrow. man, the post office wasn't too bad. I thought the life of the writer would really be the thing. it's simply hell. I'm just a cheap twittering slave.

Univ. of Chicago writes they want me to read there in the fall. well, that's something. I'm fighting a slow desperate retreat, my mind, money, resources slipping away. [* * *] I have to write a lot of poems to keep from going crazy; I can't help it. I often write ten to 12 poems a day and then top the whole thing off with a short story. I may be going crazy but it has been all hell on production. I just hang on top of this typer and scream it out. wrote the novel in 20 days. 120,000 words, 30,000 of which I pulled out on the re-reading. one outfit in Germany tells me that they will buy the novel "unseen." *Notes of a Dirty Old Man* out in Germany, translated in the German. got a good review in *Der Spiegel*—equiv. to *Newsweek* here—one million circulation. photo and all. only they had me down as a native of Bavaria or something. poor Andernach. anyhow, for all this shit, there isn't any money showing.

meanwhile there's great violence in the streets here. men shooting each other, bombing each other. a guy tried to run me over in an empty parking lot last night. I just leaped aside in time. the stuff is catching. much hatred, confusion. [* * *]

Robert DeMaria was editor of Mediterranean Review, *published in Orient, New York, to which Bukowski had submitted some poems.*

[To Robert DeMaria]
September 2, 1970

"How come my x-wife thought Robert Graves was the greatest man alive?" Well, you see, my x-wife was a snob and she touted Robert Graves and other such cumbersome creatures because then people would think (she *thought* people would think), surely this little blonde creature must have BRAINS. Got it? O.k.

Definitely a pain to send poems to such places as Spain or England or hell because you have to get those International Reply Coupons and the clerks don't know what they are or how many you stick in, and I won't ask them. You know.

Will try you with another batch of poems soon. Your remark, on your last rejection, that my work was not carefully worked-out left me on high dry ground. Of course my work is not carefully worked-out and hastily written. that's the point. I write down what I need. poetry has long ago dulled me with its tricks and mechanics. or maybe the poems I sent you were just lousy. I write a lot of those.

[To John Martin]
September 4, 1970

like you know, you've been a big help to me, allowance, the Univ. of Santa Barbara thing, typewriter, paints, many things. And I can't expect you to worry about me day and night. don't want you to. you've got a one-man operation going that takes all your energy, and you've just finished straightening out my novel and mailing it off, so to bug you or put an extra weight on you is not my point. but it has been a real frozen mailbox lately. I don't know what the hell is going on out there (the magazines), and the bankroll is dipping, I'm far from starving to death, but can't help feeling concerned. I know how fast money goes when it's not coming in—the allowance is a lifesaver, of course, but I can't help thinking—and here I am bugging you—that the Blazek letters have been out about a year. It does seem an overlong time for no results. We had such a hell of a battle getting them from Blazek in the first place, if you remember. Also Dorbin told me he got paid his royalties on the Buk biblio. Didn't you tell me that I was also to get royalties on this? I know that there are answers to all this and that you are an honest guy, so I've hesitated. I realize that you are so damned busy with everything that you can't worry about my precious little irons in the fire—like I say, night and day, but hell, that mailbox worries me, and if you don't *ask* you don't find *out*. yeah, I know, I worry too much and I've got it made. o.k.

now I suppose I've spoiled your day. I'm Carol Bergé. writers are a shitty lot, I guess.

so here's another short story. don't rip it up but file it away as per usual, o.k? Celebrating Marina's birthday tomorrow so she won't have to come over on Labor Day. She'll be 6. good god. well, I'm doing a lot of writing but it's any good or not, I don't know. anyhow, I feel like writing and when I feel like writing there's some bit of warmth in the words. meanwhile, don't be pissed...

[To John Martin]
September 7, 1970

I WORKED labor day. see enclosed.

Marina had a nice cake Saturday, 6 candles but asked that we didn't sing Happy Birthday To You. the kid has some sharp. mama packed off to Synanon and we played for 8 hours. mostly she was Batman and I was Robin. then we painted, went for a long walk. then I played dummy. a familiar role.

where are your eyes? she asked. (I think of that sometimes too.)

and I'd point to my ears. my eyes? dose are my eyes.

no, no, Hank, *those* aren't your eyes! your eyes are here! (poking fingers into my skull)

hey, hell, kid, that hurts!

now, where are the pockets on your shirt?

pockets? shirt? well, I'm a pocket, you see ...

no, Hank, look ...

anyhow, it was a nice birthday, for Marina and for me.

and you're 40 and I'm 50 and my landlord's 60 (and built like a bull) and we're all going to die, and that's o.k. too. that gives us whatever beauty and power and grace we might have now. you know this. and, also, that this has been the most magic year of my life. it came late, but it will never be forgotten—even the horror of it. that's why I hang in now, fighting for a bit more horror. it may be beyond the imagination but by living carefully—fighting the slow retreat—I hope to squeeze out 3 or 4 years more before I have to get a job as a janitor or a dishwasher or go on relief. I'm sure you understand the picture, big Jawn, and even when the end comes down and I'm swinging that mop in the lady's crapper or facing some unloving creature across a desk in the frig. relief office, that the 2 or 3 good years will reside within me and they can't take those back. it's been a beautiful ball and a beautiful hell, and I'm talking too much.

when that brush gets too smooth in the tape machine, might as well replace it, you're going to get nothing but water on the tape and the frig. tape won't stick to the box. also when you're cutting a box down to size, cut *up* from the inside so you don't damage the merchandise.

the old shipping clerk, Henry.

[To Carl Weissner]
September 8, 1970

[* * *] I am coming out of about a month of deep black pure depression. one day I had to actually hold on to the mattress with my hands to keep from going into the kitchen where the butcher knife was. mixed-up situation, what? I've been in this court too long. stir-crazy. got to get out, walk somewhere, drive somewhere, do something. [* * *]

[To Carl Weissner]
September 18, 1970

[* * *] maybe I'm going crazy but I'm thinking of writing another one, *The Horseplayer*. a novel, I mean. don't know where I'll be able to dump it, but I guess write it first is the idea. in *The Horseplayer* though, once I write it, I will insist that all the bad grammar be left in and past and present tense be left in at the same time, if that's the way it happens to be. Martin claims that very few changes were made grammatically in *Post Office*, and I believe him, but I wish the few changes had not been made. everything counts. But I've read *Post Office* twice and even liked it better that 2nd time. that's a good sign. well, like I said, we'll see.

yes, most revolutionaries just love to talk and talk and talk. yes, there's a bomb now and then but sometimes I wonder *which* side plants those. my revolution is a one-man revolution and almost everybody is the enemy. I may not be doing a great deal of damage, but at least I'm not bullshitting. [* * *]

[To Carl Weissner]
September 21, 1970

[* * *] After a bit of a dry spell, things are looking up over here. A few sales to the mags for stories and even got *paid* for

some poems. jesus. also doing a series of columns, short, called "Hairy Fist Tales," for *Fling*, a Chicago sex rag. [* * *]

You know, I've tried the starving writer bit. I guess it works with many. I write better with a few bucks in my pocket. Give me a half mile lead on the wolf and I'm tough as hell. I call it STAYING ON TOP OF THE GAME. This doesn't mean that I write for money; this means that I'll have money so I'll be able to *continue* writing. Of course it's going to end, but since I gave away the first 49 years of my life, this part is very strange. Indeed. this morning I stood on the front lawn, sun coming down, I was barefoot, nobody around, all these highrises, everybody off somewhere on their fucking crosses, and I stood there in the sun, haven't shaved in two weeks, hair uncombed, ripped shirt, 4 buttons missing from the fly of an old pair of army pants somebody had given me, and I smoked a cigarette and grinned into the world, knowing its shit and its blood and its plan, but I was in this special space somewhere for a moment, and it was quite good, quite. by god. of course, the butcher knife is still in the kitchen and I keep it good and sharp on the stone steps and that's part of it too. STAY ON TOP OF YOUR GAME, BABE, STAY ON TOP OF YOUR GAME. and a little bit of luck is nice too, but don't look for it.

[To Lafayette Young]
October 25, 1970

[* * *] I have to drink and gamble to get away from this typewriter. Not that I don't love this old machine when it's working right. But knowing when to go to it and knowing to stay away from it, that's the trick. I really don't want to be a *professional* writer, I wanna write what I wanna write. else, it's all been wasted. I don't want to sound holy about it; it's not holy—it's more like Popeye the Sailor Man. But Popeye knew when to move. So did Hemingway, until he started talking about "discipline"; Pound also talked about doing one's "work." that's shit, but I've been luckier than both of them because I've worked the factories and slaughterhouses and park benches and I know that

WORK and DISCIPLINE are dirty words. I know what they meant, but for me, it has to be a different game. [* * *]

[To Lafayette Young]
October 28, 1970

[* * *] frankly, most editors look at the writer as some kind of idiot, and in many ways he is. I've met quite a few of them and I've been taken on some deals myself. the writer, the real writer is only concerned with writing, writing that NEXT thing. you know, it's quite like that good fuck you (or I) had 3 months ago. who cares? it's tonight's or tomorrow's or the last one that counts. it's NOW. NOW IS THE ONLY LIVING BREATHING REALITY. when somebody tells me, "Bukowski, I really liked that poem 'The Priest and the Matador,'" I say, "yeh." who cares? I'd just as soon piss on it. that's why at poetry readings I read only the stuff—with one or two exceptions—that I've written in the last month or two. everything else leaves me dead and I read it dead. [* * *]

jesus christ, I've even been printed in the Dutch. DRONKEN MIRAKELS & ANDERE OFFERS. just got book in mail today. nicely done offset. Title means something like DRUNKEN MIRACLES AND OTHER IMMOLATIONS. combo of two poems "Rain and Transport" plus "Kaka and other Immolations." I was only sent one copy so can't send any to you or Jimmy [Pitts] or Katz, who have all been very good to me in my times of hell shit fire gloom. but don't think issued in many copies (really don't know) but if I may sound like a prick, it will prob. be a collector's item worth maybe 25 or 50 bucks in a couple of years. see, there we go talking money again? see how they suck us in? let's be careful. it's just a funny odd book and you can probably get it for a buck as a curio piece for the crapper. let's take it that way. no price listed. if you get one, mail to me, I'll sign it. [* * *]

Linda King, whom Bukowski met in late 1970 and who was "destined to become Hank's longtime girlfriend," had four sisters who shared her literary bent. See the letters of January 12, 17, and 18, 1972 and Hank, *pp. 211 and 216.*

[To the sisters King]
October 30, 1970

My dear sisters King (or however it has been changed):

    you have put much energy and time into writing me; I have no way of knowing, but I would judge that you are both living together, off of child support, something went wrong with the men, but the courts are fair, aren't they? hmmm? very well, diddle with Bukowski. wouldn't it be nice to put him in our female cage and poke him with sticks?

> kill a coward and be
> brave. that's
> unity.

look, girls, it's nice to have you visit. I like girls about. an old dog like me should. and I do. just to look at. but even sex, that's no big go to me. after 2,000 pieces of ass, what's one more to me? one more strip of tinsel on a tired xmas tree. I pay child support, voluntarily, and gladly, I love my daughter. but sex to me is almost so much bog. I mean, you do it, that's nice, and then it's over and then what have you got? 2 chunks of flesh looking at each other and waiting and resting for the next trip. I write about sex like I write about anything else—mainly because I think it's tragic and funny. if you want to know more about the game, do try reading *The Decameron* by Boccaccio. *Notes of a Dirty Old Man* or all my poetry are nothing compared to his explicit laughing understanding of the thing. he's in your public library. me, I'd rather just talk to women or rather listen to them than fuck them. if I must fuck them, they must do most of the work, most of the coaxing. maybe I am queer? call me queer if that makes you feel better. they always call strong men queers. I've heard Hemingway mouthed as a queer. this is society's way—they won't leave a man alone. I'm a loner. I want to do my work, drink my beer and die. It's nice when the ladies knock on my door and are pretty, as both of you are, and giggle. but actually

116

there's only one thing less predictable than a horse and that's a woman. don't bet on either one unless you want to take odds-on when you should be getting one hundred to one on your chances.

about dumbness (stupidity), ya got me all wrong—how can I have anything against it, when I don't know anything about it?

now, girls, let me get back to my business. you must realize that I am just an old guy with no visible means of support? now let me turn on that red light out there and spread my cheeks with vaseline ... ok?

your in deepest penetration
and understand and love
and looove and broken
ladders

Robert Head and Darlene Fife were the editors of NOLA Express, *an underground paper published in New Orleans.*

[To Robert Head and Darlene Fife]
[? October 1970]

have been drunk for some weeks ... this is no brag shit thing ... don't like it ... mind very heavy, fog-shit, you know. but grass and various other shit ... speed, so forth, not worth a cat's ass. death of Hendrix did not bother me. Janis Joplin death particularly saddening, terrible to me because to put it shittily, I related to her. she had the courage of a mountain, understand? don't worry about vocal chords ... wrote an 8 or ten page tribute to the guts of Joplin but so filled with love, I had to destroy. [* * *]

Listen, you know I am high here or I wouldn't go on like this with this shit ... yes, got 2 copies of ... what was it ... the issue ... I asked for. many thanks. the archive shit pays off. I'm lucy, not lucy, lucky. or maybe I'm Lucy? eh? all right. they used to have a thing called Lucy and Desi Arnez, perfectly sickening ... barely remember it, but knew right away, 2 people sucking at anything they could get at any price and fooling everybody, almost every body. That Desi Arnez, he had such a bad band (that's what they used to call them in those days: "bands"), how'd he ever get hold of Lucy? And, so what the hell, Lucy just began to look sillier and sillier, playing stupid parts, eyelashes getting longer, and more lipstick on and more slapstick on, and I don't know, this isn't hatred, it's just high, and I knew the cocksuckers of the world would bring them down, so fake them, so fake all, the final gods are very hard to fool. all right, how did I get into this garbage except to explain what it is? [* * *]

If you guys can line me a couple of readings in N.O. to cover plane fare and room and booze, would be nice ... would like to meet you both just for chicken-ass kicks ... no hatred. have long gotten over hatred drunks when I used to clean out houses full of people. now quite gentle even when totally loaded. took me a long time to learn. [* * *]

[To John Martin]
November 1, 1970

[* * *] they tell me your Wakoski is reading at Pomona College Dec. 7, flying in from N.Y. She has a nice loose and human style which I think she learned from me, but that's all right. if she has a weakness, it is the inability to write a good short poem. but few people can. Jeffers couldn't. Pound could. In fact, the shorter he got the better he got. I always liked him for that. But when he got long—*The Cantos*—he shit himself. the test of a good poet is one who can write any number of short good poems. W. C. Williams did it once, as we know. I haven't done it, prob. won't. I'm not a great and yet the greats bore me terribly. there really haven't been any strong people on earth yet and maybe that's the way the game is built. an ant is an ant and what can you do with an ant? there's an occasional flash of something now and then, but the guy who flashed hardly comes up with any more. it's hardly right, is it? when the fucking soul is trying so hard? and then you end up looking at a face like Nixon's and he's the same guy who flunked you in English I and with as little reason.

but there have been strong men—the same ones I have mentioned—Fyodor Dos, Celine, Artaud, Kafka ... arising out of the

118

billions and billions and zeroes produced and reproduced, almost for nothing—I do suppose that there have been stronger men, but circumstances simply drowned them away from future communication with the centuries. or, you take a man really strong enough, he can look around at the age of *four*, take some instrument and kill himself. swimming pool, anything else. [* * *]

[To John Martin]
November 6, 1970

[* * *] just think, someday after I'm dead and they start going for my poems and stories, you will have a hundred stories and a thousand poems on hand. you just don't know how lucky you are, babe. remember Marina. shouldn't be so serious, I know, but she is to be my literary executor, or whatever you call it. all royalties should go into a *trust* for her until she reaches the age where she is entitled to it. That name is Marina Louise Bukowski. [* * *]

all very serious, I know, and all the poems and stories may well rot, but it is a dark afternoon, and one thinks certain things...

[To Neeli Cherry]
November 20, 1970

[* * *] Guggenheim, all those prizes and grants—you know how they go—more money is given to people who already have money. Shit, I know a prof, friend of Corrington's, can't write a cat's ass...he wins a prize every year...usually the same one... and he goes off to some island and works on some project, meanwhile still getting paid half salary for doing nothing at the Univ. he's supposed to be teaching at. on one of his island trips he put together an anthology, even put me in it, but didn't even have the decency to send me a copy. "Old Man, Dead in a Room,"

119

he used. now, that took a lot of imagination, didn't it? I'll be an old man dead in a room soon enough as long as they keep baby-spooning these literary idiots. [* * *] I don't even know where to get the *papers* he fills out to win his shitty prizes. and if I did, they'd only write back, "Sorry, but…"

well, it all helps keep me pure, yeah. [* * *]

[To Lafayette Young]
December 1, 1970

[* * *] it was good meeting you, you know that, and thanks for all … that fine motel bit, the transport, you … all that. you are a gentle and easy man … I hate to see them laying it into you down there … hope you've come out of it by now and are eating a little … but your family lays it into you because they love you, man; nobody understands an alcoholic … I started drinking young … at 16 and 17, and the next morning I'd always get it—those looks, that hatred. of course, my parents hated me anyhow. But I remember saying to them one morning: "Christ, so I got drunk … You people treat me like a murderer …" "That's it! That's it!" they said, "what you've done is worse than murder!" they meant it. well, what they meant was that I was socially disgracing them in front of the neighbors, and there might be an excuse for murder, but for drinking … never, by god, no! They must have meant it, because when the war came on, they urged me to join the murder … it was socially acceptable. [* * *]

[To John Martin]
December 15, 1970

[* * *] Celine's *Castle to Castle* a horrible book. Of course, they really kicked his ass … threw him in a stinking pit … cancer ward afterwards … stole all his books and manuscripts, kicked the shit out of his motorcycle … what a grand chance he had to lay it into them by being objective … but he had to bitch and rail

120

right down to the last stitch. he had all the tools to crucify the sons of bitches, but he couldn't do so: too close to his belly-button. well, it's too late.

all right, everything here is a mess too. papers all over the floor. gloom like spiderwebs. I seem caught in my own corner. It's round ten. and they're pushing me off the stool. I'm behind on points. Face of a madman. lace on left glove undone. can't see out of eyes. who started all this shit anyhow?

p.s.—next day—yesterday's phone call was nice but now that we're off the free $100 per month, life will get grimmer. christo-mighty yeah. so we've got to start scratching. [* * *]

[To Lafayette Young]
December 21, 1970

well, the amateur drunks have taken over and will hold this town until Jan. 2 ... driving on the wrong side of the street, run-ning red lights, bellowing the same songs. figs of people, twigs of people, shits of people ... MERRY CHRISTMAS, HAPPY NEW YEAR. Christomighty, yeah.

I drove down to get Marina today—Santa Monica—we're still in tune. The few people who knew always laughed at me because I talked to her like an adult. I still do. she's 6 now but it's the same as when she was two or three. this had nothing to do with trying to elevate her mental hygiene—I'd be the worst for that. the worst one, I mean. but she's gotten used to talking to me and I've gotten used to talking to her and we listen to each other; we're serious about it but we laugh a lot too. like today, we decided to get some wrapping paper [* * *] and I said, "Now, look, Marina, see all those people trying to get into the Thrifty drugstore parking lot? The lot is already full and they are just going to sit there for hours, or maybe ten or twenty minutes wait-ing for somebody to pull out so they can park. So, we're not going to do that. We'll just park across the street a half a block away and *walk* in." Which we did. [* * *]

Marina was so beautiful and happy at her grammar school xmas program ... Christ, all she wants is love, to be *noticed* ... she glows and I glow back; it's almost unbearable ... not to bring out the crying towel, but both my parents hated me. But that has nothing to do with it: she brings the miracle to me, and *I* respond.

O.k. man, to hell with kids and Christmas talk. [* * *]

[To John Martin]
December 23, 1970

[* * *] There have been some pretties coming around in their minis, flashing me all that leg, smiling from the couch. I just sit there and glower, thinking of the trap. "I'm through with women," I tell them. "My pecker still gets hard now and then but a little cold water takes care of the problem." They just laugh. They think I'm joking. "Oh, hehehe, you're *so* funny!"

One of them wants to sculpt my head at her place. I told her, "O.k., give me a ring sometime in Jan. or Feb. and I'll trot on over. Where we gonna sculpt? In the bedroom?"

"Oh no, we have a nice secluded place in the backyard ..."

Thanks for not sending me the Creeley xmas card. Not to be a bitch, but after I've read one of his poems I really don't know what he's said, and then my next reaction is, "O, what the fuck. Forget it."

Hello to my dear telephone-relay message girl, my Barbara; don't ruffle the Sparrow's feathers, he's been bitten and smitten by the poet lice ...

hang in.

[To John Martin]
December 27, 1970

have been crawling through one of those depressive fits that seem to fall upon me. please believe me, I am not trying to play the sensitive Artist bit—that's sickening. I only wish it wouldn't happen. It's just like all the walls fall down upon me. I've almost analyzed it—it happens mostly after I have been on a drunk with 2 or more people. I don't understand it—I can drink more, all by myself, and don't even awaken with a hangover.

[* * *] 1970 was my most magic year. the horrors increased and the joys, and the typewriter became more real, instead of an afterthought. I don't know how much longer I can g.d. sluff off those most real ghosts with sharp teeth … age and booze dull the soul … But the post office would have killed me within 2 more years. my thanks to both you and Barbara for understanding a lot of it. [* * *]

●

• 1 9 7 1 •

Laugh Literary and Man the Humping Guns, published by Hatchetman Press, was the literary magazine that Bukowksi edited and published in collaboration with Neeli Cherry from February 1969. It ran for three issues until February 1971.

[To John Martin]
January 6, 1971

only one poem enclosed. those crayon drawings have drained my ass. went down today to cash a check for one dollar from Univ. of Calif. at Berk. girl looked at deposit book—it said: *Laugh Literary and Man the Humping Guns*; also, Hatchetman Press. she started blushing and giggling... "pardon me, sir, can I ask you what this is?" "it's a magazine. as you can see, we are going broke." "o, I think that title's terribly funny, sir." "that's nice. I only wish somebody would buy the magazine...." the girls always react to those titles; they really get heated as if they wanted to be raped.

last time I went one of the girls told me, "O, I think this is so *cool!*" then she walked over and showed it to another girl and then they both heated up.

what the hell. after centuries of magazines being named *Circle* and *Ante* and *Blast* and all that dry grease, we finally break the mould. what happens? First a letter from Blazek, inflamed, claiming that we were corny, exaggerated our purpose, on and on and on and so forth and so forth. what the hell. so what

125

happens? now all the new mags coming out are named like this: *When John Rode His Bicycle West to Fight the Indians,* and so forth and so forth....

anyhow, I took my dollar and walked out of there and came back here, walked into bedroom and here are two women's legs sticking out from under the covers. a dead body! that drunken bitch from ... I threw the covers back. just 2 legs. my landlord is a very funny man. he's so god damned funny that some day he's going to give somebody a heart attack.

all right, unward, I mean *on*ward and upward and out....

[To Lafayette Young]
Jan 6, 1971

[* * *] the book I guess will be out soon. I am playing with my little crayons. Look, pal, don't expect a *War and Peace.* well, that's lousy ... I mean, don't expect another *Journey* by Celine ... no excuses, shit. I wrote it in 20 drunken nights and I mean *drunken* ... just a flash of hell. a lifetime shot and nibbled at in a decaying room by a decaying man. I'm not a novelist; it's too much WORK, and so it really isn't a novel. oh, hell.

some girl in her twenties, just out of a madhouse, rather hanging around now and then. I find her *quite* sane, quite lovely ... especially the color of the eye and the way it looks at me. she's quite nice to me but most women are at the start ... then they trap you in, and BOOM!!! ... the wake-up ... and you think, after all those others, you should have known better ... men are too adventurous ... esp. old men like me ... whiskey, women, horses ... same old song ... then you're in the cage, wondering what happened. [* * *]

Post Office *was printed in January 1971 and officially published on February 8.*

[To John Martin]
January 22, 1971

I sent the ad (flyer) on to *NOLA* and asked that they run it. I guess they will. It should swing some sales. Don't forget to send copy of book to Ben Pleasants. There is a possibility he may review it in the *Times,* though we have no way of knowing. He has tried to run stuff on me before but they always cut it off. But there's a chance. There's definitely an anti-Bukowski thing going on, has been for years. For instance, I'm supposed to read at The Other Side Wednesday night (the 27th) but the dear old *L.A. Free Press* didn't run it in their Calendar section, which means I'll be reading to an empty house, which would be all right with me except the poet gets the entrance fee per head $1.25 minus ten percent. Los Angeles has always been the roughest town on me because I am basically an isolationist ... well, enough bitching. so I'll have to go through with it anyhow, so leave Wednesday out as a signing day. [* * *]

Now there's something else going. I didn't get all the names. Katz knows this publisher, so forth. all the letters I've written Jimmy [Pitts], Katz has them. they are locked up in a vault by Katz and no human eye sees them. JESUS! there's your laugh for today. anyhow, the human eyes that have seen them think that they are pretty good, along with those I've written to Lafayette Young, and Katz wants this publisher to run them—*The Letters of Charles Bukowski.* I have an idea that the letters to Jimmy Pitts were not so excellent but those to Lafayette Young, I put something into. I don't know if you ever met L.Y. but he's one of the finest people I've ever met.

So I told Jimmy I'd have to check with John Martin and then he got a little unhappy. So what do you think about this book— proposed book—John, while you're thinking of everything else? Do you have a moment to give me some thoughts on it? [* * *]

[To Gerald Locklin]
February 8, 1971

[* * *] Gerald, you can't be an honest man *and* a book reviewer at the same time. Honest men are supposed to write books and salesmen are expected to review them. Of course, not many honest men write books, but you know what I mean. [* * *]

[To John Martin]
April 7, 1971

back in after battles and love and madness on 2 Arizona ranches...haven't heard from Santa Barbara yet. perhaps the stuff is too dirty for them. we shoulda taken the 1500. a bird in the hand.

still trying to put together the book for Ferl[inghetti]. taking too long, I suppose. haven't heard a word from him. heard from Weissner who says Meltzer willing to give $500 advance plus ten percent royalties for *NOLA Express* stories plus *All the Assholes in the World and Mine.* will have to check City Lights contract on foreign rights. the problem is getting the shit to these guys. I've been cutting out the *Nola* stories—slowly—and putting printer's instructions on them. and I only have one copy of each paper. in fact, I even lost one copy with my best story in it—"The White Beard." I don't know what the hell. there aren't enough hours in the day. and after mailing this, I'm going to drive over to Burbank to play around with this woman-woman. maybe I don't know what I'm doing. it seems there has to be time to live, time to write and time to scrounge up materials and answer mail and so forth, type shit, or clip it out. I'm hardly bitching. for I'm still alive and the action is banging the walls, but—

Weissner sends a copy of *twen* (german mag) with reprint of Thurber story. W. says in the introduction to the story they say, "If we weren't sure he would turn it down, we would recommend him for the Literary Nobel Prize." See how the game goes? No wonder writers go to self-love, the way they powder them up. For me, it's pure gamble every time I sit down to this typer.

Nothing is ever easy. I never know if I can ever do it again. A man can never call himself a writer; a man is always an x-writer.

like these poems enclosed, I feel that they do not quite shake loose. It's been a bad year so far for my writing. April already. Maybe the juices will explode like mad marmalade? soon?

[To Carl Weissner]
April 10, 1971

have been back in frozen state—not getting any work done. wild hot love affair with beautiful 30 years old sculptress, been going on some months now. I don't know what she wants with an old guy like me but since she's around I give her plenty of ACTION. kind of like trying to hold onto the tail of a female tigress at times, though. she did 3 weeks in a madhouse some years back and she's plenty unpredictable. She just came off a ten year marriage and looking for breathing room. I give her room. But afraid I'm hooked in—her delicious mind, body, et al., and the way she makes love … jesus. well. [* * *]

I'm on the wagon as much as possible because I have to fuck so much now, go down, so forth … [* * *] I was fucking during the earthquake, it simply added to it.

Bukowski, with John Martin's help, had sold his first literary archive—consisting of manuscripts, magazine appearances, and letters to him—to the Library at the University of California, Santa Barbara, for $5,000.

[To John Martin]
April 19, 1971

[* * *] just 2 poems enclosed. since the luck with Santa Barbara I have decided to take the leisurely approach. the poem must work itself up without whip or bait. there won't be as many

but I feel that they will be better. the stories too will probably drift a bit away from the sex motif. for the first time I've felt I can take a breath. I think the writing will be of a higher order. well, we'll see, won't we?

I really feel that I can allow myself to feel good—for a while anyhow. it's a matter of pace and tide and hidden elements. the boogie man is drunk and we have picked his pockets.

fly. why walk?

Charley the yea-sayer

[To Carl Weissner]
April 25, 1971

ass drag from giving shitty poetry readings [* * *] and also a battle with the tigress for acting like a silly vamp. she doesn't fuck the boys but she just about tickles their balls in front of me. very highschoolgirl stuff, and I'm supposed to react to that by tickling some other gal's cunt. cheap vengeance, you know. fuck, Carl, I been around too long to play children's games. however, at this time, the tigress and I are still mating. for whatever it means. [* * *]

well, I don't know how poetry does in Germany but Martin phoned that *The Days Run Away* is now going into a *third* printing, which I understand is some kind of record for Black Sparrow. so they do read poetry out here. [* * *]

Cherry was co-editor of Laugh Literary and Man the Humping Guns.

[To Neeli Cherry]
[mid 1971]

[* * *] I also enclose the subscription order from the University of Chicago Library. Don't lose it down the envelope,

130

somewhere. I hope you are taking care of these university sub-scriptions, Neeli! I am busting ass reading this garbage coming in and sending it back. It takes hours and there are more submissions each day.

This Univ. of Chicago thing is easier. They don't ask for the quadruplicate shit. Do your job, kid.

Heard from Bennet who claims he sent a dollar and never got his copy. He was a bit nasty about it. Instead of mailing him a copy, I sent him a dollar and told him to roll it around his Hava-Havana and jam it. Also returned his work which was lousy except for one section. He's the former editor of *Vagabond*, now lives in Frisco in a $175 pad while his wife works for him. He writes, "I'm never going to work again." How do these guys do it? Where do these women come from? That support the half-ass and incompetent Artist? ah, shit!!! [* * *]

[To John Martin]
June [?5], 1971

here it is early June and I'm still batting .189, but I figure if I hit .400 through the rest of the months, the damn things just gotta climb. I believe that slumps are somehow necessary. meanwhile, I look around and notice nobody else is hitting the ball either. [* * *]

my love life is eating at some of my time but for this you must forgive me. to make writing and life and people work all right is a full time job. luckily, there's no post office. I absorb. I think it will make the writing better. trust my instincts, what the hell. I think about you quite a bit and must realize you think I am fucking off. I am always a student, John. I will die a student. it would be wonderful to continue to survive as I have. you have no idea how things have opened up. torrents rush all over me, man. everything will be there. you know what I mean. [* * *]

131

[To John Martin]
[ca. June 19, 1971]

things are difficult, of course. haven't they always been?

Packard (*N.Y. Quarterly*) writes of the poem "A Well-Known Poet and Myself," "Couldn't possibly print this poem of yours as it would blow the whistle on too many of our leading poets."

perhaps he is joking. however, I've often had the feeling that the whole game is jaked-up, jacked-off. o.k., I'm bitching.

listen, kid, who you got in my spot in left field? you know damn well he can't hit a curve off his wrists. soon as they find that out he's gonna go zero for 24 and I'll trot back out there on the green, .287 maybe but good in the clutch, rbi, and when I get a hit it's a hit, I can't run anymore.

I can't run anymore. The fight grows deep. That's the way it should be.

hang in.

[To Carl Weissner]
June 22, 1971

have been backed up in a wake of shit and my own insanity ... cops by the other night, 2 cops and a citizen carrying a shotgun. the tigress had busted loose but was gone, having left behind bits of glass and broken booze bottles everywhere. these scenes keep occurring, battle after battle and hell, I don't know if it's worth it. even a good piece of ass is only a piece of ass and when the price gets too high you don't pay it. but like she sez, things are never dull when we get together.

[* * *] right now I've got to take out the garbage cans once a week and bring them back, also must drink with the landlord and landlady to hold rent down. what I do for the world of Art, nobody's ever going to understand unless I talk right out and maybe give them a nosebleed on my deathbed. shit, I hope I end up with a bed to die in. [* * *]

[To John Martin]
July 1, 1971

[* * *] go easy on me and my gal friend. It's painful, of course, but there are benefits. and don't forget Scott had his Zelda.

"listen," I tell her, "you're not going to push my ass around because you're 20 years younger."

"and you're not going to push my ass around because you're a writer," she tells me.

a writer, I think, so that's it. I thot it wuz my good looks.

she'll do a sculpture of you for $200, John. She's pretty good.

I got my sculpture free.

(or so it says here.) [* * *]

[To Neeli Cherry]
July 12, 1971

for Christ's sake, man, enclosed this order from *Either/Or.* we can get rid of 20 copies. also those ten on that other order—that's 30 copies, that's 18 dollars! that will give us close to 70 bucks and I'm having rough shit with $$$$$. this is REAL MONEY FOR US. WE CAN SPEND IT! think about it. [* * *]

Hank Malone is a poet living in Detroit.

[To Hank Malone]
July 13, 1971

answering yours NOW of May 4th, this year, which shows my mind-state. god, yes. well, I've always been … ????? stacks of paper … dirty sheets … lost manuscripts … beer bottles and shorts under the bed, the blues, the deep down blues. peak of elation.

such shit. age, age. the streets. the dirty clouds. well.

as per a "literary conspiracy" against me, I suppose that a great many do hate me—much of it caused by my writing style which is rather unpoetic. also in my drinking moments I have caused difficult feelings, I suppose. no excuses, man. also, in my own short stories I am often the bastard-villain of the pieces. I guess I am convincing. also I don't mingle much with the literatti. literoti, eh? .... no New York City or North Beach up at Frisco, none of that. I am the loner. people come around here, I beer-up, and I have a tendency to run them out the door. all in all I suppose I have given off rays that I am a son of a bitch. they almost have me believing it myself.

I seem to be surviving, which means writing dirty stories, being lucky and giving a few poetry readings. I don't ask the universities to read, I wait on them, and although I have gotten quite a number of readings I suppose I could get more ??? if I pushed. but I am the bullhead, and so there you go. Univ. of Arkansas made me a recent $300 offer (total) but shit you put in plane fare round trip and all I have left is a used pork chop bone. so I'm waiting for some Univ. near Arkansas to toddle along and make me an offer, which prob. won't happen. I cry the blues, haha.

guy over other night claims this woman is pissed at me. She wrote me from Univ. of Wisconsin offering a year's professorship, claims I didn't even bother to answer her letter. Truth is, I never got the lady's letter and I told the guy I thought it was bullshit and the guy said, she doesn't bullshit, you want her address and I said, no. I just feel it's bullshit. or maybe I want the death-shroud. my god, what's wrong with me?

well, I guess the game will end soon enough. meanwhile I sit by the typer here writing Malone in Detroit, so all hail, and luck, may the power stay on. it is a fight in hell. but not just for the writer. but maybe for the writer it is worse because he keeps the light on, keeps studying the embankments and the snakes and the dogs and the whores and the snails and the people and the streets, and it's all bound to cut in and take a bite now and then, mostly now, and what a game, it's like getting knocked down in the first round, the lights whirling, and there are sounds and you swing, and you're brave and you're a coward, and it's the sound of the typer against everything, and everything's much, and you know this, so hang in, then, hang tough.

[To Carl Weissner]
July 13, 1971

[* * *] the tigress is in the other room writing a poem, typing a poem about the night both of us went ape-shit. I have two editors and a professor pissed at me. standard procedure. have only made it with one prof, been drunk with him and his wife 3 or 4 times, real easy nights, good talk—one Bix Blaufuss. Also one other prof, one Andre Sedricks, but he was too good a guy— Univ. of Kansas, they let him go, last I heard he was working in a bean factory. [* * *]

Saw Norse the other night, afternoon. Took tigress over and Norse and tigress talked about Spooks, Visions, Dreams, the Astral Dome of Revelation, man, I was OUT of it, but it was interesting enough. plus I have more or less been on the wagon and I have to learn how to TALK ALL OVER AGAIN WHEN I AM SOBER. I am like a baby trying to find its speech. well, learn learn, you know, that's what keeps the pecker hard.

I read at a poetry benefit for Patchen who lives in Palo Alto. Bad back, sure, yes I know. o.k. but I sat and listened to the poetry and that was bad back too, you know. had to fall off the wagon to maintain sanity. rich guy's house in hills. after the reading was over I served the folk from behind the bar. each drink I served I poured one for myself. don't remember getting on in. but here I am, several days later, looking out the window at DeLongpre ... tomorrow I take out the garbage cans to help hold down the rent. next day I haul them in. ah, the life of the Poet, sweet Jesus, but it's too late for anything else, I'm too ugly now, too insane, too old, I am just going to have to luck it. and the best luck is to keep this typewriter HOT. yes. [* * *]

we are hanging in here, we are going to make that siffed-up Papa Death work a bit to get us in the corner. Why not? That fucking coward has been picking on people, animals, flies, buildings, streetcars, stockings, shoelaces and mattresses and birds and flowers and fleas and streets long enough ...

[To John Martin]
August 2, 1971

damn, I can't think of a title or titles of proposed book. my head is empty air (smog-filled). I suppose they'll come along. a little list. but sometimes I wonder how you're surviving. all these people who knock on my door are out of jobs. and I sit here playing at being writer. it's very odd. sometimes it feels like a movie I'm watching. girls, booze, phone ringing ... hours of madness ... hours of luxury ... hours to wrestle with like an octopus in a tank. of course, it's going to be defeat, finally. but it's much nicer to be defeated on my grounds than on theirs. very important. almost magic. the magic defeat. meanwhile, the war is still on and here's a couple more poems, old boy.

decidedly yours, Henry Armstrong

[To John Martin]
September 12, 1971

Thanks for the stamps, big dad, but I see the Waldorf towers a long way off, if ever. A bare survival unto death is my dream. The life I live now is dangerous but good. And I think too that in my second year at it the writing is gluing itself together more. Although the enclosed poems are more comfortable than great, I think a few goodies sit waiting, smoking cigars and talking in the waiting room of my head. And I haven't thought of a title for the next book of poems but will work on it SOON big boss. —oh yes, the sculptress and I split continually; I always think it's over; next thing you know we're back together again. mercy, reason and logic have very little place in my life. great then.

the flying ace, Major Henry

E. V. Griffith had published Bukowski's first book in 1960,
Flower, Fist and Bestial Wail. *See volume 1, passim.*

[To E. V. Griffith]
September 27, 1971

The 50 looked good, doctor. I don't know if you know but I quit my job at age 50...a supposedly good civil service gig...a couple of years ago and am living on my luck, so all such checks contain an immense spiritual as well as practical lift. Practical in that it allows me to go on and spiritual in the fact that it allows me to go on in the way I want to. I think my writing has upped itself since I quit work; there's more energy and more humor and more life in the lines. But actually, I didn't quit the job for the good of literature, for the good of The Poem, but because the Motherfarting job was really killing me. I was in the doctor's office once or twice a week, one thing or another. I couldn't lift my arms up to my shoulders; my whole body was one mass of pain; white blisters broke out on the tops and bottoms of both hands; dizzy spells...man, I was DYING FROM THE UNHAPPINESS OF DOING THE OTHER MAN'S THING FOR 50 YEARS. I suppose a writer is not supposed to be too happy is he? I have moments of great depression now when I think I am going crazy, but I also have hours to LOLL AROUND IN LIKE BEACHWATER, and it fills, man, it fills like sunlight and love. I deserve a small slice of minor contentment; I have it coming; for this moment the gods are letting it come my way. Total suffering without relief is useless.

Then too, the love of the female is more apt to come around when one is rested, when one is a bum, when one is lounging over a typer with coffee and rolled cigarette at 3 in the afternoon, then love is more apt to arrive. Love doesn't like time clocks and some dog giving his guts to a punch press. All I am saying is that things have been mighty damned good...meaning I am surviving, I am paying the rent, the child support, the health is bouncing, the love is good...I take out the garbage cans and bring them back in to knock ten dollars off the rent. I sleep until noon and go to bed at 2 or 3 a.m. And I've learned to live with that typewriter. I mean, I wait until it's ready, or I think I wait until it's ready. I still write bad stuff but it's all in the flow, in the working, it counts, it helps somehow. Don't get me wrong, the world hasn't changed, and I know I can be out on the street soon enough. I've even gone up on the hill with the bums and taken them beer and beans and crackers and smokes. They live in the trees up there above the freeway. It's green and it's quiet and it's tolerable if anything is tolerable. But there ain't any mailbox up there and you can't very well type or write up there. But the luck is holding. The Black Sparrow books, *Days* and *Post Office* keep going into reprintings and there's a new book of poems coming up, and also Ferlinghetti says there will be a book of short stories soon. I've been lucky in the fact that I haven't gotten famous and rich through, say, a one-shot novel via a big publishing house. The gods have let me go on like this, getting by. It's good for the inner springs, the old gut mattress. It couldn't be planned better if I had chosen the way myself. [* * *]

[To John Martin]
October 5, 1971

I'm a bit depressed but, then, haven't I always been? I do like these poems, tho, better than the last batch I sent you, but, like you know, maybe out of 50 poems written, maybe one comes through as it should. I have learned to wait more and press less, and I believe that has helped the writing. I now figure that I am *writing* when I am doing nothing and that it takes a lot of doing nothing in order to write. What I mean is, that sorting mail while waiting is destructive; doing nothing is doing something...we learn so slowly and when we've almost learned it all, it's about too late.

I wanted to enclose the letter from this editor saying that Creeley stated that I was the only poet that he disliked, but can't find it. I'm plenty up on Creeley, I almost dislike all the poets. But, then, he's intelligent. [* * *]

138

Los Angeles, Calif.
Oct.31, 1000 years from heaven
one nine six two 4
                night, dak...da'k...

        Dear Jon and Louise:

                        well, since no pomes I mite as well
        untrundle the old bullshit harp, but it's not bullshit when
        I say I get your tired card and not the job has you by the
        throat, and worn, and I send a white prayer of luck and love
        for whatever good it might or might not do, and yes, send
        a page if you get around to it. there's nothing like bein-
        tired and tired and tired so you can't sleep or think or
        hope, but if this book comes anywhere near what you did
  with IT CATCHES I will know that the good angels are near you
        even if they refuse to do the slave-rote work of drudgery and
        guts. I wish I could say something to help you through except
        that I am so often in muddled state and tired too, but if it helps,
        and it might not,--a book like this lifts my life way up into light
        whether I deserve it or not. I used to have a theory that if I
        could just make one person's life happy or real that would have
        been otherwise then my own life would not have failed. It was
        a good theory but a few whores ran me through the wringer for it,
        but I do think that for a while a few of them enjoyed not being
        spit on for a while, and so this made it o.k. for me. --if
        this seems mixed up--worked overtime last night again and
        out to track without sleep, traffic, heat, blurs of horses
        and numbers and sweating flanks and thighs of sad wild
        women, o, --andnow I am pouring POURING down the beer
                the beer
        listening to some opera in the kitchen
                                I'd like to open you a
        can now but I am afraid I must drink for both of you--Frances
        and Marina Louise drinking up each other in the bedroom--a real
        love affair, and you should see M.L. look into my eyes while
        I carry her around--that intent frown and open clear-eye look
        so unbought staring into my dazed life and I feel edgy a bit
        as if she could spot the fink in me but she just seems to keep
        looking looking looking... a powoful bread, those little blue &
        thinking veins in that soft curving perfect dome. o.

        if this letter seems drunk ignore it, I do not intend to
        tear it after I let the easy river flow, I'd feel drunk anyhow
        now on water; I sense powder-landen ##### dogs trotting the streets
        but better than all this I knew that fools and creatures of
        dread here must die too... along with sparrows and fullbacks.

        my god, that track, os, ow, ugg, listen, !!!!*****I think the worst
        part of America, and we live in AMERICA??? don't we? I think the
        worst part of America is out at the track and they stink and
        scowl and push and scratch and pick pockets and piss and drink
        and walk around with thimble-eyes, and along about the 4th. or
        5th. race with the BIG DREAM about vanished, money almost gone,
        tricked and hammered stupid again and hammered stupider, they
        walk around they look--back in rags o never out of rags back
        in the alley o never out of the alley, and where you and I
        don't particularly want to get out at any price, they do, and
        they've been stunned and stung again and I'm in there #####
        #####walking with them. and listen listen the worst part of
        AMERICANS IS THEIR TOUGHNESS; or their bluff, they intend it
        as bravery but it's not bravery it's ###########snot bluff

and I'd admire them more if they'd CRY when they hurt but
they have this silly conception that good people simply do
not do this, it's square, kosher-not, and so they go# around
with these queer almighty quare square faces of wood until the
wood becomes flesh and the flesh becomes wood and it's no
longer an act, and the soul's gone gone gone gone forever--
whatever there was of it. Of course, this happens to
all of #us finally. so. yet it seems best to hang on a
while. and then they crash out in their ##cars, their
last feeling of POWER, and sweetheart, don't get in the
way. o my no.

        I don't learn much at the racetrack. I only learn
        that everything is almost impossible and it gets me
        ready to die.

                        it's Verdi tonight. Rigolette or how-
                ever you spell it.

                I used to write letters to Martinelli, and
she'd write back, "Buk, I jus' don't have time to decipher your code...
when you write drunk I just don't have time, I am in touch with the
gods, this will be a bad year for us all but it will pass, but I
just do not have TIME to figure out yr drunken ramblings...

                                love,
                                Sheri

Well, I am pretty near drunk now and cracking
another can (of beer)and I don't want to be a
gossip a gossip but maybe I am so I will say I am
worried about Sheri palying plaÿing important which
she undoubtably learned from a master at this paly
play... Basset just on phone, phoning in drunk
from New Hampshire. Where was I? What I mean is
that if Sheri is right o.k. but if she turns out wrong
(with all the pose) she's nothing but a dirty joke. And I
don't like dirty jokes. She writes a damn good letter and
a lot of it has electricity in it but a lot of it is a learned
stance too, and I guess it comes down to how much each of us
are stancing.??? what? everybody's drunk tonight.

        what next? the paper opera goes on here no I mean the one
                        on the radio, and I've got an idea everybody's
                        drunk tonight, even Ezra, even Herbert Hoover
                        in his new bones, even Barry in a quiet place
                        protected by machineguns and vultures....
                        the kid said he lost $800 at the tables
                        but he's got years left yet. He can lose
                        50 or 80 times that. And it's krist just a
                        sniff who cares? and there you are down
                        there belting it out with the rats so you
                        might possibly if the strength is there
                        publish my poems 3100 strong. It is
                        something to think about while sitting in
                        a breakfastnook on the last day of October,
                        1964.

        4th.act Rig. coming up. where are you where ar

you tonight?

    I was going to send you my paperback
SAINT GENET via edu. materials but all envelopes
outsize weird clumsy... Not that I mean u
should read it.

    on the pomes don't worry, and I know that
if you send them back
                    they are
                              of course
                  still
                      good(?)

I am not going to read this sillyass letter but
mail it right out before I sober up

        but I am tired enough to quit this one
        everything has pretty much
        caught me up
        I just heard my wife fart in the
        other room

        very little means so much to
        me

        I remember the bayonets and
        the mud ridged and
        gaw#king brown in dead
        sunlight.

        and the ####snake crawled across the
        belly of the love of that which was
        left of me
        and that which was left of me
        was not very
        much

        and it
        died.

I just awakened with my head on the typewriter, what a sweet horrible
feeling there is hearing the breathing of this steel and fragile harlot.
nothing of woman and babe. radio still on. no police. what the h*ll.
####suppose it is all right. better than rape? better than the
ok old days? breaking anything that refflected your face, mentioned your
#name?

      fuzzy golden dull wings that will not fly
      warmth that is not really warm

           my og my,
                do hold to the tomble-wavering
                symb#ls of a greater and simpler
                reality,

                Buk

Charles Bukowski

12 - 31 - 63

"SUNRISE"

Charles
Bukowski
5-25-65

Los Angeles

December 9th., 1964

Dear Jon and Louise:

     great on the trainfare!!! my god, I hate to do it thi
way but when I got to figuring expenses I began to see
knives digging into me everywhere, and look I will bring
plenty of BEER money for us (now I can, of course!) and
enough for food and rent for myself. As I said, I'd
prefer not to stay with anybody and that includes you
good people, because we all have our ways and its best
to be alone some of the time (or alone with whoever you
live with) to let the flow of yourself flow back# in.
I won't use your floor, although (seriously) I like to
sleep with animals; it gives me a feeling of peace. My
thanks, anyhow. I hope to stay out of your way when you
are at something but I also hope to be able to lend myself
in labor, wurk, if there is any work I can do without
destroying things or wrecking the routine or making you
unhappy or getting in the way. Then too, I'd like some
time just to wander through the city one or 2 nights, a
drink at a bar here and there, not too much, and a look
around around around. now, hell, I am not interested in
picking up any women. I am not a visiting American
Legionaire or an Elk or a Moose. I've lived there twice
before--New Orleans--and it wasn't the French Quarter
because I didn't want to get up against any amatuer
artiness or misleading romanticism. I didn't. I was
on the other side of ###Canal starving with the wines.
I don't feel any different now than I did then. a
3 month's old baby girl, a magically designed book,
IT CATCHES, & 44 years on my back, but I am no more
certain of anything than I was then, not even more
calm--none of the balms that are supposed to come with
age have come along for me. I do look plenty forward
to the trip, coming back to this place of my youth,
looking around, seeing you, working with you. my thanks,
my thanks.

          bear for Marina Louise arrived in great shape and she
###went for it, Lou, and more thanks here again, and do
          you know what, the strangest thing, seeing that name on
the wrapping paper: MARINA LOUISE BUKOWSKI. 2 bears now, or what do
you call them: bruins? anyway, all great.

     also photo#s--good photos--Jen how do you do it? I'm no good at
that sort of thing, balconies etc., looks fire fun and wonderous, and
it's like Frances says: "Give these people the materials and they can
do anything."

     and the article too by Lou. you write here the way you talk, Louise
straight and easy, and don't think you weren't driving me crazy with all
these trips, I didn't know where to send the poems, the god damn poems,
and I felt that the minute I sent to one place you'd be in another, and
for the first time I thought of keeping carbons which really showed I
was cracking.

Alan Bevan appeared to like my review of LAUGHING
ROOSTER by Layton and he says maybe Layton will get
his turn when CRUCIFIX comes# out, so I guess I get
it coming, eh? No, I didn't tear that much meat; liked
many of the poems and was able to say so. Yet, on
the other hand, there was no use of laying on the
butter when acid cut# the pattern#of some of my reactio

Beecher has a nice beard. Why don't you put him
and Corrington in a paper sack and let them scratch
each other to death?

It's overtime and no days off until Xmas and this
will pay for a 6 pack and my auto insurance. building
full of wild-eyed, no-eyed dull and laughing and
frightened and gibbering people. I come in in the
morning here, I am slugged and ungathered, and there
is Frances and the child and they tell me that life
is hard for them, and it's true, it is. Then in
January I've got to pass a scheme examination that
takes hours and days of study to hold a job that I
don't want. weep for me! I pour the beer in until
I can't see anymore, trying to wash it away, but
later, it's still there. weep for me, indeed! pity
me, pray for me, burn candles, yes... France's
poetry group knocked on the door again this last
Sunday, 2 males, one short and figety and egocentric;
the other tall and dull in necktie, a comfortable
well-fed slab of meat. What do these people do with
their time? Wandering around, knocking on doors,
sitting on chairs, talking about nothing at great
length. I don't have any TIME! where do all the
        dead come from? I don't understand! I can't
        run them out because as Frances says, "They
come to see me because they know that I am
lonely." or, "They come to see the baby," and I
can't run Frances and the baby out. It all comes
to mathematics and I am Mr.Zero. weep, weep.
--anyway, #####between this and overtime and the
scheme, any poems are due to be short and splashed
with blood and weak.

You 2 hold the line while I wail. You've got
enough strength for an army.

        time going, I've got to cut this. somewhat
sick but no more blood.

    March, if it gets here; if we get there. March,
March, March!

            LOVE,

            Buk

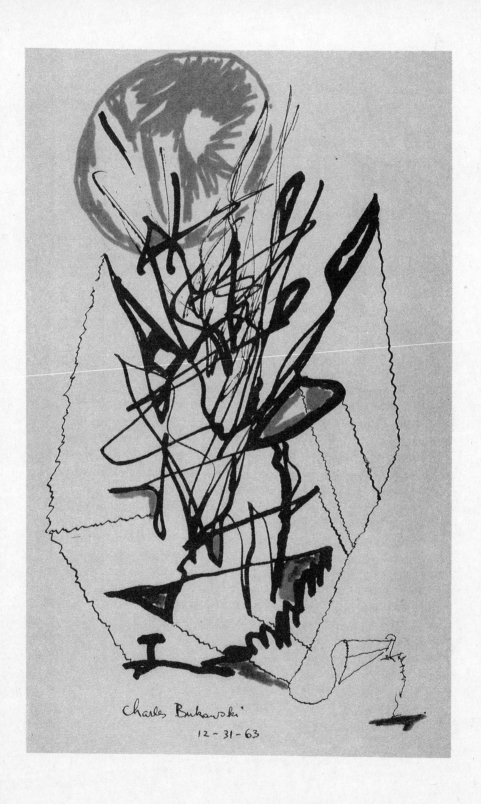

Charles Bukowski
12-31-63

Charles Bukowski

12-31-63

Los Angeles, Calif.
Feb. 17th, 1964

OUTSIDER of
YEAR
1962

Dear Jon + Lou —

I have BEEN in BED FOR past 4 DAYS WITH
COLD, HAVE BEEN POPPING useless PILLS INTO MY
STUPID JAWS — ASS BLOODY, AS USUAL (NO STOPPING
THAT) AND DRINKING BEER.

Naturally, I'd LIKE A NEW BOOK. ANY MAN
WOULD, AND WILL KEEP SENDING YOU NEW POEMS AS
I WRITE THEM — all of them — good + BAD, BUT
HARD TO SEE YOU WITH ENOUGH NEW POEMS
FOR A COLLECTION, EVEN A SMALL ONE, BUT YOU
KNOW MORE ABOUT WHAT YOU HAVE ON HAND
THAN I DO. I WRITE THEM AND FORGET THEM.
I SHOULD TELL YOU THAT MY COLLECTION OF
(REJECTED) POEMS COLD DOGS IN A
COURTYARD NOW RESTS WITH Jay
NASH of CHI. LIT. TIMES + OFFEN + PUECHNER +
CYFOXTH PRESS, AND I AM TOLD THEY ARE GOING

TO TAKE A VOTE ON IT and I SHOULD KNOW IN 2
WEEKS. I SELECTED THE POEMS MYSELF OUT OF THE
MAGS, POEMS THAT DID NOT APPEAR IN OTHER
4 COLLECTIONS. I FIGURE THE POEMS OK. IF
THE OTHER POEMS FIGURED OK, BUT THEN —
I MIGHT BE **MAD!** anyhow, I wrote a
FORWARD, did a drawing of a line of miserable
dogs — AND NOW THE JURY IS OUT. **ANYHOW,**
I WILL LET YOU KNOW HOW THIS WORKS OUT
BECAUSE IT MIGHT HAVE SOME BEARING ON WHETHER
OR NOT ~~you~~ you CARE TO GAMBLE ON ANOTHER
BUKOWSKI IN A FLOODED MARKET. — SAYING THEY
TAKE "THE DOGS." ANYHOW, GOT A CARD FROM
JAY NASH YESTERDAY SAYING HE'D READ The DOGS
AND THOUGHT I THOUGHT LIKE HEMINGWAY. SO,
I GUESS THAT'S ONE VOTE AGAINST ME. ON
THE SAME CARD NASH ASKED ME (ALMOST demanded)
THAT I DO AN ARTICLE ON THE STATE OF
THE CONTEMP. POETS AND THEIR PUBLISHERS. I
DID, BUT LEFT THE PUBLISHERS OUT.

So, I WROTE THE THING, BURIED 5 OR 6
PEOPLE AND DRANK A BEER.

MAILED YOU TAPE (3 HOURS WORTH) YESTERDAY AND
ALSO 4 NEW POEMS. I DON'T KNOW ABOUT
THE POEMS, BUT TAPE WENT FAIRLY EASY AND
LAZY, SMALL TALK.

IF YOU DO DECIDE ON NEW BOOK I
HOPE TO HELP YOU A LITTLE WITH $,
MAYBE NOT MUCH BUT SOME, DEPENDING ON
MANY THINGS — I HOPE 50$, ANYHOW, BUT
MAYBE NOT ALL AT ONCE — THINGS TOUGH
HERE NOW — 10$ OR 20$ AS IT COMES

UP UNTIL WE HIT THE 50. I WILL NOT FIGURE I
AM BUYING YOUR SOULS — MAYBE ONLY A LITTLE
PAPER AND A BEER. MY ONLY **CONCERN**,
IN CASE YOU DO THE BOOK IS

HOPING THE POEMS
ARE THERE!!!

AND A GOOD TITLE. BUT ALMOST TOO MUCH
TO THINK OF ANOTHER BOOK RIGHT NOW —
IT CATCHES STILL ALL FIRE IN MY FINGERNAILS
AND HEAD AND BALLS AND SLEEP; I STILL
GET IT WHEN I BITE INTO TOAST AND/OR
SLEEP OR WALK DOWN THE STREET.

SHERI M. WRITES. SHE IS STILL, OF COURSE,
IN POUND — CAGE, + STUBBING HER TOES ON
"H.D." BUT CHRIST, THIS IS ANOTHER
LIFE !! — THE "IMAGISTS" HAVE HAD THEIR
TURN AT BAT.

IT IS EASIER FOR SOME PEOPLE TO LOOK
BACK THAN AHEAD BECAUSE THEIR MISTAKES
HAVE BEEN SIFTED OUT FOR THEM. I
WOULD NOT TELL SHERI THIS BECAUSE SHE IS
JUMPY AND HAS THIS "I-AM-A-GODDESS"
IMAGE BUILT IN HER MIND, WHICH IS OK. WITH
ME SO LONG (AS LONG?) AS SHE DOESN'T
LORD IT TOO MUCH; HER HEAVENLY STANCE IS
$\frac{1}{2}$ OF WHAT MAKES HER MIND INTERESTING AND
I UNDERSTAND SHE HAS A GOOD BODY TOO.
(ASK OLD MAN POUND.) ANYHOW, SHE LIKED
IT CATCHES, GRUDGINGLY LIKED IT — YOUR
JOB + MINE AND WANTS ANOTHER COPY

BUT I SENT HER TO YOU. I THINK SHE OUGHT TO GET UP THE 5#

JUST LIKE THE

non-goddess PEOPLE. UH??

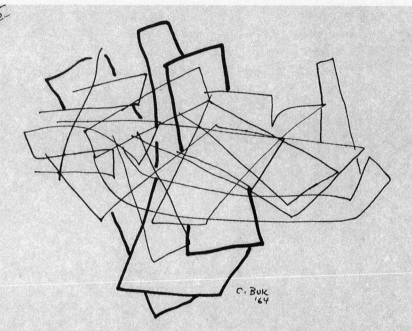

C. BUK
'64

OF COURSE I MEANT IT WHEN I SAID NO NEED
TO SEND TOTAL OF 50 IT CATCHES. YOU'VE SENT
PLENTY PLUS THE SPECIAL, THE 2 SPECIAL COPIES...
BUT I WOULD LIKE 2 MORE OF THE REGULAR, IF
YOU CAN MAKE IT, AND I HOPE TO HELL U CAN
SELL THE REMAINDOR FOR 5$ A PIECE SO YOU
CAN BARELY SURVIVE.

FRANCES SAYS HELLO. SHE IS READING "THE
POVERTY OF HISTORICISM" BY KARL POPPER. SHE'S
IN BAD SHAPE. SHE ALSO SAYS SHE HAS TO
TAKE HER TIGHTS OFF AND MEND THEM
PRETTY SOON TOO. YOU SEE WHY I DRINK

SO MUCH BEER!!. LUVVE,
Buk

[To Steve Richmond]
November 5, 1971

sure, o.k. on *Laugh*. outa sentimentality I'd like to see it go an issue or 2 more. I think our covers were the most immortal part of the magazine, but—. also, we lost our files. that is, the subscribers and libraries, and when we had them, our good friend N[eeli] ignored them. the only way I know about them is when they write us. I am trying to fill some orders now. so, everything is fucked up but I don't think we owe anybody anything, so if you want to take over this leaking laughing boat, fine. I'll presume that you will and I will forward all *Laugh Lit.* mail to you, o.k.? although lately I have been telling the submitters that *Laugh* is dead so they prob. will not come around again. no loss, from what I read.

ah, Steve, the FEMALE. there is no way. don't wait for the good woman. she doesn't exist. there are women who can make you feel more with their bodies and their souls but these are the exact women who will turn the knife into you right in front of the crowd. of course, I expect this, but the knife still cuts. the female loves to play man against man. and if she is in a position to do it there is not one who will not resist. the male, for all his bravado and exploration, is the loyal one, the one who generally feels love. the female is skilled at betrayal. and torture and damnation. never envy a man his lady. behind it all lays a living hell. I know you're not going to quit the chase, but when you go into it, for Christ's sake, realize that you are going to be burned ahead of time. never go in totally *open*. the madhouses and skidrows are full of those. remember, the female is any man's woman at any time. the choice is hers. and she's going to rip the son of a bitch she goes to just like she ripped you. but never hate the woman. understand that she is channeled this way and let her go. solitude too brings a love as tall as the mountains. fuck the skies. amen.

god, I talk more about cunt than I do about literature. literature is a hairy cunt. I know how to love a woman but a good poem will last longer, and almost every man can have a hairy cunt. put your chips on a winner—on the inner-gut sight. if you treat it well it will never betray you. and

laugh literary and MAN THE HUMPING GUNS, baby.

[To John Martin]
November 19, 1971

Thanks for sending the Wakoski books. I should get into them soon. I know that she has a nice loose line that does not restrict her thinking like most of those slick-ass men.

I am still going through a certain phrasolegy (spell?) that is taking some of the energy from my writing, but it's explorative, and, I think, hardly life-taking—say, as the Post Office was. I think, in the end (if I last) it will pay off in the writing, not only now but later, and it will also pay off as a chunk of real-ass living. Of course, I'm making a lot of errors. I always have. It's almost that by going wrong I get to the mother light. I think you know what I mean.

I just turned down two offers to drink tonight—their booze—too many good-time Charlies like to suck off of my energy. All right, like I say, after the Jon Webb* memoriam thing, we walk back into the buzzsaw of the poetry-prose blaze, and HOW IS OUR NEW BOOK OF POEMS COMING ALONG, DEAR FATHER? I need a new book of poems ... it has been quite some time. get to work on it, get to work, get to work, get to work, on it ... [* * *]

[To Gregory Maronick]
November 26, 1971

Thanks for the letter. I think that if some of your students hate me, it's a good sign. I think if they all hated me it would be a better sign. If I ever get as loved as Rod McKuen I'll know I'm as bad as R.M. What defines a poetry as poetry or any art form as an art form is puzzling. I suppose it takes a century or so and then, even then, I feel we're often mistaken. All a man can do is write what he feels like writing. This isn't as easy as it sounds; to get down to yourself takes all manner of things, but bad luck, madness, such things help. Don't let me preach. All right. I won't.

I ran out of the post office to a typewriter to try my luck. At

---

*Jon Webb had died on June 9, 1971.

140

first, it was all right. Readings, stories in sex mags; poems on the side. Then along came the tight money situation. The readings stopped. The sex mags, which used to pay 30 days after acceptance, have not only halved their rates but I now have 2 or 3 stories on the stands and I haven't even received the purchase orders yet. On top of this I have met this mad woman 20 years younger than myself. She is a tremendous flirt, hits on men continually, dances like a hot whore, but she doesn't fuck the guys, but it's such a drag, and she's nice in bed and when she's nice she's nice out of bed, but she's schitzi, has done time, and she has these tremendous runs of ups and downs, plus and minus. I get down plenty myself. I can look the other way on a lot of things except maybe just simple rudeness and unfeelingness. I don't mean to slop all this over you. But it's been one god damned battle after another. This eats into creative time. This eats into everything. We split 2 or 3 times a week. Simple madness. But it's destructive and I'm trying to work my way out of it. Like yesterday, I lay out 15 bucks and here's this big turkey on the table and all the other stuff, her two kids have eaten, my kid has eaten, next thing I know we're at each other and I'm walking out the door. She phones collect at my place 3 hours later, pretending she is another lady (?), but it's her and she claims she's in Phoenix. Goodbye, I say, and hang up. I mean, this goes on and on. It eats. If she found another guy or I found a kinder woman, we could both let go. It's killing. I don't mean to be unfair but I do think she came by because she had read my books, some of them anyhow, and she thought it might be interesting to see what this writer was. That's no way to move in on a man. She sees me sitting in a chair, she doesn't see me, she sees a Charles Bukowski. I can't perform Charles Bukowski for her, I am sick of that son of a bitch. I swear, if I ever meet a *kind* woman I don't care if she has a wooden leg or a glass eye or both or all, I'll run off to Alaska with her or China or East Lansing and we'll live together and die together. By kind, I don't mean a woman who will kiss my ass, I mean a woman who is simply gentle by nature. All these L.A. women are HARD. Their eyes are hard, their movements, their calculations. Maybe they have to be. maybe I'm hard too. I don't think so. My poems, maybe, but me, no. ah ah ah. [* * *]

Big crazy kid over last night. We got to talking about PAIN, about the world out there and about going on, how hard it was

141

just to go on, you know, the way the women were, the way everything was. And I told the kid, "Listen, you know how it happens. Sometimes I'm in the bedroom, just kind of walking around, like I'm looking for a paperclip, and it hits me—PAIN—it's like a guy has punched me in the stomach—I double over and hold my stomach—I can feel the spot—I can feel the HOLE—it's pain, the terror, the not understanding—I've had ulcers, that's not it—this is just the thing coming down and getting you ..." "I know," he said, "I get the same thing. Sometimes I cry. It's a silent crying but I can feel the tears running down ..."

So, you see, Gregory, the way isn't easy for any of us. Dylan drank his way out. Hem and Van Gogh liked shotguns. Chatterton rat poison. I can feel it now as I am typing. I am saying to the sounds of the typewriter, make it go away, make everything go away, but it doesn't. I can see it out there now. DeLongpre Ave. The world. A spiderweb of dung. Survival is an indecent dribbling spittle. o.k.

[To John Martin]
December 3, 1971

Gertrude Stein, eh? Who's that? While all us young writers starve ... God, it's dark. It rained last night. I got out of a warm bed in Burbank and drove home in the rain and when I got there the wind Gertrude Steined through the broken glass of my front door and I sat there shivering and drinking my tiny bottle of Schlitz wondering when the elephants were going to come along and kick some decent shit literature out of me, and meanwhile, here's the enclosed.

•

• 1 9 7 2 •

John Berryman committed suicide on January 7, 1972 and Kenneth Patchen died on January 8.

[To Carl Weissner]
January [?10], 1972

[* * *] well, Patchen left and John Berryman jumped off a bridge last Friday and they haven't found him yet. They say Berryman was on a quart of whiskey a day, or so somebody told me. I never saw him or it. The field narrows, babe, and there doesn't seem to be anything else coming on.

I heard from one of your buddies, Joris, in London. He's on some kind of onion, trying to translate me into the French. Another guy I know is fumbling me into Italian. Also, some guy teaching French at U.C.L.A. is working on getting some poems of mine into the French, so, shit, it's buzzing... Recession here, and mags like *Knight, Adam,* have more than halved their rates ... which means I gotta write twice as many dirty stories. This writing game is more desperate than holding up liquor stores, yet I'm snared in now and there's no out. A man's ass finally gets lazy, too lazy and the mind gets too crazy to do any damned job. Now I'm almost too lazy to write. An empty belly and rent due might stove that up a bit, though. Norse pulled out of Venice and went weeping up to S.F. in search of kinder souls ... I'm still on with the sculptress and it's unsolvable... I judge everything—women, no women, booze, no booze—on

143

my writing. I'm writing better but less. There, that's sensible.
[* * *]

[To John Martin]
[from Phoenix, Arizona]
January 12, 1972

Well, I'm out in the desert and I can use the check. Mother, it's hot in here, they turn the heat too high ... well, tomorrow I'm going to try to set up in the cacti somewhere with this machine and get into some poems, stories, the novel ... I've been lax long enough. There are 4 or 5 sisters and a friend out here; they're all writing novels.... every place you turn you see another writer. blind guy came in—he's writing two novels. writers, writers, writers—I leave DeLongpre to get rid of that gang and here I am surrounded again. Well, there may be a story in all this; meanwhile I'm with Linda, which is fulfilling when we're on. gangs of children running through, dogs, relatives, tv going, but it's all fairly nice—they tend to ignore me which is a good way of being accepted. [* * *]

[To John Martin]
January 17, 1972

[* * *] I don't understand this desert out here. It looks like something that wanted to give up but didn't know quite how. The brush is yellow, no, brown and tired and desperate. And the horses and cattle, they just don't care. They lay or stand and wait, wait, wait, Everything here is waiting. That's the feel of it. Or like this is the last edge of the world and it's all too tired to fall off. The cowboys, too, seem indifferent. The people. They walk around and their faces show neither pain or concern or worry. They are like their horses and cattle. Well, that's good and a change from L.A.-Hollywood where everybody is hard and on

144

the hustle and with the front, and most of them not having it at all. Well, hell.

[* * *] There are 3 typewriters going at once here. Can I have set these sisters on fire? Hello to Barbara. Bukowski marches on. He'll live to be 80. I always wanted to die in the year 2,000. Of course, the whole gang of us may leave at once before then, or almost at once. A cat below where I am typing just grabbed my toe, bit and scratched it. There's something cooking in the kitchen; the love is good, the cat climbs my leg now, purring and digging in his "fingernails," as Linda's daughter calls them ... Is this the literary life? Why not? The fire from the devil's beard stews the afternoon air. Don't give up on me. uh uh.

[To Carl Weissner]
January [?18], 1972

well, god damn, here I am in Phoenix, Ariz. [* * *] and I ought to be here until Feb. 10 or 12th this year, if I don't go giraffe ... like one time I was out here and couldn't bear up under conditions and I took me a 3 hour stroll in the desert. It seems easier this time—so far. staying here with my gal friend and her sister, and there's another sister on another ranch across the way, and I play the poet-writer but so far as writing goes I've done little, have made local racetrack—Turf Paradise—3 times with moderate success driving my gal's polka dot car with Calif. license plates, and I now got me kinda long hair and a shitty beard and there is madness in my eyes, of course, and I like driving around in the polka dot, the locals don't get the angle—there isn't any.

by the way, you see Herman, you tell him I ain't pissed because my girlfriend kissed him goodbye when he came over to see me. I made her kiss 5 guys at the end of one of my parties to show them what they're missing; of course, I frown upon anybody else fucking her—I tend to like the unmolested pisshole. [* * *]

these 3 sisters are all mad, sexy, intelligent, liberal ... and they're all writing novels ... about sex, oral copulation, insanity ... and the cactus is out there, and there's beer and smokes and

145

change and evenings when you can see the bored stars, I stand, old companion, with you in the battle, we will have both victory and death, fire and water, love and hate, noon and midnight, I wish you plenty, well, hang in.

[To Carl Weissner]
February [?5], 1972

got your damn good letter, it was a laugher.

meanwhile, one of the sisters got down on me because I didn't accept her writing or her as a mighty good thing and she screamed and screamed, many things, like, "my children are my novels," and so forth, then she railed against my writing. I got on out. she's 41, never been published. well, that's all right; but even if she were published I'd still think she was a bad writer. well, so I left early. back here. Linda looking for a place—2 children and a dog. not easy. we are jammed in here. can't walk around. no way to write. well, man, it's all for the good of the fire. [* * *]

I'll try to get the City Lights book to you when it comes out. I do think the stories fouler (better) than *Notes of a D. O. Man.* Instead of calling it Bukowskiana (not my idea), I have retitled it *Erections, Ejaculations, Exhibitions and General Tales of Ordinary Madness.* At the printer's now, says L.F. He calls it a great book. I agree. I don't think that since Artaud or Nietzsche there has been anybody as joyfully mad as I am. well.

well, this is just to let you know the bare things & that I am alive and your letters are always a pleasure, works of Art, my friend, and yes, I know how it must be with the ladies, we must give them all the extras of tongue and touch, because that's a creation too, making a lady truly hot, and, at the same time we must get away from them long enough to create … I think the man who said, The strongest men are the most alone, was right.* I

---

*Perhaps "The strongest man is he who stands alone," Halldor Laxness, *Independent People* (trans. 1945), quoted by Brad Leithauser, *New York Review of Books*, May 11, 1995, p. 44. But see the letter of November 15, 1974, below, where Bukowski attributes the remark to Ibsen.

146

suppose I will have to get back to that. Even though I believe I love Linda. We tear ourselves apart for the typewriter, for those one or 2 lines. and it's worth it ...

The book being referred to in the following is Mockingbird, Wish Me Luck, *published June 1972.*

[To John Martin]
February 6, 1972

[* * *] I've done ten of the drawings for our book of poems. I don't say much about it but each time a book comes out I get just as excited as the first time. I don't suppose this is very professional, but isn't this what it's about? I mean, a book, a tabulation? it makes it much easier to die, somehow, except you don't want to die because you want to do more. getting published in the magazines doesn't raise up much in me, but a book is holy [*sic*] another matter. I have a feeling that this book of poems will be the best. I warm up all through the arms and chest and belly thinking about it.

[* * *] this is a difficult life—because I am more open to things that happen—but compared to the Post Office and the hundred other jobs, it's life lighting up near the end, and it's worth it all—the gamble, the doubt; at least when I get my lazy ass up and at it, my energy is going where my feelings are, and there's no way of short-selling a value like that. Cheer up, Sparrow. [* * *]

A. D. Winans edited Second Coming *magazine from 1972 onward.*

[To A. D. Winans]
February 16, 1972

Yes, thanks for copy of *Second Coming*. I had a second coming myself the other night, which is fairly fair for my age. Re: your *Second Coming*, I thought the content all right but too much emphasis on prose. I like a balance between prose and poetry, *plus* one or 2 very nasty reviews of life, books or anything. As much as we look down on the academy, I always remember the old days, coming off the park benches and into the libraries and reading those very phoney yet bitchingly beautiful reviews in the old *Kenyon Review*. But never mind all that. [* * *]

An Anthology of L.A. Poets, *edited by Bukowski, Neeli Cherry, and Paul Vangelisti, was published by* Laugh Literary *in 1972.*

[To John Martin]
March 14, 1972

[* * *] Neeli, Paul and I are going to put out *An Anthology of L.A. Poets*. I think it has long been needed. This town has been smeared long enough both as a place to live and a place to create. Of course, it *does* have Hollywood attached to it but L.A. needn't be a Siamese twin. Many people live here and ignore Hollywood, Disneyland and the L.A. Dodgers completely and also Alvera street and Broadway and Hill and the Rose Parade and the Santa Claus Parade. L.A. is really still the Grand Central Market and Alvarado st. and Main st. and E. 5th and E. L.A. Watts is fairly Hollywood. Watts has been tricked. But may bounce back. [* * *]

[To John Martin]
March 31, 1972

[* * *] Regarding your phone call, I have some down moments but I don't think I'm about to go just yet, especially if I stay away from the whiskey. You know, the writing must come out of the living, the reaction to living. If I get a little scorched now and then, it's all for the good of the barbecue. And when the leisure time is needed in order to get it down, that time is there and I think it makes the writing solider. Forgive me if it doesn't.

On Linda, it has to end sooner or later. In 9 more years she'll be 40 years old. I just can't tolerate them thar old women, dude. [* * *]

[To Carl Weissner]
June [?20], 1972

[* * *] The sculptress and I split. She went back to her hometown in Utah. But there seem to be a great many long distance calls and letters going back and forth between us. I didn't wait long. I jumped right into bed with a 43 years old gal who is president of some record company. My personality isn't very good but I throw good fucks for a 52 year old guy. "You just couldn't wait," says the sculptress, "you just had to go jump into bed!" "But, baby, I thought…"

The new one is very kind and says she loves me but it just doesn't seem the same as the other one, it just ain't, and I don't know what the hell. The sculptress phoned and I was going up to Utah and then the new one heard and swallowed a handful of sleeping pills. I stuck my fingers down her throat and made her vomit, and called the trip off. I am caught in between all this. And there's no solving it, it will never be solved. [* * *]

remember when you came to the U.S. and I couldn't pick you up at the airport? I became stricken? airports and space were beyond me, I hope you understand. since then I've flown a dozen times and I bounce in and out of space ports like a human flea. too bad I wasn't ready for you. I grow so slowly. Sorry.

I truly don't understand the ladies, Carl. They seem to exert terrific pressures while asking a kind of freedom of their own. I am puzzled beyond puzzlement. Any clues? My problem is that I seem to care too much. How the hell can I get out of that?

[To Lafayette Young]
June 25, 1972

Thanks plenty for the clothes for Marina. I'm going to see her the monday from next and you just don't know how happy she'll be with them. She doesn't have much to wear, I suppose I should do better, but anyhow the clothes and purses, all that great stuff will be put to a mighty use: to make a beautiful little girl more beautiful. thank you, friend.

the human race? god jesus, save us from it, somehow. I hang in and wait to die. just got off a bad experience—16 months— with a woman. trying to put myself together again. I'm now with another. it's gentler but hardly as stimulating. well, it's a day at a time, and it has never been easy.

hang in.

William J. Robson edited and published Holy Doors: an Anthology of Poetry, Prose, and Criticism *from Long Beach, California (1972). He had previously, in 1970, published* Looking for the Giants: an interview with Charles Bukowski.

[To Bill Robson]
July 11, 1972

Now that Richmond and Fox have me down as failing, a liar, a sell-out, so forth, it's curious that you still want to hear from me. Don't you believe them? Don't you realize that I am a ruined man? That I have forsaken the truth, all that shit? I don't know how to answer these boys. They both seem to be staking a claim as real writers, overlooked, for this reason or that. Whatever the grounds of their bitching wails, I only ask that you measure the totality of all my work against theirs and make a judgment.

Poor Fox. He claims Black Sparrow published me because I was "known" and didn't publish him because he was "unknown." He claims the quality of his work had nothing to do with it. I have no idea of John Martin's worded rejection of the Fox manuscript. It was probably kindly-worded and Fox read into it what he wanted to read into it. The real fact was that the poetry probably was simply bad stuff.

This bit about the "known" and the "unknown" is ridiculous. No writer is born "known." They don't know us in our cradle, or in our rompers or in our schoolyards. We have to become "known." And if a writer remains "unknown" long enough there's usually a good reason for it.

Fox and Richmond seem to think I have "sold out" because I make my living with my typewriter. I have even labeled myself "a literary hustler," but where is their sense of humor? The story in *Rogue* was not crap or some cheap little bullshit formula story for a buck, as Fox might say. He might read the story again. He likens me to the prof in *Blue Angel*, egg broken over head... Christ, these little snippets, these tiny little quarter talents... they really want to do me in... They know that my work is better than ever and that I am getting *paid* for it, and that's their attack—I make the money writing: therefore the writing must be a sell-out.

Fox from his professorial post advises writers to go get a job and write on the side. I've had a hundred jobs and I wrote on the side. I worked until I was 50 in the most slave-labor and demeaning jobs imaginable. That doesn't create literature; it only tires your ass out. Fox chirps to his students and Richmond lays in the sun outside his beach cottage, claiming to be worth only $300. All I say is that the real ARENA is CREATION. Let them get into that arena instead of bitching like neurotic housewives over the backyard fence. I'm afraid that the small presses, the mimeo presses have kept alive too many talentless darlings, and have made life difficult for their wives, their children, their girlfriends.

I don't believe that in getting paid for what you do, that being a professional, necessarily detracts from your art. It may detract from yours, it doesn't from mine. Many people get paid for what they do. And they do all right. Starvation and obscurity are not necessarily signs of genius.

151

Let Time itself answer the attacks on me by Richmond and Fox. As for me, I've wasted enough time on them. Oh, my little friends, how you cry and weep and bawl and puke and slobber over yourselves. May I suggest that you use more of your energy on what you pretend is your craft—that is: writing. There seems room for improvement. Some day you may be men.

[To Patricia Connell]
July 31, 1972

Hello Patricia Connell:

Thanks for your letter. Very interesting stationery. Too bad you didn't come along with it. It's not every day that this dirty old man hears from an airline stewardess—though most of them piss me off for one reason or another when I ride them, or rather, their plane. I suppose it's because they're all so god damned casual. If only one of them would break a leg some day or drop a uterus. Still, I suppose somebody *does* read my column and/or my books. I'm largely underground with a red nose from drinking beer and I'll be 52 in August, the 16th. That doesn't leave much left over. I just broke off with a 31 year old girl, a looker, 16 mad screaming months, and I've told Liza not to love me. There. Tah tah taha.

If your pilots tend to go my stuff, there's a large jumbo collection of my stories just out, *Erections, Ejaculations, Exhibitions and General Tales of Ordinary Madness*. It goes for $3.95 via City Lights. [* * *]

[To Patricia Connell]
August 3, 1972

So you're 27 years old! I'm just mad about young women, they drive me ape, completely out of context and/or reality, but I don't give a damn. Don't know if I've mentioned but I just got over a 16 month affair with a 31 year old sculptress. We fucked

152

and sucked and loved and slept together, ate breakfast together, lunch together, everything together—fighting, mortally wounded, she was a Carmen, that one, beautiful and cruel, a flirt, a vamp. a woman, a most wondrous woman. She finally ran off to Utah when I walked out on her once too often. With Liza I'm honest, I tell her, don't love me, please don't love me ...

I'd like to come see you—you haven't invited me—but my dear old 62 Comet needs a bit of repair work ... Manhattan Beach?—that's where my wife split when she divorced me—she was a millionairess—I married her through the mail—sight unseen—when she kept writing that no man would ever marry her—there was something wrong with her neck—she couldn't turn her neck—I said, kid, I got scars all over me, I look like a punchboard, I'll marry you—she was all right, for a while, until she knew I didn't love her. Manhattan Beach. That's it. Yes.

I hesitate to phone. Phone conversations are difficult. Just think how we'd look together? I could pose as your father. Until we got to bed. I do all right in bed. Not that I'm exceptionally hung but I go down on that thing with some artistry and believe in the long ride.... Is this what you'd call shooting the shit? I know that most men who claim to be great lovers are nothing but on and off jackrabbits. Listen, how did we get into all this sex bit?

I worked most of my life on dull labor jobs but 2 years ago quit and layed it all on the typewriter. I'm not getting rich but I'm still alive. 7 year old daughter in Santa Monica. I volunteer 45 bucks a month child support. I like lobster, beer, and occasional racetrack (computer data?), young women, especially those around 27 with a job dishing out those two drinks in the sky. I am emotional and kind and ride around in a big tank so people won't stick pins into me. The sculptress said, I don't think I ever met a guy with a line like yours. And Liza says, "I never met a man who made better love." So there you have it, plus and minus. I don't think I have a line. Well.

I don't expect you to like all my writing—prose or poetry. No matter what you do. some people are going to like it, some are going to dislike it, and the vast majority aren't going to give a damn one way or the other. [* * *]

The man-woman relationship is fraught with pain and glory and warmth and wonderment. It's certainly worth the trip. I've liked your letters, they show insight. I'd like to see you some time. For all my talk, I'm very slow. I don't like to rush. I don't want to get into anything that I don't want to stay in for some time. I'm sentimental as all shit. It's my nature. I'm tough too. I can be a son of a bitch when I have to be and sometimes I have to be.

Save these letters. They're worth money. You may need money some day, dear, when people stop flying United and fly angels. I'm really not a male chauv. pig. Be good, Patricia.

Bukowski (fly me!)

[To Patricia Connell]
August 8, 1972

You're right—there's a lot of self-destruct in my relationships ... The sculptress and I practically lived together—but there seemed two violent whirling flaming battles a week—break-up, make-up—it was vibrant enough and the love was great and the sex was great, and when it was all going well you couldn't beat it—but ... Now with Liza there are hardly any arguments, it's all very smooth, but, at least from my viewpoint, it's not the grand flame ... so I asked her not to love me. The sculptress was coming back to me from Utah once or twice and Liza acted up quite badly—I won't go into details but it was a mess, and I don't want to see her get that way again. Oh, I'm capable of love, my child, I've been in love twice in 52 years. I didn't love the sculptress but now I realize that something in our personalities will never leave us at peace. so I had to tell her that I had given up on our relationship. That's the package.

Oh, I'm Buk, not Buck. Pronounced Buke.

Ah, the seriousness of old age, you say. Well, I don't know. A certain lady says that no man has made love to her like I do. I'm the best of the bloody lot, and she's known hundreds. I can't help taking some pride in that statement. I intend to live until 80 and to ball until 80 and to go down until 80, and if this seems crude, so be it.

It was good talking to you on the phone. I liked your voice and you had an easy manner, you made me feel comfortable.

Yes, I'd like to have a beer with you some time. We needn't

make a large thing of it. I don't believe in trapping people or chasing them down, or vice versa. Also, there's no rush, although I have to leave town in Sept. a couple of times for poetry readings—one for Ferlinghetti at S.F. and one at the Univ. of Arizona. Meanwhile my poor car is getting a blood transfusion. Somehow it feels good to hear from you and to rather be in touch. I hope to hear something from you, and to eventually set up our famous meeting over a beer... Size? I'm 5′ 11″ and ¾'s, 210 pounds. I'm Leo. Like beer, boxing matches, horse races; like to drive women crazy on the lovebed. Or so says the computer. I'll always try to fly United, so help me, little one. I'm influenced by Celine, Dostoevski, Kafka, classical music, myself, the miracle of the female and the general weathers of life. Hell, write me when the mood moves ye.

[To Patricia Connell]
August 11, 1972

Oh, *Post Office*. I wrote that in twenty drunken nights on scotch and cigars. Don't expect too much.

I phoned the sculptress last night on a lark. She's moving back to town in Sept. "I'm not coming to you, Bukowski. I'm going to think of all the evil things you did to me. A week before I come back I'm going to get some guy to fuck me for a week so I won't need you."

Well, the female is a clever creature. She knows how to regulate her affairs. Most often it is the man who falls apart; it's the man who jumps off the bridge. When we give over our feelings they run off with us. There's no regulating them. I give over my feelings too easily, and it's not all relegated to suck and fuck (as the sculptress calls it). I get as much, or more, out of the other parts. Small talk. Breakfast together. Sleeping while touching. Waiting while the other goes to the toilet. Love-making after a stupid argument. Drinking beer with maddened friends. Hundreds of tiny things. I am never bored when I am with my woman. I get bored in large formless crowds. Bored, hell, I get desperate, I lather and blather at the mouth, my eyes roll, the sky shakes. What am I talking about here?

And you're strange. Why do you want to meet a 52 year old man? (I'll be 52 this August 16th. Wish me a happy birthday.) Is your father dead? Or didn't you have much of a father? If we like each other somewhat I can be your father, but on the other hand, I'm very horny. Was your father very horny?

My guess is that you've gotten too much attention and found it wanting—jackrabbits, fly-by-nights, so forth. Young men are too stricken with themselves to be human. I can stand by you while you wait for the arrival of the proper one. My god, we're getting serious here, aren't we? Uggg. Well, it's hot, the weather's hot and I went to the boxing matches last night and spilled beer on myself. Then over to Liza's. I must be careful not to hurt Liza. She's a kind and a good woman but I don't love her. Anyhow, the boxing matches were good. Everybody screamed. Even the fighters enjoyed it. And there you go flying to Richmond, Virginia. I think we should meet but I don't want you to meet a stranger—hence the letters, a bit of talking. I find myself thinking about you at odd moments during the day and I don't even know who you are—flying out there over Richmond—all those oilmen dandies and insurance dandies, all with that satisfied look, twisting the rocks in their scotch as the satisfied pilot gargles some inanity over the intercom, yes, yes, perhaps we can meet and perhaps we can hate each other right off, get it done with, clean the deck and look for the next pink cloud, what? But your letters have been warm, and I have the feeling that you've been through some things and come out better for them. Keep in touch, Pattie, you make the mailbox look good.

[To Patricia Connell]
August 16, 1972 [52nd birthday]

'tis very stimulating to get a letter from a woman, and a very young one at that. I got in about ten thirty and there was your letter, very fat, warm like a glove, the bit on the back, this girl looking inside this man's head and kind of playing with him spiritually. ah. there was some other mail and I read it first, then got a beer and opened yours. there had been a postcard from England, "have just finished your city lights book and have found it the best writing of short stories since Cervantes and Dickens and Walter Scott ..." now, uh huh, that's high praise, as they call it. for dirty stories, that's o.k. anyhow, I went through your letter to try to find out who you were, and if you're a little sarcastic, that's o.k. I like being insulted, it charms me. that's what got me going with the sculptress. she was sitting there doing my head and she looked at me and said, "My husband said when I divorced him that he hoped I would meet a real crud, and now I have." I laughed. it was too delightful. I've got to have this woman, I thought, even if she's only 30, I've got to have her. well, we lasted 16 months, but looking back now I see it was mostly sex and battle. we went 4 or 5 times a week, right on through periods and all and fought and split forever twice a week. it was total flame and madness and it finally broke wide open. I phoned her last night and finally ended up hanging up on her. there's no getting together. all our ideas seem opposite. she said before she moves back to town she's going to fuck some guy for a week so she won't need me. And, to me, that was the tipoff—I am just a sex machine for her servicing. to hell with that. I've got nothing against sex, I'm all for it; there's nothing I like better than to really satisfy a woman. It's an art and I like to be a good artist. But I also like to feel some warmth outside the sexual relationship.

I think we should meet. I am not a pushy person. And I'm *very* EASY to get rid of. Liza calls me a bashful madman. Maybe I am. We should get a few drinks between us when we meet ... easing of tension, you know. it's really a very difficult thing. you are a stranger to me. you *know* something about me because you've read some of my shit. Can we meet during a day sometime? Frankly, I'm over at Liza's each night, and I don't want to hurt her. She's in love with me, for one reason or another she's in love with me, and she knows I don't love her, yet still I don't want to hurt her. We had one or two split scenes where she almost cracked—the suicide bit, you know and I've been on the love-end and I've been hurt by the other, and the pain is intolerable, unbelievable, so I want to be careful with Liza, yet since I don't love her I still feel I have a right to see some other women. does this sound like bullshit? well, it's not.

I'll be in Frisco Sept. 14 giving a reading and at the Univ. of Arizona Sept. 28, reading, and outside of that my time is my own. But that's Sept. this is August and I'm 52 years old writing a half a love letter to a 27 year old airline stewardess, o, the world

157

is mad, isn't it? but great too. can you tell me when a good day would be? Sat and Sunday, I think, would be bad days. can you draw me a map, how to get there? my car's running but best to stay off freeways. no auto insurance. do you believe in sex, or do you just want a talking relationship, or what? or do you want to see what happens? let it flow? tell me things. I'm selfish, you know. I think a sex-love relationship with you would produce a great many poems, love poems. the whole last third of my last poem book, *Mockingbird*, are love poems to Linda. you see all I want you for? just for my typewriter, Pattie Connell, just for the ticking of the keys....

I think it's good for a woman to meet a great many men, in bed and out of bed, so that when the good man comes along she'll know why.

I enjoyed your long letter, even though you seem a little evasive. Is the man you're going with very jealous? Do you love him? Does he go down on you? Does he do it right? I mean, are you getting anything out of it? or are you just going through some rote thing for lack of anything else to do? you know, many men are satisfied with their women because they satisfy themselves upon them, but few men really satisfy their women. they're simply too selfish. that's why I didn't mind Linda being 30, because I took proper care of her.

I celebrated my birthday a bit early yesterday. A lawyer dropped by, and then Liza, and we had a few drinks. A few too many. "Look," I said, "here I'm sitting with a corporate lawyer and a record executive, and I'm a starving poet. What the hell are you people doing here?"

I haven't been to the racetrack in some weeks. Del Mar is such a long haul... Linda is going with a homosexual now. I told her it was a cop-out. that she should get a real man and face the fire and the glory.

All right, Pattie, I think we should have a meeting. nothing oppressive or up-tight, maybe a little nervous, but with nobody owing anybody anything. loose, you know. you might hate me on sight. I'm hardly pretty and hardly a normal type human being. In fact, I'm pretty badly fucked up. Crazed, Liza calls it. but I'm hardly dangerous or maniacal or any of that shit. I suppose you'd call me a kind person. well, my god. some out of work actor just called up and wished me a happy birthday. he's stuck in some factory, working the swing shift. we're all trying to make it, this

158

way or that, trying to find love, trying to find sex, trying to find peace and meaning before we hang it up. I look at these 52 years gone by and I know now that I don't know any more than I did at 18. That's not much growth, is it? ah, let me hear from you on all matters. I'm sentimental and I get attached to women but I wouldn't force anything on you. I have an idea I couldn't. you must be fairly sophisticated, running up and down those aisles, jostling and chatting with the passengers, getting pinched by the pilots. I'm more raw and clumsy. maybe you can teach me some polish. when I get up to read my poems I sound like one of those old fashioned victrolas, running down. but you wouldn't know about them. there are no bluebirds in my skies, Patricia, and the sun blinks on and off. looks like rain, last night I had all these rain dreams. it kept raining and raining and raining. do you think I'm out of my craw? christ, well, write me, little one. I think all this is quite wonderful.

some kind of love, Buk.

[To Carl Weissner]
August 16, 1972

[* * *] I just got rid of a bad one, and once again I seem to be making moves toward 2 young girls. one is 27, the other I think is 20. I shouldn't. I must be going crazy. the one I'm with, she's 43, treats me gently. gave me $70 for my birthday the other day. Needed tires for my car, various parts. a good woman. but I'm so used to bad women, whores, flirts, vamps, sluts, liars, mad-women. when I grow up I am going to break off from all of them. that's the system, that's the out. [* * *]

[To Patricia Connell]
August 18, 1972

Thanks for the birthday card, 'twas touching. You're still on *Post Office*, I suppose. You should read *Erections*...via City

Lights, a better work. Either/Or [bookshop] should have had it. I haven't read Kosinski but he was put on me. A gal came by one time, she used to dance with a ten foot boa constrictor on the Sunset strip—she's in Berkeley now—and she put the book onto me but I passed it on without reading. The boa constrictor lady was ready for consummation at the moment, and still is, but I wasn't ready.

I'm supposed to go to Del Mar this Weds. or Thursday. With Liza and a couple of guys from a tv station. they want to put me on an education television thing. They seem serious but last time I saw them we all just got drunk. It's supposed to go on 65 tv stations across the nation but so far there hasn't been a click of video tape or whatever. such non-going shit can last into eternity.

So you're a sadist, eh? God, the sculptress was a cruel woman too. It seems quite standard, doesn't it? I suppose men beg too much and this gives the ladies this feeling of power. You've got all these little men on your shelf. O.k. When you gonna put me on your shelf?

I really should do some work with this typer today, but wanted to thank you for the card. Write when you feel free to do so.

[To Patricia Connell]
August 21, 1972

It's noon, slight hangover, coffee on, going to Santa Monica soon to see my daughter—she's 7.

Yes, I suppose we should meet. I lay claim to being the world's ugliest man. Perhaps we can meet, hate each other right off and get it done with.

A relationship without love is comfortable because you are always in control if the other person loves you. But the one who is in love really has the benefits because (he) (she) is thriving, throbbing, vibrating. I would certainly rather be in love if I had a choice but one doesn't always have this choice. I've only been in love twice in 52 years.

For a person who is supposedly afraid of people you are very open with me. And it would take guts to meet me. It would not

160

be an easy thing. I don't think you have too much fear of people.

I've been going with Liza since May 2nd when Linda and I split. I jumped right out of one bed and into another. I suppose that makes me a bastard. I don't like to sleep alone.

We could have a friendship. Or let it start that way if it wanted to. Sex is damned nice but not necessary. A Thursday evening might be nice. But I won't want to drink too much because I have to drive back and already have one drunk driving rap. Liza goes out and has drinks and dinner with these 2 guys every Thursday night. Yes, I have a nightly vigil by Liza's side as you say. But there aren't any chains on me. I just don't want to mess her up. If you and I ever got anything going she would have to fall by the way. But it seems senseless to hurt her without that. She's a record company exec. and plenty of men are after her. I'm rather honored that she preferred me to all the young handsome men but she'll hardly be alone if we ever split.

A little luck in the mail today. A German publisher wants to translate *Erections, Ejaculations, Exhibitions and General Tales of Ordinary Madness* into the Hun. But we're waiting on Rowolt—the largest German publisher—and if they go it I won't be driving that 62 Comet much longer.

I enjoy your letters very much. Get relaxing with that Bloody Mary soon and tell me some more things.

[To Carl Weissner]
August [?30], 1972

[* * *] The sculptress is back. Saw her yesterday. "Listen," she said, "you're in a triangle now. You're trying to hold 2 women at once. It can't be done."

"They do it in the movies sometimes," I said.

Anyhow, we got into an argument and I cut out of there. her face looked strangely hard after that 4 month's separation, and her eyes too. I'm afraid something has gone out of it for me. I don't love the other one either. Krist, I'm not in a triangle at all. I'm nowhere. the female is a monumental puzzle to me. I must be strong enough to do without them, without her and her and her. A lot of dirty laundry and haggling. [* * *]

[To Patricia Connell]
September 13, 1972

I've been into a lot of shit and so I'm late in getting this off to you. Up to Frisco tomorrow—PSA—Hollywood—Burbank to give a reading. They claim it's the largest SF crowd since Yevtushenko the Russian poet. The auditorium holds 750 and they claim to be sold out. I hope they are. I get half the god damned take and at 2 bucks a head maybe I can afford a cold beer when I get back. 750 for Billy Graham ain't cat's turds but for poetry it's something. o, yeh, I write poems too, kitten.

A fine photo thanks. Youze is a lovely lovely thing. I gotta meet ya some day if only to look at ya. I mean, look, I wrote you all these letters. That's work.

I broke off with Liza and went back to the sculptress (Linda). Liza took it hard. She read me off good. I talked to her for 7 hours about it, during which time she beat the shit out of me 5 times. I let her beat on me because I felt bad about what I was doing to her. But she'll make it. She has a good job and plenty of men are after her, or her money. She's really a fine person and should never have put her trust in a slob like me, but the sculptress has this immense pull on me, I am helpless. She just walks in and I'm finished. I don't have any excuses except that I might love the sculpt. and I didn't love Liza.

All that sounds like vomit in the beef stew, doesn't it? A mess. Well. Anyhow, I'm not much good at triangles so I had to pull out from one or the other.

You sound like you're getting love-security from a man you want and don't want. I'd rather imagine you're shopping around for the spark, that's why you're dating other men. If your man doesn't walk out on you it may be more from weakness than strength. Or maybe I'm wrong.

I've got to line up the poems for the reading, so this will be fairly short. —I enjoyed your telling of the Tom Jones bit. Those jackasses get *so* spoiled.

We ought to meet some day when the climate is right for both of us. Easy does it, you know.

You exclaimed that my letters were too short when I phoned you. Listen, kitten, if I wrote mine in longhand like yours they'd look pretty long, you know. Ah, our FIRST ARGUMENT!!! Isn't it great?

162

[To Patricia Connell]
September 18, 1972

ah, I am back with Liza. Went north with Linda for the reading, came back all scratched up. I broke it off with Linda on grounds I'd rather not go into. anyhow, she threatened to kill me. Liza has also threatened to kill me. interesting life, what? Linda's schitzy and when she's up or right I love her very much but when she shows the other side, it's too much. Liza is really a fine woman, though I don't love her. channel 28 is doing a documentary on me and we had cameras and sound men on the plane up and during the reading and on the plane back, so forth so forth. I felt like your Tom Jones although I didn't get anybody in the crapper.

actually, tho, ART is the matter, the crux, and with all the shit going on I keep this in my head, the real ACT, the form, the holiness. I love women but they are hardly the center of the universe.

I've suggested to Liza that she play it looser this time, keep some backups. She's going to the movies tonight with some guy. it's o.k. with me. I don't want to ever leave her totally ALONE again. they tell me she had a rough go when I was with Linda. also if I can get her to go out with men, then when I want to see somebody—say for a night or a couple of hours—I will be able to do so. say somebody like you.

Linda broke in while I was at Liza's last night and stole her sculpture of me back. That's all right, I trotted one of her paintings over and put it on her front porch. As long as I don't get murdered here, everything will be fine.

I read at Univ. of Ariz. on the 28th. Liza will prob. fly out with me. I don't know if the cameras will be along on this wing. It's a little different situation. U. of A. is rather uptight and I won't be able to drink very much. will prob. make a dull reading. I also have a tentative date at Cal State Long Beach Nov. 29, once at noon and again at night. If I'm still alive.

Yes, yes, I'm "hot to trot" to meet you. Your photo fine, fine! I might say I'm in love but how can you fall in love with a photo? and when I'm 52 and the photo's 27? You'll probably be disgusted when you meet me. I'm not a very good talker; in fact, a rather dull fellow.

Luck with your new love, but remember that few people hold

163

up over the long run. Weaknesses begin to appear all over shit. It depends upon how much weakness you can love along with the good parts. It's good you keep shopping. The only way you can know what you have is by comparison.

Should we get together a bit it might be better if you come out here. (You almost found the way once.) We could go to a bar for a few, then maybe come to my place and have some drinks and talk. I live in a *very* beat-up front court. I am lazy and a shitty housekeeper. But there is great freedom here. The landlord and landlady are my friends and overlook a great many of my inconsistencies. Somehow your letters get me horny. Is it the pink paper? Not that we need make it. I don't want to do anything that you don't want to do.

You make my mailbox warm. Lemmee hear words from you....

[To Patricia Connell]
September 22, 1972

a short one until later—very hectic here—you won't believe it—I'm back with Linda. it's my last move. if I break with her it has to be somebody new. this going back and forth doesn't get it, it's cowardice. for a few days I was with one in the daytime, the other at night. now it's Linda. very stormy with Linda, but the love is high high high there, both physically and spiritually...

I haven't been doing my work, so must get into it. Univ. of Ariz. next week. not a drop off the typer.

Linda's very violent. She kicked down my door in S.F., clawed my face, bit a hole in my arm. But what love we make together! She's 32.

This is just to let you know that I am still together, it's hardly a letter; will write when I have more time.

Yes, you got left alone on your own doing... left with the tv tube, but I'm happy for you that you were able to have a few drinks and write to me, for you weren't entirely alone then, and you know me well enough to let loose a few things. I wonder which of our love-life's the most fucked-up? You with all your beauty and youth, you have troubles too. me, I'm extra

164

emotional, my mind's half gone, I expect trouble, I may even create it. But with your equipment you should have things under control.

well, listen, my invisible love out there, I really have some WORK to do. keep touch. I'll write again if I'm alive.

[To Patricia Connell]
October 2, 1972

It rather cheered the old man up to talk to you today, all these low dark clouds, and somehow you got me to laughing. I guess that reading at the Univ. of Ariz. looped me down. such a staid gang...afterwards there was a reception...cookies and some kind of lemon punch...Christ, and me with my tongue hanging out...I mean for a *drink*, Connell, a drink...

yes, the sculpt. is a looker, a vamp, a tease...a bitch...a schitzy, and, at times, a wonderful woman. I don't suppose it will ever be smooth with us and I don't suppose I'll ever stop breaking up with her. but it does me good to break off from her because it gives me more area. but, I must admit, this last get-together, it was my idea, I did the work, I did the talking...but we're still always on explosive ends. the male-female relationship is almost impossible, yet one keeps looking, trying...so many things fuck it up, small things really, like not getting together on a Thursday night...some small offhand thing can crash it all down. nerves, maybe. or looking for an edge. it all seems to keep crashing. and it's not just me; I look around and everybody is in trouble. and now what am I doing writing a 27 years old woman? you're 25 years younger than I. I gotta be crazy. but I guess we ought to have a drink together sometime just so we can laugh each other off. you might think, why that ugly old dog, what'd he think he was gonna do? and I'd think, why, that stewardess, she ain't got no SOUL like me. you know. something.

Liza I did wrong to and there's no excuse, except I know that if somebody dumps me now I have no need to cry in my beer— I'll be getting just what I gave.

How are all your loves going? You may have too much going

165

at once. It might make it lively but it might make it hard to level off so you can see where you are. It's almost impossible to have a steady relationship going with one man while carrying on side relationships with others. Me? I'm different. I'm the dirty old man. I can do what I want.

I got an offer for a reading in Canada. Do Eskimos really kiss with their noses? What else do they do?

ta ta, this is your invisible lover.

[To Carl Weissner]
October [?3], 1972

[* * *] Made the San Fran reading, 800 at 2$ a head, I got $400. I suppose there were various expenses. They put a refrig. full of beer on stage with me. After a while I mostly stopped reading and sat there drinking beer. Split with sculptress up there, went back to Liza. Then split with Liza, went back to sculptress. At moment am with sculptress. There's no rest, there's no victory, there's no meaning, and love comes in salt-grain size. Well, you know this.

There's this airline stewardess, 27, maybe she's the one. Maybe I can drag her ass down to the Bukowski depths. but the sculpt has quite a hold on me; maybe not as good a hold as she had 6 months ago, but it is some kind of hold.

Speaking of a "hold," there seems to be a hold on my writing now. Is this the end, old buddy? Has Bukowski coughed it up? I'd suppose not. I suppose it will be along. No telling, though. That's what makes the madness good.

[* * *] Maybe I'm just a drunk. You know, you get with the female, they get on you for the drinking. I suppose I do act the ass when I'm drinking, but there's a necessary release there. I get out into this available space that is always there to float in. No, it doesn't make any sense to anybody but me. But it puts me somewhere, and when I get back down I walk to the typewriter and the keys work better. But drinking, to the female, really violates something in them. THEY HATE IT WORSE THAN ANOTHER WOMAN. It might kill you, they say, we love you. But they don't figure it

166

might kill me a thousand other different ways to remain sober and drink tea. ah ah ah well.

[To John Martin]
October 8, 1972

Now that you're thinking of bringing out a collection of my columns—stories—you needn't feel like my energies are being taken by somebody else. I rather like to earn that hundred and a half if possible. How about the title? Can I cut loose on that too?

I still need to work with my old pal the poem, tho, and I enclose a few more. The novel? Well, I believe it will awaken soon...faith, faith. Everything must work by itself. I don't know why I tell you these things—you already know them. Hello to Barbara. yes, yes.

old 52, Henry Charles

p.s.—I'm on the comeback trail. Linda seems to inspire me *when* things are going well. B.

[To Gerard Malanga]
October 27, 1972

Man, you know, I am under it too, under all that any of us are. this doesn't mean I am too weak to respond, but basically I am fucked...I mean, fucked with what I am and how to work it and not work it.

Signs, counter-signs keep working, they keep working me, I don't know how to work them. there's neither humility or artistry here (in me), it's just a working of a process and it is more clever than I am.

I've gone through, I think, plenty, but there'll be plenty more.

I suppose this all sounds very holy. I am supposed to be the tough guy, the battered Bogart with a typewriter. that's their idea.

there's very little to subsist upon. all this grist we are supposed to create an art upon. sometimes I think that the greatest creators have been the greatest liars. well, inventiveness, that counts, doesn't it?

too precious, too precious, I know.

well, shit, hang in.

Copyright by Charles Bukowski.

[To Carl Weissner]
December 7, 1972

[* * *] I am still in this female battle, and I can't quite figure it, they are entirely too clever for me. it rips me up and makes me late answering to good people like you who are only trying to keep me together and you together while trying to make whipcream out of mudshit. (Life, ya know.) I never met a guy who fought harder for me while getting as little via $$$$ so I just know you've got to like what I am writing down in a line of words.

all right, I say let's get it all going. I wrote Ferling to accept all offers, but he is strange, he runs hot, he runs cold, yet I can't bitch he put out a fat book of my screams. whether he likes me personally is another matter, it doesn't matter because it's my work I'm selling not my drunken days and nights and fits and panics and dreamatics [sic], swans with knotted necks singing Elvis Presley ... [* * *]

like I say, I'm sorry I'm so long on this answering but you know what a woman (women) can do to a man. at 52 I've taken some guts shots that my mind (and experience) should have warned me to ward off. not that I'm crying: maybe that piece of my soul that was blown off needed to be. but it all weakens energy and is a pissing upon my barricades. so much for excuses ... I don't know if I've said anything relevant here, but the two bottles of beer were good, and I still remember the unexpected birthday gift, the cigars and the bottle. I've kept the box. I'm soft on that kind of shit. and feel justified being that way. I hope your life isn't going too bad. Tell Andernach I said hello.

168

Martin had been urging Bukowski to write an autobiographi-
cal novel based on his childhood but Bukowski found the mem-
ories too painful. Several short stories based on this material
had been published in Confessions of a Man Insane
Enough to Live With Beasts *and some more would follow in*
his book of short stories South of No North.

[To John Martin]
December 16, 1972

   on the novel, you know, shit, we stumble. I've decided that I
must enclose parts that were printed in earlier mimeo editions to
fill out parts. otherwise, it can't be done properly. yet the writing
will be different, better. I do believe I am writing better than
ever. how long this will hold has much to do with the gods and
luck and the way I walk down the street. o.k. so I'll start the
novel up again. I've hardly felt like writing the immortal novel,
maybe I never will. if I do I'll probably be 65 or 70 or 80. I think
of some of Hamsun's tomes. he did some living. that has to be
there first. I suppose that's the trouble with professional writers
—they become so professional they stop living. well, I mean they
live as writers, consciously live that way, they stop living haphaz-
ardly as humans. well, I don't like humans or writers but I think
I'm still loose, I'm not a professional writer and if I ever become
one I promise you first boot at my ass, hemorrhoids and all. yeh,
they're back. o, yes. poems enclosed.

p.s.—I get good rays off your Robert Kelly, he is basically a good
sort although he has maneuvered himself into a strange area
where it becomes more button than bone. he reminds me of a big
dog heavy with water that he wants to shake off. but he's kind,
that counts. I think he wants to sing on and on, throw words like
pebbles. that's all right, you know. he's a little too holy but most
of us are ...

[To John Martin]
December 29, 1972

[* * *] Got your good check today. It's a lifeblood thing and always appreciated. I suppose I'm into you for a bit now but maybe it will work your way, finally. I think the writing has gotten better since I got out of the post office—except for the first frantic months ...

Creeley's all right. He's been sniped at too long. We've got to allow him an occasional tantrum or bitterness. the rancor that's out there is unbelievable. I rather enjoy their knocks but that's because I'm a little punchy. That is, I don't mind their knocks when they are published in magazines or newspapers, so forth for everybody to see. what I object to is little hate letters, little jealousy letters to Linda about me from various mimeo editors and poets (?) ... meanwhile, look at their poems, and who are they trying to write like? ta, ta.

[* * *] you tell Barbara that I'm still punching this machine. Harry Truman's gone, Ezra's gone, but I'm still here. laying down the line.

———————————————————————

•

• 1 9 7 3 •

[To A. D. Winans]
January 18, 1973

Excuse the delay but I've come off a 4 day drunk that damn near did it all the way... still shaky... but alive. I'll get some work to you soon for your project. I've changed my mind on answering my critics. I did that in the last *Holy Doors* bit and I think one can only go so far in answering that way... it gets you down there wallowing in all that shit: kind of like a COSMEP conference. I'll just let them have their say, all right? by the way, I'm *honored*, if I didn't say so before, to have a special issue [of *Second Coming*] on this Charles Bukowski guy. [* * *]

[To Joanna Bull]
January 19, 1973

It's bad to be down but we all get down, I get down all the time. Break-ups are bad because 2 people just don't realize how much they fill in for each other until the bust-up, then you feel it all. There's no advice I can give or no wisdom. I drink when I'm down but it only makes it worse. I suppose you'll make it through—women are tougher than men.

I could come by to see you some night. Wednesday night is a

171

good time. But it would just be talk. I'm 52 anyhow, and been
going with a 32 year old sculptress-writer. We have some hard
times but basically I feel like playing her fair. Not that I mean
we'd fuck or such anyhow. just to mention, I could drop by...
where the hell's Ocean Front Walk?

Thanks the poem...You speak of reading a book. one of
mine. which one?

I've been in a writing slump of late. I mean I haven't written
for a week. no, I wrote a column last night. I forgot. I had a fight
with Linda. Confusing.

I don't know. the human being is really durable. I've actually
felt pain crawling all over me like a dark skin, meanwhile the
same motherfucking shimmering knife in the gut in the gut in the
gut in the gut...again and again. but sometimes durability ends.
I tried one suicide and failed. gas.

and a new involvement hardly ever solves an old involve-
ment. there's no escape, and damned little hope. but we have to
laugh. jesus we have to laugh.

as far as writing goes, other writers, they don't come through
much to me. it may be ego. I've got tons of ego and tons of self-
doubt. I'm in good shape.

you hang in,
Buk

[To John Martin]
January 23, 1973

Iz u still alive? don't worry about the novel, the novel is tak-
ing another breather. the fat must stoke up and then I will skim it
off. you understand: everything at its proper time. meanwhile,
some more poems. I hope you and Creeley have patched up your
broken knitting.

everybody's dying—Truman, Johnson, some old jazz great
today at 87...name slides past...we are still working the keys.
My master plan is to live to be 80 but that last drunk damn near
did me in. I can handle a one night drunk but if I hang 2 or 3 of
them together my system just can't take it. I'm 52. that doesn't

mean I have to stop living but it does mean that some of the living must be channeled away from the old bottle. I think too many writers have let it eat them up, kill them. if I can hang in 28 more years of fair writing, I'll be satisfied. don't forget, I rather more or less began at 35 so they owe it to me on this end. o.k. let's see what happens.

[To John Martin]
March 8, 1973

[* * *] listen, I have the most expensive dentist in town. I don't know where I found him. he has these nurses that crawl all over you (me), rub up against one (me) with tit and flank, stare deeply (platitude) into eye (mine). this costs (me). in the old days they called them dentists, you walked in, opened your mouth, stuck your finger in there, said "get that one." you sat down and he yanked it out. now they're called dental surgeons, have these prostitutes around, you just get hard-ons—no teeth pulled. consultations, x-rays, clever jokes. an appointment once a month. meanwhile you're charged and nothing done. also I lost at the track the other day. [* * *]

I checked out Eshleman's poem on the spider. do you realize that he is invading my sacred and private grounds? my poems are full of spiders. spiders, horses, beer and gentle and innocent lament.

[To Carl Weissner]
March 23, 1973

Well, it's all not so bad here, I'm drinking a bottle of calif. rhine wine—cheap shit, granted, but not too cheap—smoking a rolled Prince Albert (and I still can't type) ... we waste some time playing the horses but not too much money ... I'm waiting for the Muse to grow giant-size.... Linda wrote a one-act play, pretty good too, it'll be on the boards in May, I think. no cash but a

173

start. I've gotten some $$$$ offers to do a play but maybe I can't do a play and I just don't want to limp in with some lines ... the force and the mood just gotta precede me. there are some wars here with the lady but then I'm a little crazy in my thinking, or maybe I'm not crazy in my thinking. anyhow, I'm still here, it's a good change, and I'm not going to say LOVE too heavy because that might jinx it. [* * *]

as I write this Linda stands by the typewriter reading over my shoulder and scratching her beautiful ass. now she laughs. now she rattles papers. now she rattles papers and laughs.

now she says Bukowski will you please shut up about me? she's such a modest kid.

o.k. she says the book of the year is hers not mine, and it's called *Sweet and Dirty*. and it is. maybe I can get her to send you a free autographed copy. o.k.?

where was I?

all right, I've got to get into some work, work, work, but I hardly think of it as work especially after a long layoff (6 or 7 days) the words build and the ideas climb like hornets about the walls, ah. the divinity of our lives is majorly amazing ...

I must roll another cigarette and watch the blue smoke curl and curl and curl and let myself feel good for a few moments. I never used to let myself feel too good. now, for some reason, I feel like I deserve to feel good. I've paid the baker, the druggist, the gods, the cops, the pimps and the whores ... now, look—see how it works? Linda just came over and got some of my wine. a little shot, she says. little? there went half a bottle ...

Love Story. yes, I saw it on tv. I never laughed so much in my life. what a ridiculous hunk of pretentious phoney shit but looking at it as pure comedy it was magnificent, if you know what I mean. I guessed each scene before it arrived. you know, the world is really a long long way from solving ANYTHING when they gulp in this kind of tripe and admire it. no chance, friend. we might as well give up. just saw off a corner of the action, a very tiny corner and sit there and wait for them to come and get us. [* * *]

174

[To A. D. Winans]
March 23, 1973

Listen, here is a photo of me. Didn't you want a photo of me? o.k., here's one. is the Bukowski issue still on? I want to get famous.

When do you want me to start working on a cover idea? How much porno can you handle? when in the hell are you coming out with this issue? summer? will I live until summer? I think I'll get a statement of sorts to you. I think maybe a longer statement, bio and rambling, will be better than a short story. I'll get a couple of bottles of wine and sit down one night to the typer. we'll get many imperfections that way but I'm not against imperfections. I think that the literary people are too smooth too careful, cover mistakes. we'll piss on that. all right? after all, it's *my* old ass that is going to be exposed.... [* * *]

[To A. D. Winans]
April 2, 1973

sounds like you did it up but there you go, it's the price and pain of drinking and it's like the price and pain of women— you've got to pay hard sometimes when you least expect it. I've been in so much trouble, jail jail jail jail jail jail jail jail jail jail jail and fine, fine and jail, drunk driving, getting beat up while drunk, all that, well, it's the same for most of us but one of the best things I learned *was to stay out of the bars* and also to try to stay off the street. I fail sometimes to stay off the streets but not too often. the finest place on earth to drink is in your own place and *alone*. you probably know all this. all right. [* * *]

so now look I've got to scrape myself together and work the typewriter ribbon a bit. some real dead creeps over last night, brought no energy, and I had to split with the beer though there were 4 of them. taken again. they ate my time. nothing to do, they had nothing to do, and there are billions like them.

[To John Martin]
April [?25], 1973

[* * *] they're rough on the P's lately. Picasso gone, Pound gone, it's hardly false humility when I say I'm not in their class, but it's still good going on a while, working with the word and the way. there's no other life and when I realize and look back on all those years working for other men for their way and their profit and their glowing beings, I realize that this is a very magic and lucky time, indeed indeed indeed, and you had very much to do with making it so. sometimes I awaken at night and think, my wrists are here, I'm here, my toes, my body, there's the walls and there are the streets outside, dark hard blood-tasting streets, I know them. And I think, just a few years more like this and I'll be paid back for all of it. well, now we have been very somber and serious. let's let up. you balding red-haired devil, don't get run over in the streets, I won't know which way to look.

[To Joanna Bull]
May 1, 1973

I'm still living with Linda. Some rough battles. I don't know if we're going to make it. I don't know whose fault it is. Some of it might be mine, but not entirely.

Anyhow, Linda makes her annual trek to Utah around mid-June, stays about 3 weeks, and I'd like to see you a few times then. I have good memories of you—so far. So, around mid-June, if you're still there I'll try to contact you. I hope you're still there. We needn't push too hard at each other. I have nothing to prove. It's just that I feel that the Linda situation won't hold up, and it would be good to know somebody. I have male friends but it's hardly the same thing. You be happy if possible.

176

"SPR" is the Small Press Review *published quarterly by Dustbooks from Paradise, California, from 1967 to 1974, and later as a monthly. Nikos Stangos was the editor of the Penguin Contemporary Poets series, in which Bukowski shared a volume with Harold Norse and Philip Lamantia.*

[To A. D. Winans]
May 16, 1973

I think the SPR was a hatchet job to begin with, Fulton leading the tribe. I don't mind Norse; I think he's truly mixed-up on what has occurred, he's basically honest and stung, it's just that the eyes that see out of him or whatever sees out has it wrong. It's like Martin said when he read Norse, "But, Jesus, you *told* me to print him!" Al, things happen to us all and when things don't work we tend to point to others. I've been in the same room with Norse when he has made his accusations to me and they were so out of the way and ridiculous that I didn't respond except to take another drink. I still think Norse is a fine poet but he has become a great big grandma weeping into the towel. I don't know what to do with him. I suppose the best thing to do with him is just to let him go on writing his poems while I write mine. His claim that he got me into Penguin 13 might have some truth. He was a friend of Stangos, one of the editors. If I wanted to be a bitch I might suggest that Norse got in the same way. But I'm sure that Stangos and Penguin and Norse himself wouldn't have wanted me if I hadn't shown them a good spitter, a good slider and a fair fast ball.

I thought Packard did a good professional job, and Linda King's was amusing and Quag's was drab o.k. but most of the others were in with some kind of buildup or bitch or grind, trying to make a climb upon the Buk myth or mystique or Buk bullshit or whatever. It was an attempt at a personal advancement of sorts—saying: if he's no good and I know he's no good, I *must* be good, even great. It's all right. Watergate poetry. These tiny shit climbers bug me, hahaha. Winans, too much time used upon talking about them gives them what they need. I don't want to go into them or out of them anymore. Except to say, that frankly, it's not bad being attacked, it was expected. long ago, when I first started writing poems at age 35 to Jon Webb: "I know when I get

177

them angry that I am getting there." These aren't the exact words. I just went over to the bookcase to find them but didn't want to bother. Tra la la.

[* * *] listen, criticism is all right—if they can break it down and say it's wrong and why—I think I did that with my review of Hemingway's last book *Islands in the Stream* for *TV and Fine Arts Guide*. There is a way of doing things. but the cheap shots never pay off. I have given a few low shots—for sake of caricature—but not too many cheap ones have I dealt. I don't run cheap; I keep it strong and clipped and even, and that's what pisses them.

I am glad that there are *some* littles that play something besides the lonely heart and diminutive talent game. these few show that there's a chance somewhere in all of us, a human easy decent chance. that's plenty, that little chance. the whole god damned nation of the United States of America is now wobbling. failing, failing, with all that power. think of how some 19 year old kid in his mother's bedroom, just getting over acne and going to college and having his 25 buck Sears Roebuck mimeo machine sitting there must feel? he can reject Ginsberg if he wants to because Ginsberg likes to send to such shit rags. 25 dollars doesn't make an editor, though it can. there are just too many non-things playing as things. I do suppose it's the age of super-fluousness. everybody is something, or thinks they are. what a vast can of *shit*. how are we ever going to get out of it?—mean-while, while I write this I'm not writing something else. [* * *]

[To Joanna Bull]
July 1, 1973

All right, after the first week in July I'll phone and see if I might come by with my tiny bottle of beer.

Things very tenuous here. I once loved Linda very much and I believe she still loves me (love is an easy word to use here for lack of something else) but it is slowly breaking off, it has to be final, eventually. I don't want to break your back with my side of the story. Perhaps, someday, I can write it down—novel form. Somerset Maugham wrote something near to it, but hardly near enough and he seemed to lean towards homosexual proclivities and I think it takes a man to write about a woman. A woman can't do it either, and maybe not me. It's so difficult to tread center in the female-male Emote. But I am obsessed with the Art-form, it's the only religion, the only beastly breath of air left. It purifies shit, it explains it; it lets you sleep at night, finally. I'm not a moralist and I don't believe in conscience but in matters of feeling one should be careful. I am careful because feelings are holy and humorous and three-quarters of the sun. I don't trust the mind unless it's run by the bellybutton ... god, how I go on! what am I saying? I said that I wouldn't break your back.

I suppose with Linda I filled the father-fixation process or whatever the fuck you call it? Ask the Calif. School of Psychology. Are you ready for a father-fixation process? My darling beautiful Linda goes into all manners of fits and fandangos when I reject her final innards and make moves to leave—mostly violent, very, physical attacks which I handle as best I may. Which means getting her under control with as little injury to her as possible. I am what you call a very cool cat under fire. Some other men would have killed her long ago; I am looking for material for a novel, and I once did love her; besides she came out of a madhouse and they haven't put me into one, yet. That makes me master, doesn't it?

Look, you say obsessions die hard with you? Is that what men are? Obsessions? Don't you ever want to give up the game of hurt and hunt and chess and cheat? Can't you make a value judgment? Can't you choose anybody? To lay down with and look at the ceiling with and listen to music and smoke cigarettes and talk and laugh and flow? Wouldn't it feel good to you to become something? Shit, I'm not saying it's me. I'm your father. But it should be somebody. Somebody for somebody, even if it's only yourself. That's what I'm working on: me for me, easy at first, and then maybe I can open a door for somebody else.

[To John Martin]
July 4, 1973

Well, shit, I don't know, I'm heading for some foolish Utah mountain, I might be gone from two to four weeks and I suppose

179

there might not be much work done. Linda wins again. But don't worry. I'm making a study on her. If I ever get it down right some day you'll see the female exposed as she has never been exposed. Very difficult to do, though; the tone of the writing must be impartial, exact. The more it's that way the better it will be. meanwhile, haha, there's still *Factotum*, isn't there? [* * *]

[To A. D. Winans]
July 16, 1973

been on a week's beerdrunk, back from Utah, Linda and I have split, I have to be out of here by the 29th. I've got a little book with 3 or 4 numbers but I'll be damned if I quite want to get involved again, maybe never again, kid, I'll be 53 in August, and this battling with and living with the female has kept me trim in a fashion, but so much of the game is run on trickery, chess moves, false moves, ticklers, blasters, farts and one-tenth feelings …Ugh, I'm too simple to comprehend, understand…I think most of our women have been raised too much upon movie magazines and the screen. They've learned game-playing and dramatics but my head just wants to go where it is.

yes, run the Norse, I haven't had a good belly-tickler in some months. I think that what has happened with Hal is that he has put total importance upon *poetics* and what a poet is supposed to be. a good poet never knows what he is, he's a dime from the edge, but there's nothing holy about it. it's a job. like mopping a bar floor. I can't rail too much against him; I suppose that the things he has imagined in his mind seem very true to him. who is the judge? I rattled around his place in Venice a couple of nights drunk but it was much more in energy and clowning than malice or a wish to destroy. I'm an asshole in many ways, I even enjoy my assholeness. I can tear a man in half in a short story; I can also tear myself in half, but I'm no knifer, I don't whisper things into editors' ears. I'm no destroyer. Nothing can be destroyed that has the power to move forward into its own thing. fame or acceptance or politics or power has nothing to do with it. nothing is needed but self going-on as self must. one only need realize this small realization. [* * *]

180

Mich[eline] is all right—he's one third bullshit but he's got a special divinity and a special strength. [* * *] I can't think of another poet who has more and who has been neglected more. Jack is the last of the holy preachers sailing down Broadway singing the song. He's right: they'll find him after he's dead. [* * *] Jack has it; through all the bullshit and con and hollering, Jack has it. may the gods give him a good woman who understands him, and a better Age to live in than this castrated, de-emphasized, titless, toothless, anti-human, anti-word, anti-feeling 20th century, amen.

the split with Linda isn't easy. I never go into things with just a toenail. but we can't fall down on the rug and die. we came up too hard and too slow. we are dumb but not quite damned. and most of the things that happen to each of us happen to everybody. not that it lessens the feelings but we have to keep remembering that we aren't especially singular or especially precious. [* * *]

think how low we'd feel without even the word to bounce around? well, there's beer and a rolled cigarette and my radio plays a touch of Brahms. I haven't grown much. I don't know how.

[To Carl Weissner]
August 11, 1973

sorry the silence but as you can see I'm at a new address, Linda and I have split and I am a little bit out of my brain, guts dangling ... [* * *]
I am really down low. can't even get the word down. forgive.

[To Carl Weissner]
September 10, 1973

sorry I dripped the blues on you last letter, I've got the pieces put together better now, still trouble, trouble with women and trouble inside of my head, but I guess that all the rumbling and shit and insanity counts, let's hope so. if I ever get stable I might as well sell my ass to the peacocks. [* * *]

actually, though, I do have my UPS. I sometimes sit around thinking, god, some people think that I am a writer. How did I ever fool them? I can't write a cat's turd. I am still alive. I can lay in this bed for 4 days and nobody will bother me. That's fine. I can masturbate, I can kill myself. dear god, I have all kinds of freedoms. I can even read *The Rebel* by Camus, that book I bought the other day at Martindales except I lost my glasses the last time I was drunk and I can't read the print. I verily can even open a can or bottle of beer.

all right, baby, the hard rain falls for all of us sometime. take Job. take him a long ways away. I am tired of his wails. take me a long way away.

you hold too. all this lightning, she gotta stop.

[To A. D. Winans]
October 7, 1973

listen, Micheline did get me at a bad time. Some of the stories were all right but he does get too much into this MOON— GLORY—I AM A POET trip and it tends to sink the whole thing. like, poor bastard, he's a poet. well, there are a lot of poor bastards—interns in hospitals, garbage collectors, dishwashers, factory workers, farm hands ... if anybody has divine rights they probably have them too.

[To A. D. Winans]
October 24, 1973

you write a letter like a man who knows where it's at.

yeh, we all come out of areas. Lefty O'Doul. boy, what a hitter. he was an old man when he was managing the Seals but he still pinch hits against the Angels down here, and damn, every

time I saw him it seemed he got his hit... but, like you, all that
has drained for me. you keep seeing them coming and going and
there are all the screams and then it vanishes. I think Ezra played
a better game even though he denied it at the end. I think he
realized he played it a little too fancy and too heavy but he had
guts enough to admit it and realize it.

getting over the documentary BUKOWSKI and making love to
the ribbon again. I, shit yes, look forward to your special Buk
edition, and with that maybe I can get back to the holy grind
(poetry). ah.

you appear on the right road in. beware the blood-suckers.
beware the friends. beware, especially, the poets. even me.

[To Gerald Locklin]
December 5, 1973

Well, readings are like women, they're good and they're bad,
and you go on to the next one or you give them up altogether.
But readings are only an aid to survival and I can't in anyway
judge them as a creative act. It's closer to carnival and you need
some luck and a few drinks to come out close to even. I think
even guys like J. Dickey know this; he charges two grand, reads
once or twice and goes out and shoots something with a bow and
arrow. A man needs his basic strength in order to move that
typewriter ribbon into good action. The idea of the game must
never be forgotten: the laying down of the line.

The '49-er bar is as close to literary bar as anything I have
seen; but, luckily, it ain't snob, the rays are good and easy. Now I
gotta fly up to S.F. and do my little act. I pretty much feel like a
whore selling quicky snatch up an alley. Well, it beats being mid-
dle linebacker for the The Dallas Cowboys. [* * *]

•

• 1 9 7 4 •

These two young writers had founded a magazine entitled Aunt Harriet's Flair for Writing Review, *only one issue of which appeared, November 1974.*

[To James Whitaker and Ebenezer Juarez]
January 3, 1974

got your ten. hot cha. you've got an immortal title to your mag. the problem is in setting the pages on fire. I know. I edited a mag once. 3 issues. I dwarfed out. just not enough around. o.k. I wrote these poems yesterday. look them over. let me know, plus or minus. I still got your motherhumpin' ten. you seem to show style. do send me your first issue whether I'm in it or not.

p.s.—you needn't drop a check on him because unlike me he's got money and *plenty*, but it hasn't seemed to diminish his humanism (whatever that is) or his artistry (whatever that is) but I'd suggest you write him for some poems...he can lay the line down: Steve Richmond [*address follows*].

[To James Whitaker]
January 14, 1974

help, help, help, help, help, now LISTEN: tear up poem "sitting around listening to Bach"!!! wrote this on split with my woman, was bitter and vindictive; may be good writing in there but it definitely is from the wrong source, especially now ... wouldn't want woman I'm back with to *read* that poem ... DESTROY. I've destroyed my copy ... stamped enclosed envelope to let me hear from you that you've done likewise, AND, I want to THANK YOU, MIGHTILY. o.k.?

no, haven't read anything by Jim Harrison; that isn't saying that he couldn't quite well have it, though.

the millionaire's daughter and I lived (for a while) in Wheeler, Texas ... the place with 7 lakes and wild turkey and *green woods* ... Frye Interceptor, World War II plane, planned and put together by her father. Gramps owned the land and the farmers did the work for ½ the profit while the son's planes sprayed the crops and were paid for it. on and on. like you know, we didn't make it. if I remember, Wheeler very near to Oklahoma border and voted by a panel of experts as the last place in U.S. anybody would care to lay an atomic bomb upon. pop. then about 2,000. [* * *]

[To A. D. Winans]
January 21, 1974

Went to the p.o box today and there it was—Vol. 11, no. 3. I don't go to the box often, don't know how long it has been laying there, but to let you know—much more solid than *The Small Press Review*. better writers writing. I guess it *was* needed to get some of the grit out. I think the best part was that most saw me for what I was—fucked-up, battered, battering, punchy but durable, trying to get out, trying to get it on down. Literature has always had this sheen of dignity, it's disgusting. I'm glad if we put some dirt and blood on the carpet. even those who were always crying for a changed literature, a better literature, a more *real* thing, guys like Pound and W. C. Williams, they *still* worked out of the formal, stilted cage. I hope we've now gotten some freedom for those who follow. Maybe I carry it too far. for instance, I've always advocated that they serve beer, play music, maybe have strippers at our museums. think of how much better *and* more real the sabre tooth tiger would look? o.k., you know what I mean.

I liked the Richmond. He knows how to give due to the object without destroying the object involved. this is no easy thing. Steve also knows how to write a *sentence*. Most can't. [* * *] I have said for years that Steve Richmond is the most underrated human and writer and painter that I know. perhaps it's best that way. he's protected. he may be lucky too if they leave him alone. a man must have time to build certain walls so if they finally come with their pompoms he can take that, and still go on.

Micheline was fine, god damn romantic hustler, he turned on high, he sings those lines, he's in rhythm and breaking through. [* * *] when Jack is turned on high he is capable of writing a better poem than I could ever write. I write more good poems over the long haul but when he is totally high and singing I can't touch him. if he stays at it and stops hounding the publishers and just does his work he will be found again long before he is dead. [* * *]

Norse? I understand his viewpoint. we simply come out of different poetic backgrounds. [* * *] And when I'm drunk I am generally rude and boorish and stupid to everybody alike. I just don't select Hal. If he could understand this he might feel better. before a man can ever meet the gods he must learn to forgive the drunks. [* * *]

Alta. I understand her viewpoint and it certainly must seem plausible and right to her, but creation, art, is the breakthrough. we hardly do what is proper or kind, though often, in life, we are kinder than most, much more. without flying flags about it. Alta does not know how to write a sentence down. it hurts her pitch. I don't want to rape Alta. I don't want to rape anybody. I never have. But if an artist wants to go into the mind of a rapist or a murderer and look out of that mind and write down that mind, I don't think that is criminal. furthermore, I didn't say my stories in *NOLA* were "sarcastic." I don't apologize for my work. If I write a story about a shitty woman then that shitty woman did exist. one form or another. blacks can also be shitty as can whites. I refuse to be restricted in the materials I can paint with. it's really all so ridiculous to defend anything as *just* that thing, can't they even understand that? Oh, Alta, I *have* love … that's why I can write of other things. [* * *]

Hugh Fox, as usual, uses the opportunity to advertise himself. that's all right. if you got the talent to back up your breakthrough. see: Hemingway–Fitzgerald. When Fox claimed he had been beat about more physically than I had, that's untrue. [* * *] no man knows what a physical beating is until he gets one. getting off your knees in a dark alley with 14 drunks watching and before you can get your hands up to your knees he lands again and gives you a knee in the nuts as you go down. Nothing to do but get up. finally it becomes a matter of breathing. you can hardly breathe. and neither can the man who is murdering you. and finally, as you start to come back on him, they stop the fight. you get in 7 or 9 of these, you know what a physical beating is. and the factories and the farm labor market. Fox is a dreamer. he's never had a physical beating. I looked at his face. he still hasn't had one. I can tell by the way he writes.

All in all, Al, it was a very good issue, and the stuff I wrote and the way I lived was mostly for me, but I see that if some have picked up a certain style and meaning in it, good. But I never mean my way to be their way. they can have theirs and I don't think they'd fit in mine. that's fair. I do much of my stuff out of tune, out of one ear. we don't want a mythology or a hero. it was just a way to go. and there's still tomorrow. Shakey's tomorrow &&&&&&. then Dashiel H's, or was it somebody else's Big Sleep. ah, hahaha. after I'm dead Hal Norse will be able to eat his soft-boiled eggs and his Egyptian parsley in peace.

[To Carl Weissner]
May 17, 1974

I got the *Gedichte die einer schrieb* … your signed copy, plus 5 others from the publisher. You put it together so well, babe, you make me feel like Bogart Bukowski Bukowski Bukowski. I like it. I like to like things sometimes. You know I've gone a hard route and have put down some words and you don't mind admitting it.

all right, it has been a good circus, and I'm lucky to have you over there to transmute me. ah. the book has the warm feel of burning and there. you've done it. You know you have. I won't brag anymore on the book—except to say the good things you've done for me usually arrive at times when I need them most. Like you know, hahaha, I am rifting with my woman again; it is such a slow process, these many breakups, but it's necessary to finalize it finally. the woman's thoughts and feelings are continually against mine and the other way around. she seems to understand my enemy more than she does me, so there's only one thing left to do—let her go to the enemy. it's not easy, but she belongs with them; I've only borrowed something from them. tra, la. tra, la.

Big shoot-out tonight. I guess it happened just as I left the racetrack, a loser, after the 9th race. I passed very close. The SLA* Army, it seems. Trying to look for some symphony music on the radio I passed upon the news. Nothing finalized at this moment. But much fire-power. Where they were holed-up caught on fire. There are so many angles to this thing. One is that DeFreeze was allowed to escape from a minimum security area when he was in jail. whoever knows that and what the truth is? who knows who squealed? Who knows who is who? Who knows what it finally really means? Maybe just the tv screen brought into the streets? maybe an overdose of Marx? Christ knows I am one of the last who knows what's going on around here, and I hardly adore it. But I don't know if I love the SLA anymore than I do the USA. It's all a manner of hard hunger and wanting control. Each side pushes so hard that they become dehumanized. religion and the popular vote, of course, are the softeners. but, babe, I've got to believe that *we* are in the right slot—creation is the greatest and purest revolution of them all, and it finally causes everything else to move behind it. Maybe too far behind it. But we are the prow. we know the death and the waste and the glory, and some of the way, and we have Eye enough to see the Revolutionary, the Capitalist, the Fascist and the cabbage. We have trouble with women, but give us a new typewriter ribbon and some of the rent paid, we get the courage up, and getting the courage up and moving toward the sun, that's fair enough in this time of bending funnels.

---

*The "Symbionese Liberation Army," a terrorist group best remembered for kidnapping Patty Hearst and converting her to their cause.

since I got kicked out of the lady's house for not caring for her parties and my friends (she *likes* my friends), I came on over here, and there has been much trouble here, I inhale and they phone the police, I scratch myself and they beat on my floor (I'm up on the 2nd) and the little man came around and said, Inflation, gave me a notice of a rent boost and also my friends below and all those about this frog-in-the-garden-pond-vine-death-cement endurance of quiet posing and pissing and murders; how they HATE the sound of my typewriter... [* * *]

so the town is half burning down again over here. and I'm *still* on my second novel... Let's hope that the German female and the German life is fairly good to you over there. if I ever get enough money, which I won't, I want to come over and see you, have you lead me down the streets of Andernach, I will weep and we will drink beer somewhere and my mouth will form into a round toothless and insensible hole, and you'll think, great god, what've I got on myself here? Bogart turned to mulch and butter. I shoulda translated Douglas Blazek.

Winans published Wantling's 7 on Style *in 1975. Bukowski's foreword was not included (see letters of July 25 to Weissner and November [?] to Winans, below).*

[To A. D. Winans]
May 21, 1974

Have been in bad mental state so have not responded to yours.... sobered up now and on better spiritual grounds.

Yes, I know about Wantling, Ruthie phoned me about it some time back. Like, we're always ready for the death thing yet when it happens we're still not ready. I picked up on Bill, all the way. So, sure I'd like to do the foreword to *Style*. Wantling had been sending me some of the poems but I can't seem to locate them. If I do a foreword, of course, I'd like to see the poems. Can you manage to send me xerox copies? [* * *]

On Bergé, she's down on me. We had a bit of a haggle when I was editing *Laugh Literary*. Nothing much. She wrote what I thought to be a letter that was a bit precious when I rejected her poems. I mailed the letter back but she returned it. I had no recourse but to publish the letter. I guess she hasn't forgotten. She's never met me personally so her knowledge of me is through my writing. Enough. [* * *]

Bukowski is here reacting to an advance copy of Burning in Water, Drowning in Flame, *officially published June 21, 1974.*

[To John Martin]
June 17, 1974

I react slowly... it's my nature... but your (and Barbara's) (and my) Selected Poems book is a marvelous creature. I have not lost my wonderment toward very good things. Grace and luck to all of us. New poems enclosed.

[To A. D. Winans]
June 24, 1974

Well, here's the shot at it. I had to wait for it to pull together. If it doesn't work for you, send it back. See enclosed s.a.e.

I'm single again, trying different women. They're all pretty good if they don't stay over two days. [* * *]

Kitty Foyle *(1939) was a novel by Christopher Morley.*

[To John Martin]
July 16, 1974

on the Linda split—she could become the 3rd novel if I ever finish the 2nd. I don't know if I'm man enough to write it straight. S. Maugham did something similar—what was it? Kitty Foyle? No, something else, I believe. o.k. [* * *]

[To Carl Weissner]
July 25, 1974

[* * *] no, Prince, I don't take the ups and downs of women very good; I am a *very* emotional fellow, I get to like almost everything—even mosquitoes. one thing, though, I've never gotten much of an affinity of attachment for is the roach. only Kafka's marvelous roach, poor fellow. but I *do* take it hard because when I go, I go. I throw away the oars. I know, I ought to know. hahaha. the female is generally *very* good to me. I haven't known a great many but most have been long runs. I'm not a chaser or a hunter. If one doesn't arrive, I don't search. But upon arrival, my guts generally go right down the mother drain, they're spilled in there, helplessly. I am tuned-up to this inside roar and when this inside roar touches upon something—it flicks off in a rather helpless state. it feels very good but the headlights are sometimes dim. what happened this last time is that I kept compromising in order to hold. she began to drift, at first, spiritually elsewhere because she thought she was beautiful and maybe she was, but this type of woman needs constant outward attention from many outward sources. she needs feeding from many. I might need feeding from one, and when the chips are really down that one might only be me.

so there you had it. a Loner in bed next to one who needed the constant adulation of the Crowd. no way, Prince. the crowd drained me; it bucked her up like puffed wheat rice cereal dropped into milk. she found all manners of fascinating aspects

192

about the crowd that to me only seemed pig-farts and creeping lies and game-playing and obviousness. she wanted parties, she wanted to dance and chat and giggle. she was Marilyn Monroe the sex pet, she modeled herself after her. she drove and whirled and gambled, wiggled her tits and ass, drove the men crazy. and I thought, christ, how did I ever get into this? it was simple: she had sought me out and I had sucked in. now she wanted me as the strong man springboard that she could leap off of and return to. she had her parties, she had her way. I held my ground, cooled it, looked the other way. she moved again. she started fucking guys, two in a week, followed quickly by another. same old shit—claiming she had only done it in reaction to me—the time she had caught my car outside Stella's house, the time I had gone with Liza Williams to Del Mar and slept along the shore with the waves breaking under us.

Prince, I found that she was too swift for me. She looked better than I did—to most people. She could get fucked more often and more continually. Does this sound like a bitch? She was. So she took off for Utah for 3 months and left me her television set. She told me that she would accept a Summer man but that I would be her Winter man and that it was only fair of her to tell her Summer man that.

How much shit can an old dog swallow? I wrote back and told her in three sentences that it was over. What the 3 sentences were don't matter here. but I cut the knot, Gordian or otherwise. it's finis. her tv is in her closet, the key is on the mantle and the birds piss into the wind. aloha. [* * *]

supposed to write foreword to one of Wantling's last books, *Style*. I did but his old lady came out here and we didn't make it at all—total opposites. It wasn't because I didn't fuck her, that wouldn't have been nec. It's only that all our ideas were reversed. I met and knew Wantling—we were on similar waves of a sort. Down in a motel in Laguna one night I snarled at his x-wife (death is divorce, isn't it?), "No wonder the son of a bitch had to take the needle for 9 years. He was living with you." Then I walked out drunk in my shorts and jumped to the bottom of the pool. came up. as you guessed. but at 54 I ought to wear water wings to pull shit like that. anyhow, she'll prob. nix the foreword, which is all right. I was only talking about *Style*. [* * *]

No, nobody has my tape. *Terror Street*. it has vanished into the languishing cunts that once spoke love. and there are a few new women about. I've fucked a few but the one I cared for I was afraid to fuck. I didn't want to make any mistakes. She had these rays shooting out about 30 feet from her body—I can't explain it, very difficult, she looked good but without push. everything I said she understood and I tried some wild areas. she got it, I could tell by her counter-answers. I left her alone. I let her sleep on my couch; I slept in my bed. neither of us slept all night. wide-awake. it was very funny. when I took her to the airport, everything was a generous high ... no cancer. I'm going up to see her in August. I know that things are seldom as they seem, but I must find out ... *again*. we're suckers to the last, Carl, cunt-suckers, soul-suckers. [* * *]

Carl, there has been a great emotional and spiritual spring-back since I cut myself loose from that Marilyn Monroe so-called good luck thing. she claimed that I restricted her artistic complexities. let her do well. you don't know how many of her poems I worked over to make them o.k. She'd read them to me. I'd say, "Now, look, don't you think you'd better just *drop* the 3rd line down? And the ending—what do you mean by that? It's useful to you but insensible to anybody else. Why don't you just say: ..." and I'd give her the ending and she'd use it; one of them even rather immortal, talking about what a jackass I was ... called "The Great Poet." an ambitious woman. they pop their cunts over you and their lips over your dick and expect all the answers.

Have written a hundred and ten poems in the last two weeks; a few of them are shit; 7 or 8 of them are immortal. [* * *]

[To John Martin]
August 2, 1974

Yes, that letter was from one of those modern sicks—thinks it's clever to steal a $35 or $15 book from the library and then write to the author and brag about it. hell, the best thing about a library book is that more than one person gets to read them (it).

And I'm to come by and eat dinner with him? Such an immense stupidity. Ow, ow, ow—and we're both poets! He says.

[To Carl Weissner]
November 7, 1974

Thanks the good letter. You over there in Germany waving
Bukowski around feels damned fine to me. Glad you like *Burn-
ing*. It's been a long hot journey but I want to go on a long while
yet ... typing ... and I hope the gods let me. Meanwhile my life is
about the same—fighting the women, the horses; getting fright-
ened and brave, up and down, low and high. [* * *]

Just in from Utah and Michigan. Michigan reading paid
$500, plus air, plus room and food and booze. Cost 'em a grand
to hear me sing. Stopped off in bookstore after reading. They'd
advertised in the *Detroit Free Press*. 700 arrived, massed-in, ass-
hole to asshole. I signed books, danced, read, drank and insulted
people. It was crazy but I was so damned high I didn't care. Slept
in hotel 200 years old, stayed 3 nights and days. Awakened one
morning sick, retching, phoned down to switchboard lady:
"Look, I have a complaint. I wake up sick here every morning
and the first thing I've got to look at is that American flag out
there. Can't something be done about it?" She got very pissy-
assed and asked if I didn't LIKE the American flag. "Look," I
said, "I just told you. I'm sick and it makes me sicker. If that
makes you uptight, just forget it's a flag. It's just a matter of
white and red stripes waving in my face. And the stars. I've got a
bad stomach." They didn't take the flag down for me, Carl.

Guy came over and got drunk with me last night. He wants
to buy the movie options on *South of No North*. I drank his booze
and then turned him over to Martin. The other guy just renewed
his option on *Erections* and the guy who has *Post Office* says he
has high hopes. If just one of these turns into a movie I'm going
to buy a new pair of shoes.

Like you know: stay in the trenches and lob some out. I think
we're wearing those sons of bitches out. ya.

195

Hello editors:

Regarding the Lynne Bronstein letter of Nov. 15 about my story of Nov. one:

1. The story was about pretentiousness in art. The fact that the pretender had female organs had nothing to do with the story in total. That any female made to look unfavorable in a story must be construed as a denunciation of the female as female is just so much guava. The right of the creator to depict characters any way he must remains inviolate—whether those characters are female, black, brown, Indian, Chicano, white, male, Communist, homosexual, Republican, peg-legged, mongolian and/or ?

2. The story was a take-off on an interview with an established female poet in a recent issue of *Poetry Now*. Since I have been interviewed for a future issue of the same journal and for future editions of *Creem* and *Rolling Stone*, my detractors will get their chance to see how I hold or fail under similar conditions.

3. When the narrator lets us know that he has Janice Altrice's legs in mind might infer more that he is bored with the poetry game, and also might infer that he could have a poolhall, dirty joke mind, at times. That the narrator might be attacking himself instead of trying to relegate the lady back to a "sex object" evidently is beyond the belief of some so-called Liberated women. Whether we like it or not, sex and thoughts of sex do occur to many of us (male and female) at odd and unlikely times. I rather like it.

4. That "she is indeed speaking for Bukowski himself, who has expressed a similar contempt for unknown poets who give each other support." The lady spoke for herself. Her "contempt" was toward poets not academically trained. My dislike is toward all bad poetry and toward all bad poets who write it badly—which is most of them. I have always been disgusted with the falsity and dreariness not only of contemporary poetry but of the poetry of the centuries—and this feeling was with me before I got published, while I was attempting to get published, and it remains with me now even as I pay the rent with poesy. What kept me writing was not that I was so good but that that whole damned gang was so bad—when they had to be compared to the vitality and originality that was occurring in the other art forms.

—As to those who must gather together to give each other support, I am one with Ibsen: "the strongest men are the most alone."

5. "Now that he's well-known and the only southern California poet published by Black Sparrow Press, he thinks that nobody else is entitled to be a poet—especially women." My dear lady: you are entitled to be whatever you can be; if you can leap twenty feet straight up into the air or sweep a 9 race card at the Western harness meet, please go ahead and do so.

6. "A lot of us think there's more to write poetry about than beer drunks, hemorrhoids, and how rotten the world is." I also think there's more to write poetry about than that and I do so.

7. "Female artists, on the other hand, try to be optimistic." The function of the artist is not to create optimism but to create art—which sometimes may be optimistic and sometimes can't be. The female is bred to be more optimistic than the male because of a function she has not entirely escaped as yet: the bearing of the child. After passing through pregnancy and childbirth, to call life a lie is much more difficult.

8. "Could it be that the male is 'washed-up' as an artist, that he has no more to say except in his jealousy, to spit on the young idealists and the newly freed voices of women?" Are these the thought concepts you come up with in your "ego-boosting" sessions? Perhaps you'd better take a night off.

9. "Poetry is an art form. Like all art forms, it is subjective and it does not have sex organs." I don't know about your poems, Lynne, but mine have cock and balls, eat chili peppers and walnuts, sing in the bathtub, cuss, fart, scream, stink, smell good, hate mosquitoes, ride taxicabs, have nightmares and love affairs, all that.

10. "... without being negative ..." I thought they'd long ago ridden this horse to death; it's the oldest of the oldest hats. I first heard it around the English departments of L.A. high school in 1937. The inference, when you call somebody "negative," is that you completely remove them from the sphere because he or she has no basic understanding of life forces and meanings. I wouldn't be caught using that term while drunk on a bus to Shreveport.

11. I don't care for Longfellow or McKuen either, although they both possess (possessed) male organs. One of the best writers I knew of was Carson McCullers and she had a female name.

If my girl friend's dog could write a good poem or a decent novel I'd be the first to congratulate the beast. That's Liberated.

12. Shit, I ought to get paid for this.

Charles Bukowski

[To A. D. Winans]
November [?], 1974

[* * *] About the foreword you yanked, o.k. That's what an editor's for ... you either promulgate the thing or you reject it. In this game we all get stuff back, and sometimes get things taken and published that would have been better tossed away with the used condoms.

Been on the reading kick ... the old survival suck ... Detroit, Riverside, Santa Cruz ... Ginsberg, Ferlinghetti, Snyder at S.C. Drew 1600 at 3 bucks a head. Benefit for Americans in Mexican jails ... after the poets got their bit of cream. There was a bomb threat and old Allen's ears jumped. He got on stage and improvised a poem about the situation. Linda read too. Next day we hung around town testing the bars. They seemed to be a cut or two above the general slop pits of L.A.

Ginsberg was all right, he seemed a good sort. [* * *]

Haven't written too much while on this poetry reading tour. The juices are there; simply have to get into the habit of sitting at the Royal Altar ... keeping letters short and staying away from the track ... a bit ... might be an aid.

Bukowski was now writing his novel Factotum.

[To John Martin]
December 4, 1974

Hard times are a-comin', kid. I hope we loop through. Let's get lucky against the tide. Why not? Meanwhile, these which I cracked out last night.

By the way, saw some of the work of this Tom Clark in *Poetry Now*. He really flows and gambles and plays it loose. I like his guts. Good, very, that you are publishing him. He's the raw gnawing end of the moon.

I know about the novel. Next envelope will prob. have a couple of chapters. I reread the fucking novel and get depressed; it doesn't quite have the spring and mox I wanted it to have. but as an easy whorehouse journal of madness I do think it scores. It's all the angle you want to look at it at. I think, though, the best thing to do is to finish it even if I finish it badly. Getting it published seems much more secondary.

[To Louise Webb]
December 23, 1974

It's about the same with me. Confusion, abject and candy-colored. Got Brahms on the radio ... Thinking about Jon now. He gave me a powerful lift. He loved my shit. Those two books you guys did will never be topped. I look at them now and it's all so hard to believe. And now Jon's gone and the rare book dealers are raking in the green leaves. [* * *]

---

the screenplay shit was just some teacher wanting to do a stu-
dent film. a) he doesn't seem to have the money. b) it's from
Erections ... a .45 to pay the rent ... and Stone has the option on
that. and c) he wants to come over and drink beer with me.

here's some poems. the novel will soon be done. I'll ship you
4 or 5 chapters in a few days. [* * *] If I don't get murdered I fig-
ure the novel will be finished by the end of January for better or
worse. I don't think it's a great novel, but I think it's an odd one,
a curious one and it reads easy. well, we'll see. did Hemingway
talk like this? [* * *]

times are going to get deep hard and this machine is just
going to have to toughen up. let's hope the Sparrow keeps flying.
ah, I got a teaser for you. want to dedicate *Factotum* to John and
Barbara Martin. now that's lard for the pan, isn't it?

•

• 1 9 7 5 •

The documentary Bukowski *was made by Taylor Hackford and first shown in October 1973. See* Hank, *pp. 239-240.*

[To Carl Weissner]
February 19, 1975

[* * *] The documentary film on *Bukowski* just showed at Whitney museum along with one on Henry Miller and I'm told the *Bukowski* got a good write-up in the *New York Times.* I even get quite a few phone calls at night now from drunken young girls in Mississippi, Cincinnati, Philly and New York City. Those young girls just want to suck the soul out of a literary sort, right out of the top of his cock. I'm tougher on most of those calls than most would be, I'm sure. It feels good to send those chicks scattering back to their lead-weight boy friends.

The depression is here although the govt. prefers to call it a "recession." Which reminds me of the old one: a recession is when your friends are out of jobs, a depression is when you're out of one. It's at times like this that I'm glad I trained myself throughout a lifetime to detest a job of any sort. All these poor automobile workers sitting around glassy-eyed with homes half-paid for and cheating wives. They trusted that a hard day's work for a good day's pay would get them through. Now as the govt. tries to pump blood into the corpse they sit around and work crossword puzzles and look at daytime TV shows programmed to the female ... the only thing that will cure this is the same thing that has cured every capitalistic depression since 1940—another war; a big war, a little war, a hot war, a cold war, but war war war, and so we arm the Arabs and we arm the Jews and we send scout planes out once again in Vietnam, and I write my poems and drink my beer and try to get through the last 4 scenes in *Factotum*, and I fight with my girlfriend, hop a plane to Santa Barbara, pick up 300 bucks for making them laugh at Baudelaire, and I find myself on a house boat the next day with 3 crazy people and we're laughing at the ducks and the boats and the sky and everything we say, smoking that bad shit, and we're still alive and we walk down the docks later and all at once all the boat owners honk their horns at us and we wave our arms and wave our arms and the horns honk and honk all over the harbor, one picking it up after the other and not knowing why, and we wave our arms among all the honking, and as we get into the car and drive off they are still honking, you can hear them over the engine. You see, when I read in Santa Barbara, Carl, I even turn on the abalone fisherman and the mallards. somebody taped it with real professional equipment. it was a good crowd that night, drinking out of huge mugs of beer. if this guy spins me off a tape I should spin one off for you. charms.

[To Hank Malone]
April 20, 1975

I am still zonking on the poem and the story, no quitting, I guess. They're going to have to come get me, I can't do the Hemingway no matter how much I admired it. I guess I got started so late that I'm still trying to save ground.

Still trouble with the ladies; what a dirty, hard and relentless game that one can get to be.

Finished the 2nd novel. prob. out in Sept. it's a little rough and maybe a little corny but think it has some saving graces in the halfass mad desperateness of ye central charcoal.

uh huh.

your blithe and non-boring presence when I was in *Dee*troit not forgotten.

Winans published California Bicentennial Poets Anthology *in 1976.*

[To A. D. Winans]
April 29, 1975

got to say I'm glad you found some—so many—for the antho.

word leaking down here that you're getting drunk up there and kicking ass. the way I look at it, Frisco-wise, is that any ass you kick is the right one.

finished the 2nd novel. [* * *] it'll be a long time to do a third novel. if it ever comes it will probably have to do with the MAN-WOMAN situation, and that's a big bite out of the lurking dark. to do it well I'm going to have to grow up more, plenty more. may never grow that much. [* * *]

[To John Martin]
May 28, 1975

You must allow the writing to write itself. I can think of one in your particular stable who has simply written herself out by not waiting for the re-fill process. It's easy enough to do, this thing of getting very professional about your act. Ez did it, Ernie did it, and it didn't work, finally. You've been much more than an editor to me, and that's all right. But you have to trust my instincts. I make enough errors, that's part of it. But I think in the final addition the luck holds. Do you know what I mean? Sure you do. Relax.

p.s.—the drink won't get me. I know that monster too well. if I don't get murdered by a woman I'll burn up a hell of a lot more typer ribbons. yeh.

203

[To Mike —?]
June 22, 1975

[* * *] maybe you're writing too much the way I write. I once wrote like William Saroyan for about 3 years until I decided that his content was candyass and only his rolling style had something to hang a hat to. so I took part of that. and part of Ernie and part of Celine and I had a little luck. maybe when you decide that I am candyass you'll have a better chance. [* * *]

Roth Wilkofsky was, with Karyl Klopp, editor of Pomegranate Press, North Cambridge, Massachusetts.

[To Roth Wilkofsky]
August 9, 1975

[* * *] Have had the flu and my balls actually ache and my girl friend is crying for sex sex sex, and yes I've heard the Bruckners you mention but I don't have a phono, but always glad when I get Bruck, by luck, on the radio. He's good sound listening, puts it right on the rail. I think he's terribly underestimated because he sucked to Wagner so much, but unlike his master he didn't fuck his work up so much with the human voice, which is most of the time one of the worst sounding instruments. yah. [* * *]

[To Carl Weissner]
August 28, 1975

[* * *] there's too much to do here too—meaning writing, drinking, fights with women, drinking, playing the horses, drinking, fights with women, drinking, and visits by people who do me

204

very little good. I'm going to have to get harder with the door knockers. there have become so many of them. each thinking that they are the *special* ones, that they have something to say, something for me to *drink*, something for me to listen to. some of them even have balls enough to bring their WRITING. kindness sometimes only begets pain. these people have nothing but time to lounge around in. I don't mind wasting time as long as I do it in *my* way, it's somehow still not so bad. but after they drip their tiny souls all over me it's a long time getting back to where I can even feel less than half-sick. 99 per cent of the world consists of bloodsuckers who must feed and feed and feed. I am going to send them to another bucket of blood. [* * *]

The Russian composer's full name is Reinhold Moritzovich Glière.

[To Roth Wilkofsky]
September 4, 1975

[* * *] 3:30 p.m. on my 2nd beer. rolling Prince Albert. something on the radio. what is it? I've heard it, yes. many times. can't spell it. Illeia Morovitz by Gliere? long strains and strands.

have in mind to shape up a few of the ten or 12 poems I wrote last night. when drinking one tends to use too many lines but a certain gamble comes about and you use some lines you'd probably never use when you're sober. mostly I hack out the flowers and leave in the brambles.

Bruckner and Mahler, yes. I could never quite get it on with the Bee. Don't know why. Bach was easy because he didn't have to carry around a lot of excess crap. anyhow, classical music and booze—taken together—have carried me through many a night when it seemed as if there were nothing else around. and maybe there wasn't.

[To John Martin]
September 19, 1975

Oh, John—meant to get these straight and to you earlier—
one night's work—but I've been fighting off these sex-mad
teeny-boppers. can you use a half dozen? Barbara need never
know.

---

*Charles Plymell is the author of many books of poems from
various small presses.*

[To Charles Plymell]
October 29, 1975

[* * *] My ass is really strapped for time but I burn and slob-
ber away a lot of time anyhow, and have been meaning to answer
your letter which I appreciated ... *Rolling Stone* Mag by today
shooting photos for an article on Bukowski which they say
should appear in the next issue or two. The cover of *Time* mag is
next and then I will end up sucking my own dick with my legs
strapped around the bedposts.

The whole problem is how serious a man can take what the
media does to and/or for him. What one should realize is that
the media puffs up a hell of a lot of stale fruitcake ... like Joe
Namath, Bob Hope, Robert Ford, Henry Ford, Zippo Marx,
dead Kenny's x-wife widow, all that. Most creative artists are
weak because they are emotional, and because it's hard and dirty
work even though it's most interesting work. They fall to expo-
sure, camera flashes, that grisly attention. I think that when any
creative artist gets good enough society has an Animal out There
that the artist is fed to so he won't get any stronger. Creativity,
no matter what you say, is somehow bound up with adversity,
and when you get dangerous enough they simply take away your
adversity. They've done it with the blacks, they've done it with
the Chicanos, they've done it with the women, and now they're

206

playing with me. I intend to allow them to clutch a loud, empty fart for their reward. I will be elsewhere, cleaning my toenails or reading the *Racing Form*.* [* * *]

[To Charles Plymell]
December 3, 1975

[* * *] I am riven. Female claw of ballsoul. Yet when one figures one is rifted and lost forever... there are more knocks upon the door, and here each one enters more beautiful than the one lost. I mean, what rivening shit, eh, Chaz? What I am trying to say is that I hurt in the proper places and I move very slowly toward a new person... but miracle flowers arrive and perch themselves upon me. It's as if they know that I need help. I love them, their cunthairs and my tongue dribbling in between. At my age, I ought to be playing checkers at the corner park. I'm drunk, yes. Reading in New York City, the Bowery bit, June 23, they tell me. I might round out in Baltimore... only payment I'd need would be a couple of young cunts I could eat out alive. No siffed-up shit, bastard. I've never had v.d. Just something that looks good and would might maybe diminish the minor tremblings of a tottering soul, hey hey hey...

---

*Cp. "The artist, like the God of the creation, remains within or behind or beyond or above his handiwork, invisible, refined out of existence, indifferent, paring his fingernails."—*A Portrait of the Artist as a Young Man*

*Black Sparrow Press moved from Los Angeles to Santa Bar-
bara in the fall of 1975.*

[To John Martin]
December 3, 1975

now that you've moved I realize how tremendous our rela-
tionship has been. anyhow, if you've got the guts to cot down in
a different area and continue, I imagine I might have too. tra lala.

Linda problem sloved ... solved ... I've been drinking. mis-
carriage. so we can still shoot for that 50 grand death pact.
[* * *]

lost and lousy and lovely girls coming by almost each night.
what shit. do you think they'd do this for a postal clerk? (by the
way, I keep the hard-earned bankroll *intact*.) [* * *]

The novel mentioned in the following is Factotum, *which was
officially published on December 18, 1975.*

[To John Martin]
December 10, 1975

Well, here's the new machine—$143.10, tax included. I was
out one night and came home and Linda had broken in. All my
books were gone, plus the typer, radio, paintings and various
items. Linda was crouched behind a brush and started smashing
things when she saw me, and screaming. Some of the things,
items have simply vanished, others demolished, including the
typer which she bounced against the street again and again. She
also broke my windows, so forth. I am putting things back
together and trying to start over again. I am in semi-state of
shock so please don't expect too much literary work until after
Xmas. o.k.?

Like you know, I am really waiting on the novel. As soon as it
comes out please AIRMAIL me a copy ... !

Just wanted to get this thing off to let you know circumstances. I've puttied back in all the windows and it's quiet tonight. I intend to go on. There's novel #3 you know, and more p o e m s and D I R T Y stories, and I hope you're settled and all's in order, and hello to Barbara.

[To John Martin]
December 14, 1975

things are very nice right now, and it's damn well time they should be. the health, the feelings, the flow is (are) still in good running order. my pre-training holds me in ultra good stead. carry on, rally forth, all that. shit, it's only the 8th round and I've got a good cornerman to patch up the cuts. rah rah rah. or have I finally gone nuts?

stead? is there such a word?

I would be the last one to slap you with a merry Xmas. I'd rather wish you lucky midnights and more submissive and obedient shipping clerks—than the next to last.

you tell Barbara that I'm going to answer the motherfucking bell for the 9th round.

•

• 1 9 7 6 •

[To John Martin]
January 6, 1976

here's more poems.

I'm still thinking in terms of starting the 3rd novel in a couple of months. I'm not quite sure I'm man enough to handle it. You know, tones of vindictiveness, all that. Unless the slant and the laughter and the judgement get off of beggary it's almost a waste. The problem is not so much what I feel but what everybody must feel in similar traps. Tra lala. [* * *]

The new novel announced here as Love Tales of the Hyena *eventually was published as* Women *in December, 1978.*

[To John Martin]
January 22, 1976

[* * *] Have you ever read Catullus? There's a translation by Carl Sesar via Mason & Lipscomb, seems full of butter, fire and laughter. Too bad Cat seemed to have drifted off into homosexuality. That may be a standard literary trait but it always discourages me. Anyhow, he could lay down a line, and he was dead around the age of 30. Them there war the daze; it seems

like slavery creates art. can you send me a couple of slaves, John? virginal, about 15 with golden sensitive hairs about the boxes? I wait ...

my Boswell—Pleasants—says he has discovered some typos in *Facto*. [* * *] I've heard some good sounds from people who've read the book. But get ready for critical attacks. If you can take it, I can write some more. Title for 3rd novel *Love Tales of the Hyena*. I've written a chapter out of the center. But whether I ever write the thing or how long it takes, that's drizzle out of a long spread from nowhere.

Hey, you tell Barbara that the book design was super superbia exellente....DON'T FORGET! [* * *]

[To John Martin]
January 24, 1976

Thanks for the good words in ye Calendar section of ye good ol' *L.A. Times*.

If the game ends right here it has very well been worth it, that big run right up through center banging against malarkey and piss-ants, tradition, whores, fags, schools, sharks.

I'm still at Hollywood and Western, there's a potato boiling behind me, the health is amazingly good and it's very quiet here tonight. I could go to the phone and get trouble but I think I'll just let things lay easy.

Did you see the Foreman-Lytle fight on tv? What a ball-busting back-alley drunkeroo. Well, it wasn't dull but if that's what championship contenders are made of Ali is going to be around like a Bukowski sucking a beerbottle. For a long time.

[To Katherine —?]
January 25, 1976

you are like sunlight
sunlight walking around.

212

you don't know how good
you are.
you play with my seriousness,
make me laugh.

when you comb your hair
all the gods come down
from the mountain
and watch

you are the woman
all women should have
been.

I ache with disbelief and
yearning

no matter how you turn
your body
or what you say
it is the perfect diamond
the perfect cut
the perfect glow

and when you get the blues
I get the blues
because I don't want you
to get the blues

in my life
I've told two other
women that I loved
them

I wouldn't say it to
you

one of those women
died
and another died
in another way

if I never see you again
I will always carry you
inside
outside

on my fingertips
and at brain edges

and in centers
centers
centers
of what I am of
what remains.

[To Carl Weissner]
February 13, 1976

Kaput in Hollywood, I really like that title—you're making me look good. Hope Martin goes your book of projected Buk poem translations. But I'm hot on *Factotum*, my last novel. Ya seen it yet? I think it's the best writing I've done. have gotten quite a bit of mail about it agreeing with me. In fact, today I got a letter with return address of Henry Miller, Pacific Palisades, and I thought, my my, is the old man bending to write me? But when I opened it up it was from his son, one Larry Miller. Ah well. He praised *Factotum*, part of which goes: "...I guess I just wanted to say thank you for being the first writer since reading my father that has made me feel that all is not lost in literature today; especially a sense of reality that seems to have escaped nearly everyone else..."

Oh, Cupcakes...she's got it. Miss Pussycat of 1973, she's 23, brains, body, spirit...Flaming red hair, long...she's in front of my bedroom mirror now combing that flame as I type this to you. she'll be the death of me, but it's worth it, pal. [* * *]

I'm going to swing around and read in Pittsburgh, Boston, New York City. Big time, Buk. looking out of superjet windows, looking at stewardesses' asses wiggling, ordering drink after drink ...in there with the businessmen and swindlers and killers. I'm

214

finally where I belong, Carl: the poetry-kill: I'll fuck 'em in the left ear with a distorted sonnet....

[To John Martin]
March 28, 1976

[* * *] one of my problems is with Scarlet ... Cupcakes ... we've rifted. she's a speed-freak, pill-head and on the smack. you just don't know how HARD people can get until you've met one of those. and, of course, I got sucked-in early. you've seen the poems. John, will I ever meet a woman who is good to me? I suppose a lot of my problem is EGO, and at 55 I should be laying down that game altogether. as long as I've lived I'm just too fucking soft inside. but, baby, don't worry, we'll pull through this one just like we pulled through the others. not because we don't care but because we do.

the plans now are for my first vacation. I should be in Austin April 8th to meet Katherine and stay with her a couple of weeks. that is if Linda doesn't arrive and kill me first. I've been hearing quite a bit from her via phone and mail and she seems to be making overtures. I think I should kool it with her, tho. she's simply crazy. then there's another in Texas, Suzzana. Suzzana has a load of money, wants to marry me, take me to Paris, all that shit. do you think I could write a poem in Paris, big John? advise.

meanwhile, I hope to keep going on *Hyena*. if I can write that one, B.J., people will forever stop talking about *The Ginger Man*. there are so many unbelievable layers of laughter and love and blood madness ensconced there ... you just don't know what's been happening to this old man while he's been sending you these tiny poems.

Katherine is the kindest one I've known. but you know how a writer is—he'll go for the sloppiest whore and the meanest bitch on earth—hoping to cure it or understand it or at least live with it ... temporarily. [* * *] even tho I can't spell I think my writing is getting better and better. I can feel all those words inside of me, puffing and blowing, and it doesn't even scare me to talk about it. I'm loaded to the ear lobes. both ways.

These are from a series of mostly undated, mostly holograph notes, addressed sometimes to "Pam," "Scarlet," "Cup-cakes," or "Cups," a woman who lived in the same apartment complex as Bukowski. The parenthetical date of the first one is noted on the manuscript and initialled "P.B."

[To Pamela Brandes]
[mid-1976]

Tues. night Wednesday morning [April 6, 1976]
Pam, Pam, Pam, where are you? I love you. I love you. I love you.

§

3:45 A.M., Monday
I *love* you, you bitch. I'll be gone for a *month*. I only wanted to *look* at you and say *goodbye*.

§

1:30 A.M. Sunday morning
Red death sunset blood glory gal—
Why is it that you are the one woman I have met who has not loved me entirely, madly and out of context? It confuses me. You must be my superior. Well, that's all right. —I mean, if I can win 8 races out of 9 I can expect to be upset by a longshot.
[* * *]
[*signed "blubberboy Charley" with a drawing and arrow pointing to "Tears of Agony" dropping from the figure's eyes*]

§

June 5, 1976
Cupcakes:
you've made me write a lot of poems. (another enclosed). some of the poems are nasty and vindictive, some of them are lousy, but some of them are good, so I've got to thank you, gal. I hope that we can remain friends ... in spite of some of our rough spots. keep it together.

§

Pam:
I HATE YOU FOR NOT ADMITTING YOU LOVE ME.
you are acting like a stupid cunt.
you will only suffer and suffer and suffer because there is a
difference in what you feel and what SOCIETY wants you to feel.
the best way to anywhere is the most honest and truest way.
you've been fighting it.
you say you want to be a writer.
begin at the beginning.

your friend, Hank

§

Saturday, 1 p.m.
I miss you little Reds. Come see me soon.

§

Pam—
I'm sorry I got mad. But I give you money, your mother
money, buy booze and cigarettes and dope and you treat me like
a dog. I mean, hell, look at my viewpoint once in a while. Even
though I may be unrealistic.

p.s.—your mother phoned. I suppose she's found you by now.
keep yourself together. I still *like* you a lot.

§

Scarlet:
Come on down and see me sometimes. I've got some more
Southern Comfort for your strep. I even won at the track—no
horseshit. Well, keep it together.

Hollywood Hank

§

My dear Pamela Brandes:
You *too* can be replaced.

Hank

§

217

Pam—

I didn't mean it. I still love you. It's just that you never show any feeling toward me, and Jesus Christ that sometimes cuts in pretty deep.

I don't mean to load myself on you. I'll work it out. It's just going to take me a bit of time to figure out what the hell's happening.

Hank

§

7-1-76
Pam—

Thanks a hell of a lot of shit for nothing.

[To John Martin]
May 3, 1976

enclosed some poems.

I have gone a bit mad, and there's a reason. Anyway, I will be flitting about the country most of May, and June I'll go back to work except for the N.Y.C. reading. [* * *]

I have to get out of this court for a while. Things are very hard and ugly here right now. I feel that by the time I get back that she (Scarlet) will be moved out from this place in the back.

I'll be all right. No Dylan Thomas coming up. I am in more danger of doing it right here—looking up with her window light shining down from above in back, or no light for a couple of nights. I am hooked upon her barbarity—ruthless and raw—but know it's a shit trap and must work my way out.

[To John Martin]
June 7, 1976

don't worry; nobody's going to crawl into bed with me unless she almost deserves it. about the *Rolling Stone* interview—that's just another test the mother gods are laying upon me. I ain't going to wilt to the sound of late trumpets semi-heralding a late and minor fame. please don't worry about me, boss, I am too crazy to go crazy.

about Cups—she's got a hook into me and she knows it—but she's gone too, and talks to me straight, she promises nothing. and that's a better game than any I know that's GOING around. I've been drinking. so some of the CAPITALIZATION is accidental.

about the novel—I can't take guidance or I'm fucked. I mean, let me write it choppy. that's not all accidental. novels put me to sleep because they are not choppy. when we lose the raw sloppy gambling edge, then we are truly finished—turkeys. see the Dos Passos trilogy *USA*. I enjoyed his attempt—the idea was there—but he chopped it too fine. There is a difference between a 2 year old kid beating upon the back of a saucepan with a spoon and symphony, say, by—anybody. I have the feeling that the secret or the glow or the luck is somewhere in between. what I'm trying to say here is that I'm not writing *Hyena* for the *Free Press*. it comes out like it comes out, and I'm sorry I have but only one death to give to Bukowski. I'll probably rewrite the fucking thing, anyhow, when I get the full scan of it written I can mend parts, throw out parts, glue parts, add parts. but it's fairly close to home now, I feel it more than I can see it. but let me wobble through the first course, then maybe I will be able to see my balls from my cerebellum. [* * *]

[To A. D. Winans]
June 7, 1976

[* * *] I did one reading for a grand. I ask $500 plus air and plus...for others. keeps me at home. where I belong instead of waking up in bed with a teacher of retarded children in Tallahassee, Fla. and waking up in another bed with another teacher of

retarded children in T. Fla. the next morning, no toilet paper in her crapper, I gotta write [*sic*] off my shitty bung with a brown paper bag into a beershit that will not let go. this ever happened to Ezra? [* * *]

I am in trouble with women as usual. they are getting younger and more vicious and more beautiful. they are my superiors. they kill me, almost. [* * *]

[To Carl Weissner]
July 13, 1976

[* * *] as usual, the women have me on the old cross. I am sitting around waiting for Cupcakes O'Brien's footsteps. Her shoes, hairpins, mirrors, stockings, underwear, lotions everywhere ... but where is *she*? Cups, you bitch, appear!

Off to Columbus, Ohio, tomorrow ... The *Hustler* magazine flying me out round trip, putting me into a hotel to interview me the next day. I feel like Hemingway. I hope they hustle me up a nice piece of ass. They've bought a couple of short stories from me ... they *say over the phone* ... I await the solid feel of a *check*, however. Columbus, Ohio, that's where Thurber came from, you know. I will shake his invisible hand when I land at the airport.

you keep close touch, old buddy. we are just beginning to blast the shit out of their bungholes! the women won't kill us, the booze won't kill us, the smog and the horses won't kill us, God won't kill us and the devil isn't interested. our journey through this ... will be remembered. I am drinking steam beer, fan on my ass, good music on the radio; the sky is turning red and the dead sit on their palms just as they were meant to do.

[To A. D. Winans]
July 13, 1976

Have meant to answer sooner but I've been on the road. now going again—to Columbus, Ohio, Thurber's x-hangout.

220

as per a quote for back of your book, could you use this one?:

> A. D. Winans is one of the few writers I have met (and I've
> met too god damned many of them) who doesn't *act* like a
> writer or think of himself continually as a *writer*, and maybe
> that's why he writes better than they do. I always prefer a
> man I can tolerate for more than ten minutes—that's rare,
> and so is A. D.
>
> —Charles Bukowski

[* * *] down here with women I am having much trouble. I
am over-emotional, not worldly, and my feelings get hooked in
when others might be playing games. I get burned, pal, but it has
almost always been that way. [* * *]

can you give me any advice on women, kid? they are waving
my guts on the ends of their flagsticks.

[To John Martin]
September 13, 1976

[* * *] on the novel, *Love Tale of the Hyena*, I may have to
wait a while. I think my nose might be too close to the mirror at
the moment. there's no use writing a bad novel early when you
might write a better one later. there are holy mathematical equa-
tions running through my mind—ha, ha—and I might take the
woman and mix her into 3 women. Uh, I just don't know. I play
around with these things in my head—when?—I don't know. But
maybe we'd better delay things and do them more or less right—
right meaning the taste and the flow of a good thing. I feel that
this novel just didn't start with the right... easiness of laughter
and terror. we're just going to have to wait, baby, and it may
never arrive but that's better than having it arrive asshole badly
and as journalese... or however the shit it dies. [* * *]

[To A. D. Winans]
September 13, 1976

[* * *] Things are still shitty here, I mean spiritually shitty. The redhead I was in love with for a while, the former part-time hooker told me today she has gone back to it. She did a trick last night for $100. I cashed the motherfucker's check for her. It will probably bounce. [* * *]

I am luckier than most; I have various other sources of fulfillment—female, of course. But I doubt that there is any real woman upon the horizon (for me, my mind, my need, my weakness) and I'll probably go to my death without ever seeing her—which hardly makes my life any different from another man's. Yet I keep feeling that she's out there, somewhere, but how do you get to her?

Christ, what a lack of grace, what a shit-smeared moon, night, day, noon, 3:45 p.m. [* * *]

[To Carl Weissner]
October 16, 1976

[* * *] Cupcakes and I are finished. I have 3 new girlfriends but she can't seem to be replaced—none so vicious, so evil, she was a real witch with long red hair. It's going to take me a long time to get over this one. I was thinking of coming to Germany with her but now that it's over I don't want to come. [* * *]

I can't write much more. I am sitting here with this spear stuck into my gut that Cupcakes jammed into me. pure pure blithering agony.

you hold and I'll try to hold.

222

[To A. D. Winans]
October 26, 1976

[* * *] I am still mending from the Cupcakes disaster; it's a slow heal ... the eternal beautiful witch-factor. she is killing off some other poor sucker soul as I write this. some people need to kill, it's an instinct, it keeps their neon juices flowing.

Do you think you'll ever be able to give up editing? It's my suggestion that you do ... before the dogs eat off your toes.

Get out, Al, and take a plane and go lay down next to J. W. for a week. eat breakfast together and get drunk at night. there aren't any poets; gather real valuables. get the hell out of North Beach and go East of no West.

and allah be wit de.

[To John Martin]
October 27, 1976

[* * *] not to hex myself, but anyhow I think after Nov. 13 I'll jump into this novel I have in mind: *Women*. whether it works or not.

I don't think I'll ever be able to do the childhood bit. oyee, maybe when I'm 70 but you know some woman is going to kill me before I reach 60.

[To John Martin]
November 2, 1976

oh, I ain't quite quit yet. I feel I'm in a slump, swinging at the outside curve out of the strike zone. the redhead still bites me inside my gut even though I know she is a deathly scorpion bringdown ... so I'm rather batting .143 in the minors. I get to pinch hit now and then, I hope to get the swing back. I feel I still have it. it just has to rise up to meet me.

meanwhile, the checks look great, I hope the sales hold. I

wouldn't feel good if you sent me money that didn't come from royalty sources. I'm not your son. hardly. and if things narrow down you cut the margin down. the bankroll looks *good* ... I've had to open another account next door at the Bank of America. oh, christ. what I mean is that I don't have the needs of most people and I live cheaply. this will help me keep writing. I'd rather not be a janitor in my last years. so I'm careful with my money, even though the redhead took me for about $500. a real artist, she. [* * *]

[To A. D. Winans]
November 2, 1976

[* * *] yes, watch those young girls, Al. their sincerity seems so sincere until they don't get what they really wanted, then they move on in the hunt. meanwhile we get burnt down believing that they wanted *us*. we let our egos waylay us, it's so easy. then the truth comes up and we can't believe what was obviously the believable.

on short stories, I think the best idea is to write them the way you want to write them, then look for a market. the deliberate slant automatically takes the juice out.

keep it together.

[To A. D. Winans]
November 30, 1976

My spiritual advisors have told me not to give any more mixed readings. —but no shit, they are a bringdown. I like Alta, you and Miche[line] but it just won't work. it causes a scratching I don't like. so I've got to say more. like: no. call me a shit but there's a lot of shit in the river.

Miche has never got his just due but it's as well—it'll keep him on his spring instead of turning him into a silky-haired, over-read, over-precious N. Mailer. overexposure is the toughest

224

whore of all. and one that few men can turn away for a head job.

you're right on the women. they can eat your time, they can eat you out. but, finally, they will leave you alone for a while—they make master moves on the chessboards of cunt-cock steel-wall play. but what material. I realize that I have gotten locked almost into this area. but that too will pass. and then I can write about the cockroaches, or whatever is left. [* * *]

I miss that belly dancer. We laughed for almost 9 days and nights. she said I caused the laughter but it was her, she made me feel so good and crazy. Sometimes there's luck. When there is you stock up on it and wait for the other times. [* * *]

●

• 1 9 7 7 •

[To John Martin]
January 8, 1977

everything's lovely except there's a madwoman on my bed and her back faces mine and she has covered herself with a blanket. I really draw them. she's been like that for an hour. I doubt I'll ever die a natural death. o, poems enclosed. keep it up. mine is.

[To John Martin]
January 10, 1977

I've got a reading on the 30th of this month, which means poems, so I'm going to hang with the poem until then, hoping for new juices and so forth. Then in Feb. we start the 3rd novel, *Women*. I mean, I'll start it. And if it doesn't roll by itself I'll just stop. Let me be the judge. and jury. and the killer. ah.

anyhow, I'm glad you're on a new book of poems. 1976 was one of my roughest years. since I was in my early 20's. so much happened and so much failed. It was like I had to learn all over again, and that's good. those big eyes looking into one's soul aren't always telling the truth no more than the roses are or the fish are or the mountains are. [* * *]

227

[To Hank Malone]
January 16, 1977

Lost your address, found it. Have also been going through a bit of rough time via some trollop-strumpet red haired witch. One is not too interested in literary essays when one is walking around with a knife in the gut. It's still there. But—as in your essay—one goes on. Wow. Endurance is more important than truth, I says.

Hank, the essay hits some points pretty good—the alcohol bit-need, the carry-on in face of constant shellfire, and the need —sometimes—for laughter. Sometimes instead of dying or killing myself I just go to bed for a couple of days. Shades down, swilling in the swill.

There are always more women but the one that's wanted and the one that's gotten a bit is the one that works you over good. And never leaves you alone long enough to get over the trap.

You got any advice for me on women—send right off.

Me, I'm watching James Cagney. *White Heat.* and drinking white wine. thanks for mailing me the essay.

[To Carl Weissner]
January 27, 1977

[* * *] the mailman found me passed out in bed, hungover, at 2 p.m. in the afternoon. "Charley," he said, "I got you a little letter here." he's o.k. he sees me with young girls, hags, and I'm usually drunk or drinking. got a couch outside. 2 young German girls came to see me one day. I tried to fuck both of them, finally settled on the older (22) and the other went for a long walk, and maybe it was limp dick but it seemed she had a corkscrew pussy. sometimes there are those and they work good. I say, "ah, ah, look I'm sliding way up around the left side but I'm in, somehow I'm in, I'm no boy scout, I'm in, and ah ah ah ..." but maybe I wasn't in *this* one. I kept punching at a tunnel-ending. I gave off and ate her out. they stayed for 3 or 4 days and nights until I got tired. then I drove them off to some woman's place in the hills and I drank cans of beer steering out of there, and little cans of

vodka mix, red or pink cans, the sunlight blaring in at me, wondering if I were nuts or the world has calmed, but really nothing much, I found my way back in, stretched it out, went to sleep for a couple of hours, the phone rang... [* * *]

This is the first mention in these letters of Linda Lee Beighle whom Bukowski eventually married on August 18, 1985.

[To Carl Weissner]
March 3, 1977

[* * *] have heard from Ferling.'s bookkeeper. I think his overseas cut is 50 percent. it can't be helped. but it does leave a goodly sum. John Martin is nicer. His cut is ten percent and so far he has always been good enough to waive it.

Cupcakes has vanished into space. not really. she's after the gold fillings and after a young dentist who plays with them. smart girl. got some new ladies, a little less related to the shark. Linda Lee—the # one new one (not Linda King—x) studying German. she thinks we're going to Germany. well, who the hell knows? [* * *]

[To A. D. Winans]
Late April, 1977

Thanks for sending your special issue to the Germans. Things are working up over there—4 or 5 of my books in translation. I think the Germans have me down as an admixture of Bogart, Hem, Adolf, and Jack the Ripper. I may go there this summer with my lady friend. Drink and die there. The Fatherland. [* * *]

[To John Martin]
May 10, 1977

Enclosed the bit from Germany. It's nice that you take 10 per instead of 50 like Mr. Lawrence F. He wrote me the other day suggesting that City Lights put out a Bukowski "selected poems." I haven't answered. I've told him time and again that I am in the Sparrow's nest.

The Germans are honest and I think Carl W. keeps them that way.

On the other hand there is *London Mag* who put out *Post Office* and *Life and Death in a Charity Ward* and not a sound, not an advance, no royalties. These books were issued in 1974. I wrote the editor inquiring about the matter about a year and a half ago. No response.

Well, it's just like the women—the writing's still the thing. No matter what they do or don't do to you. [* * *]

[To Carl Weissner]
May 11, 1977

[* * *] although I no longer live on one candy bar a day, life still kicks my ass pretty hard, mostly in the form of people, mostly in the form of women, a real crazy rip. sometimes very authentic and horrifying, so you see the gods are still playing with me. don't worry, old friend, if some woman doesn't kill me there is a lot more coming via the word.

Martin phones: "Weissner is the one responsible for getting you over in Germany. He is a very good man."

"Hell, I *know* it," I say, "and he even collects my bills for me. And I have the *strange* feeling that the son of a bitch *improves* my writing when he translates it."

I talk to my present girlfriend Linda Lee about you. "I've got to do something for Carl. Maybe I should send him some money."

"No," she says, "do something really nice for him."

"Like what?" I say. It's hard, Carl, for me to do something nice. I'm going to dedicate a book to you some day, hurrah. but

230

that don't buy no groceries. well, anyhow, thanks for all the damned work you've done. thanks again. jesus christ, yes. [* * *]

my 89 year old uncle is alive in Andernach. Heinrich Fett. and, did I tell you?—the house I was born in still stands but is now a brothel. I can get the address from my biographer if you want to get a piece of ass in the house that Buk was born in. [* * *]

[To Hank Malone]
May 27, 1977

Yes, I read your piece again—the altered one—and you know it's difficult for me to say whatever. You must know that I don't know who I am or why I do what I do, and that if I did know I probably couldn't do whatever I am doing now.

I don't ask you to feel guilty in choosing me as subject matter but don't ask me to feel guilty either, or to understand anything about it. You must know this. You must know that I'm unable to handle it—not out of modesty but simply out of whatever makes me functional.

I have no feelings about most writing—past or present—except that I dislike most of it, can't read it.

Thanks, anyhow, for sending this on. [* * *]

[To Carl Weissner]
August [?17], 1977

[* * *] I don't care much for the record *90 Minutes in Hell*. The title wasn't my idea. and I don't care for most of it, except for the short story that ends it. I think I did a good job there.

There seems to be plenty of people knocking on my door nowadays and they just seem to sit and sit and sit, and it's like they are crunching on the hours and I am the only one who seems to feel it. they can't take hints. finally, after much agony I politely inform them that I'd like to do a little work. you can't tell

231

them you want to take a shit because they'll wait that out.

Went down to Del Mar with Linda Lee and we got stinko in our motel room and went swimming and diving in the rough surf at 1:30 a.m. A real gasser and not a bad way to die but I came on out and we got back to the motel, poured some more, and got along that night. She's a good girl and has lived through many of my drunken, mad, unkind nights and has forgiven me ... so far.

[To Carl Weissner]
September 22, 1977

[* * *] Got first copy of *Love Is a Dog from Hell* in mail yesterday. Finished the novel *Women* last night: 433 pages, 99 chapters. I think it's all right but it will confuse some people; others will simply hate me, as usual. They may even put a hit man on me? [* * *]

Now it's back to the short story and the poem again.

That novel was a real juicer for me (*Women*). I mean it *gave* me energy, it didn't take it from me. I feel strangely lost now....

All the Germans who come by drink Coors which is one of the worst beers in America. I can't sip it without puking. [* * *]

[To John Martin]
October 9, 1977

[* * *] I sent the corrected pages of the novel off a couple of days ago. It still read o.k. to me. had to make another name change—from Ruthie to Cecelia. The woman was Ruthie Wantling and I thought that was getting too close.

[To John Martin]
October 17, 1977

[* * *] word from Carl: the blue book has gone into 53,000 copies. word from publisher: by the end of the year they will have 70,000 copies out. to me, those are astonishing figures, and so much of it is due to Weissner, his translation of the works and his getting it in front of people.

I write things because it is some kind of disease but once that's over I think it's all right if some other people get caught on the same sickness, you know? [* * *]

[To A. D. Winans]
October 27, 1977

you sound down. it's probably all those big mouths down there—up there—proclaiming their greatness. the longer I know of the poets the more sick I believe they really are—asking for decency and love and understanding from the world in their poems and, in person, being exactly the opposite of what they ask for. there's a speech for you. ah.

things here are fairly quiet. have more or less settled with a good woman, Linda Lee, after running through quite a number. getting fucked by many is not so important; it's a settling for an easy clarity that I think helps the nights, the days, the months. [* * *]

[To A. D. Winans]
November 2, 1977

[* * *] get on the white wine, A.D. beer is fattening, the hard stuff eats the gut, the liver, and it's hard to type under the hard stuff. good white wine, German, can be had for around 3.50 a bottle. 2 bottles of this can make a nice evening and you won't wake up feeling like you've been swallowing wet cat turds all

night. also, before you start to drink take a tablespoonful of metamucil or one of maalox. if all this sounds chickenshit to you or rails against the spirit, don't do it. the way I see it, I'm 57 and I've proved I can drink as long and as hard as the next. I think the time comes when the long-ignored body asks for a bit of kindness. it has waited around a long time on the doorstep....

the poets? well, I prefer the fishermen and the corner newsboys. I don't know where people ever got the idea that poets and poetry was (is) the holy thing. I think the only time poetry gets any good is when it forgets its holiness, and that's very seldom. take Ezra Pound—Pound as good as he was with the language he made that place a temple and a sanctuary. any man down on skid row would have preferred a can of beans. I'm not saying the poet owes anything to the masses; I find the masses both disgusting and interesting. it still might be good if they found us the same way? Whitman said that to have great poetry we must have great audiences. I think he had it backwards.

yes, Linda Lee is a good woman. I was due for some luck. she is a stayer with a gentle courage and doesn't play man against man as if she were some golden cow. I've had some bad ones, many bad ones. the percentages have come around and I am able to accept them. [* * *]

Martin says *Women* out in June. o.k. you're going to know many of the people in this one. I may get killed for this one. it's written as some type of high-low comedy and I look worse than anybody but they're only going to think about how I painted *them*. it's a jolly roaring blast, I think, and when I re-read it I realize that I must have been crazy from 1970 to 1977. like Thomas Wolfe, after this one, I can't go home again. it was quite easy to write and it didn't take too much guts on 3 bottles of white wine a night. oh, ah, oh ...

Martin has been good to me, I am one of the few wild cards in his deck. If your stuff comes back, realize that he sticks fairly close to poetry as craft, the well-honed line, rather like voices speaking out from behind wallpaper, the sublime traditionalism: Douglas Woolf, Reznikoff, Eshleman, Corman, Creeley, Loewinsohn.

For my money, Micheline, Richmond, Winans are closer to the blood-source, but then I'm not an editor or a publisher, and Martin has been good to me, he picked me up early and gave me a chance to get out of the post office when nobody else was listening. I can't forget this and I won't. he's my publisher. I've got the hound-dog loyalty and I don't mind; it feels good. but it is hard for me to read or agree with who he *does* print. all right, I type on. [* * *]

[To A. D. Winans]
November 9, 1977

[* * *] yes, I'm down to one woman now. after re-reading *Women* I decided I needed a rest. some aren't going to believe that novel. I can't blame them, but there's very little fiction to it.

you seem to know a lot of women who have passed into the vapor. I mean death. Linda King phoned from Arizona not too long ago. She claims she's now a lush & she's pregnant. she sounded quite sad. she gave me a hard row. after we split I met two other women named Linda. I meet a lot of Lindas and lot of Joans and Joannas—mostly names that end in "a". it's curious. [* * *]

[To A. D. Winans]
November 13, 1977

Could you tear up the poem "a very serious fellow"? I don't think Steve [Richmond] could handle it. there are many reasons why I don't think he can handle it but don't want to number them here. just *trust* me and rip up the poem. I am asking Martin to destroy the same. I think the poem is accurate but I knew Steve pretty well personally and I just don't want to have him go under the damage....

o.k.?

[To John Martin]
November 15, 1977

[* * *] listen, on the poem about Richmond "a very serious fellow"—please never print it in book form. I've written to Winans who accepted it and have asked him to tear it. Steve can't handle it. he's hooked into something besides poetry which makes him weak against almost everything of this sort. I can't say any more about it. just tear the poem or don't publish it. [* * *]

[To Carl Weissner]
November 16, 1977

slow in answering, my ass deep into horses and white wine ...
[* * *]

I do wish to hell, though, that there were some way we could get *Women* going over there. it's the ultimate novel blast of blasts, it should cause riots in the streets. mostly because they will be confused by my viewpoint, which I am also confused about. and now and then I do much leg-pulling and they'll never know when I am pulling the leg or jacking-off the truth or writing it as it is, or was. John says we gotta wait until June. I do wish he could get a copy to you, to see if you might care to translate it. right now it's not in final draft. I would like to see it again and maybe take out a few wrinkles. [* * *]

[To A. D. Winans]
December 3, 1977

[* * *] I'm still writing poems and fighting with Linda Lee. Since she's 34 I'm giving away 23 years but I'm right on in there. Interview of me, with me, in present German *Playboy* but since I can't speak the language I don't know what I said; besides, I was drunk and so was the guy who flew over here. The whole interview was a two day drunk and they layed $650 on me for it.

236

Jesus, me and Rod McKuen.... Some day I'll be writing you, "A.D., me and Rod Mc and James Dickey are going fishing in the Catskills ..." then *you* can attack me and I'll understand.

Bukowski very rarely went to movies. Here he reports on one directed by François Truffaut.

[To John Martin]
December 12, 1977

here's more poems.

by the way, I went to see the movie *The Man Who Loved Women* thinking it might be something like our novel *Women*. excuse me, but there's nothing to worry about: ours is more humorous, more insane and more tragic and—the devil knows—more realistic.

got the checks, ah. yes, I should have kept book this year but I had no idea... will begin on the first of Jan. I phoned Calif. Fed. Savings because I had torn up my earlier pass books and have no records but the lady informed me that they had no records either and... I said, "Suppose I were the income tax people and I asked to examine some of your books?" and she answered, "Well, if they subpoenaed us we'd let them see them." which leaves me nowhere.

I know what your salary to me was, that's fine. and City Lights always sends me a statement of earnings. But the Germans? Christ, I have no idea. I could write them and ask for statements but such things are slow and maybe even impossible. to top that they'd send me total earnings *before* your cut and Carl's cut. now, here's the biggy!: do you have any idea of what I got from them? I'd appreciate a breakdown (looks like I'm having one). I'd never implicate you in any tax investigation but a set of figures from you would really help this damned muddle. also, didn't I receive something from Playboy-New Visions? and not to be *greedy*, ugg, but wasn't there a second payment due Oct. 15 or Jan. 15 or something? I guess I've spoiled your day but I lay a lot of this shit on you because I need help with this and I feel that our relationship while straight on an editor-publisher writer relationship is straight, I ask you to perhaps help me with this on more of a friendship basis. next year I'll be totally competent and professional about the whole thing for my interests and everybody else's.

now *that* was one hell of a poem, wasn't it?, and not the kind I'm fond of writing.

[To Carl Weissner]
December 15, 1977

[* * *] good checks from Germany arriving through Martin via you and the publishers. you are our beloved hit-man. and the money is lovely; I drink better wine, eat out now and then; even bought two new pairs of pants and some shirts the other day, 2 new tires for my car. I can go to the track and lose 30 dollars without having a nightmare, and I'm going to phone my dentist tomorrow. sounds pretty fucking civilized but it's a good change and I have written around 200 poems since Sept., most of them pretty fair. [* * *]

Now I gotta worry about income tax. this life gets wilder and wilder, but the main thing I go on is whether this typewriter is working well or not.

•

•1978•

[To John Martin]
January 6, 1978

[* * *] I can't help now and then feeling good about *Women*, though, it's going to be an a-bomb in the novel wars when there has been so much nullity and so much peace. forgive me for saying so, but this one is going to ring down some walls and the bitter counter-attackers will at last have something to do.

[To Carl Weissner]
January 22, 1978

[* * *] oh, you tell your wife that almost all the teeth I have left are in the front. I used to live on one candy bar a day while writing my short stories; candy bar and cheap wine, then the old ten year drunk, and the years of starvation. I used to reach into my mouth with my fingers and pull my teeth out. I would just wiggle a loose tooth for a while and it would work out. or I had teeth that I just picked away at, breaking off chunks. it was interesting and not at all fearful. it really wasn't until 1970 that I started eating better and drinking better. I even went to a dentist a few years back and he looked at the x-rays and said, "I don't understand this. It looked like your teeth gave up and suddenly they decided not to give up."

239

I haven't heard a thing from the French publisher who suggested the Paris trip. Maybe my letter scared him off. I asked not to be placed into a slick hotel but into a place where the common people lived, the French ordinary, without the American tourist. I also asked not to be fucked with too much. I don't know. Maybe I scared him off. Maybe I can still make Germany. I can afford it but jesus you'd think some of those publishers would kick in a bit; I might do a few tricks for them to help sales—a few, not too many. and maybe a reading to help expenses. but I can make it without aid. we'll see. I hope your back is better by then so we can lift a few together. Linda Lee says hello. she's high on you. when I get drunk I brag on you. but don't worry, I still have the old German reserve; I won't slobber all over you when—if—I arrive.

and Carl, I know that Paris, go or not, is pretty much shit and pretty much hard but so is almost everyplace else, and that type of thing I am used to. the Left Bank means as much to me as east Greenwich Village, and Munich or wherever the hell else would be the same—people and streets and the moil. still it might be nice to have a look—a small yellow notebook to write down streets and places—New York city or New Orleans, Mannheim or Andernach, it's shit in the sewer, cunts, cocks, police, betrayal, madness, joy and something to drink.

the horses are going very well for me. I have devised a system that entails 5 numbers—I will rate each horse in 5 categories and he will have numbers say like this: 2, 7, 4, 3, 6. each contains a meaning, a compilation: on the final odds of the horse, the first number must be *lower* than the odds, the center 3 less than the odds, and the last number near or below the odds, all depending upon the first flash of the toteboard and the last. it's quite quite interesting. and it gets me out of this god damned place and away from the typewriter so I don't have to play professional writer. [* * *]

[To Carl Weissner]
February 22, 1978

[* * *] Renate Derschau brought by a couple of copies of
Stern. Poor Linda Lee Beighle... billed as Linda King. she re-
acted and sent a *cable* to *Stern*... I can't blame her. forgive me,
but she's a much better soul than Linda King, and such things
cut. the photos were good, though. o.k.

I'm still writing nothing but poems. I don't understand it.
they are all around me here, dozens of them. I have to go with
the tide. the poems are all around me here. at night I type them
while drinking wine and now I've got to type them up without
the wine stains and errors and get them out of here. I shouldn't
complain; it's better than having everything shut off. it fits my
battle plan of typing the last poem in the deathbed or wherever it
might happen...

Linda Lee and I will be leaving L.A. May 9th [i.e. 8th] at
8:15 p.m. and will arrive at Frankfurt May 9th at 3:20 p.m.
[* * *] we'll stay 3 weeks [* * *] I think one reading is enough.
Linda Lee says she looks forward to meeting you. there are some
changes. we are off the beer, just drink wine, German, mostly
white and only eat fish and poultry, no red meat. I have come
down from 223 pounds to 196 but drink more than ever. we
should try to slow down just a bit in Germany, though. got to
face the judge tomorrow morning at 8:30 a.m. jesus, what an
hour to face a drunk driving rap. but I've stood before that man
many times. I hope he's a nice old fellow. oh yeah.

we may make Paris in September *if* the Frenchies come
through with one round trip ticket. I don't mind spending dollars
to see the Fatherland but the Frogs are going to have to dance a
little before I do the Paris journey.

well, listen, friend, I have to get typing some of these fucking
poems up. and I must thank you again and forever, Carl, for
translating my stuff so that they like it so much and for pushing
Charlie Bukowski and for collecting bills and knocking down
doors. you are the miracle man.

[To John Martin]
March 9, 1978

[* * *] The trip to Germany will be low-profile, easy and I intend to avoid the hale guzzlers. I drink for my pleasure, not my image, or their image of me. My health is better now than it has been for 40 years. I have no intention of tossing it away.

Women is going to land like an H-bomb into all this literary serenity. [* * *]

[To Carl Weissner]
March 12, 1978 within the dwindling yeers
after the death of the sun leeving only
the father under der Holy Ghost...

Hello Carl—

Perhaps a little too much white wine tonight. Linda Lee in bed re-reading *A Pavilion of Women** and me out here (3:11 a.m.) smoking and sipping and lucking upon some Mozart upon the radio. And I get worried about coming to Germany but then I think, fuck it, I'll let it slide. And I remember when you came over here I was terrified to meet you at the airport because I'd never been to one and I didn't know how and I was afraid I couldn't do it. Now I've been in and out of dozens of airports (quite suddenly) and anyhow—thanks for sending magazines such as *Stern* and etc. as they come out Bukowskivana. What I'm writing about, however, is I intend to enclose $2 and if *Stern* ever comes out with an apology-retraction for the Linda King Linda Lee fuck-up (as demanded by cable), please mail said copy, much thanks. We have a German bookstore here but they drag-ass about 2 months behind time. For instance, as of this date, they are only stocked up on and up to *Stern* #3. So, if they ever come out with their thing, please mail, o.k.? Letter from Unc. Heinrich, has been in hospital for months, heart trouble, now

---

Pavilion of Women by Pearl S. Buck (New York, 1946).

out, he will be *90* years old this March 15. I hope he lasts until I can say hello to him. I hope I last until ...

Linda Lee says that we will "defile" you. I tell her that you are already that way. She says, maybe so in a German way but that we shall defile you in the American way. I hope so. Actually, both she and myself prefer a quiet and easy and gentle visit. Hello to your son and your wife. Tell your son I come to shake his hand in warmth as one German boy grown old to another German boy to carry on.

[To Hank Malone]
March 13, 1978

All right, you're my literary shrink. like, you know, living in east Hollywood is pretty damned splendid because all that messes with one are the hookers, cops, crazies—black, white and yellow, and there are poets around but only those who haven't made it and when they make it they move up to Frisco. as per the door-knockers I have lessened them and the phone has become unlisted. the problem with the door-knockers is that they are all quite similar, they say almost the same words as the phone-ringers, and it gets strange and fearful as if they had all been sent by the same Central Parrot Society. I was never one for mixing socially and maybe now that I've had some luck with the writing, that hasn't changed, although some may think my disdain for them is related to the luck I've had with the writing lately. but if I acted the way they wanted me to I'd be them and I'd be knocking on doors.

Finished a novel, *Women,* I guess I told you ... finished it last Sept. Martin says not until June 1978. he can't keep up with me. since then I've been on the poem-kick and have probably written a couple hundred. when *Women* comes out I might get shot like Larry Flynt (of *Hustler*). I'm off the beer, have switched to good white wine, drink *plenty* of that and only eat fish and poultry; my other habits are about the same, only I'm down to *one* woman now, much less travail, but, of course, I still get pretty low-down now and then; I guess the mechanism is set that way. have come down from 223 pounds and I now weigh in at 193—from a 44 waist to a 37. there are lots of fighting years ahead; working on the left hook and the counter-punch. going to take a hop to Germany in May. intend to return. they caught me drunk driving on the Harbor Freeway last month. I now go to the Drunk Driver's Improvement School. what a turnip patch that is. the instructor talks about the problems he has with his wife. last week he drew a diagram of the female sexual mechanism upon the blackboard and gave lessons on how to eat pussy, although most of his students already seemed well-versed in the art of.

... all these poems running out of my ass now ... I get somewhat worried about the short story ... have only done one since last Sept. but I go with the tide, maybe it's a rip tide but you don't fight those either.

yes, I know about Celine. they stole his bike, his hog, busted up his berry patch because of supposed anti-semitism and Nazism. Hamsun got the same hard boot. see Ezra. it's surprising how many of the good writers got caught and hacked like this. what people don't realize [is] that it is hard for a good writer to go with what is an overwhelming political Thou Shalt Believe. they have to go the other way simply out of their natures feeling that most of the people around them are wrong most of the time. I'm not saying that the right is always right or that the left is all that's left. I'm just saying that these men puked up against the obvious. ah, well ... [* * *]

[To Carl Weissner]
April 3, 1978

[* * *] The Academy awards are on t.v. tonight, Linda Lee watches and I sit with ear plugs in. movies don't do it for me; I even find the so-called pretty good ones pretty bad. they miss somewhere, they seldom get down near the bone. it's a giant shuck, the whole entertainment field, and the masses suffer brain damage from eating the shit. earplugs are a blessing. sometimes when the rock stars come on I bless the gods for these motherfucking red rubber plugs. I still prefer to select the areas I move around in and if people think me an egotist and a crank, they may be right—but I have some thoughts for them too. amen.

Mannheim dull or not is o.k. I don't expect a circus over there. I expect people to be walking around, most of them with arms and legs, most of them dressed in clothing, some of them constipated, some of them frenzied, most of them sleepwalking and a few of them all right. we, I, don't want to stay at your place for 2 days, that to me is an imposition. maybe we could find a place around the corner and take you and yours out to a few meals. you've got your work to do. I would enjoy drinking some wine with you and talking easy, lazy. I think we should room somewhere nearby, a city nearby Mannheim and we can bus about and take our little tourist photos, got another AE-1 and am trying not to lose it. also, like a god damned writer and unlike I do around here I'll probably carry a little green notebook and write down names of streets, places, so forth. I'm not much of a sight-seer, I'm mostly a lazy man except that I type about as much as I sleep. got to see unc, though, he's 90, has a bad heart and I want to go *very* gentle with him, no drinking around him, no hippies, no door-knockers. [* * *]

[To Hank Malone]
April 25, 1978

[* * *] Read at the university of Wisconsin, Milwauk., on Ape 17 but they got me too drunk before the reading and I drank during. I think I blew the whole god damned trick but I got the check, a grand plus air, so that will teach them.

I get plenty of mail, most of it thin and sick—my readers Some of them act as if they own me. Many of them claim I have saved their lives, which doesn't perk me up one tit's worth: Billy Graham and Bob Hope have probably saved some lives too.

Going to Germany in May. Taking my girlfriend if we don't split before then. You know how human relationships don't work.

[* * *] Physically and spiritually I am feeling pretty high lately; I used to be afraid of that; now when it comes I embrace it like a beautiful virgin; I know that the other—that whore—is going to come back quickly enough. [* * *]

[To John Martin]
May 3, 1978

this is probably the last writing I'll send you until I get back from Germany. life gets more curious; I peek under the edge of the tent: clowns in there, clowns outside, but not very funny. but gimme a little credit, Mencken, I ain't formed no schools or preached any directions nor have I taken guru-shape. there's hope and when a man has hope he's got hold of ¾'s of the ball of string. o, yes. [* * *]

[To Carl Weissner]
May 3, 1978

yes, it's here on the ticket: 3:20 p.m. I don't worry about the terrorists. if they think I am important enough to be killed, well, that's it. actually, I'll pass through without a whisper. no, not exactly, a German stewardess who knows us might be on the same flight and a photographer, I forget his name, will probably be clicking away. don't be alarmed, don't pose. [* * *]

All right. not much time. cleaning things up. Carl, even if anything and everything turns to shit it's still o.k. no mountain climbing. I'd like to meet your wife and your boy. sit quietly. I should be tired but I'm not. But still, vast spaces of air and easiness are wonderful. [* * *]

[To Carl Weissner]
June 6, 1978

Well, Linda took another week or so off and we layed around and drank some more and played the horses but 5 or 6 weeks at 24 hours a day together can be murderous and Linda's physic pyschic [sic] somebody says that thereby makes her a saint and I suppose she is. anyhow, this is one of my first nights alone at the old machinegun and it's good that it's still cranking... 4 or 5 new

246

poems, not too bad, I think...one about a Rhine cruise, so I know I've been to Germany. Got a letter off to Unc down on Privat Strasse 1, refused to open the door to some visitors who claim they are my friends...had a sign out: "WORKING...please call at another time, thanx, Hank..." they saw the sign, heard the typer, knocked anyhow. never catch a writer working, jesus christ, it's shameful, and if you do catch him working, it doesn't matter, he can do it at another time, he can do it anytime. Right, Carl? a plumber or something, you don't fuck with him. you don't stop a fireman or a dentist, but a writer??? shit, it's all a shuck, my god, every man's a poet...

By the way, Martin gets 20%, I told you 10. He used to get 10. Linda dislikes him, thinks he is fucking me, so I told you 10 so she wouldn't start the shit. I appreciate her concern but I don't want to end up like Celine...bitching and bitching against editors and publishers. the idea is to write about something else. by the way, thanks again for the *complete* rundown of finances... must have taken you two weeks but it keeps the air clear for me. [* * *] the radio's on. I'm alone. I've got to get alone, finally. I fill on the walls. people confuse me, crowds of people. they are all so sane. they all know what to do. what to say. the assholes terrify me. yet, I am able to write about them, about it. that's luck or I'd have to hide in a madhouse. in fact, that's what I'm rather doing. I'm stronger than the people and I'm weaker. I see what they see, only I can't use it; what's honey to them is sawdust to me. well, fuck a pig in the ass! listen to me weep! [* * *]

[To Hank Malone]
June 27, 1978

Your stuff is getting better, you are banking your shots in with more ease and laughter—that way is better because if you are telling the truth it's done without preaching and if you're telling a lie you didn't mean it because you weren't trying. so. [* * *]

Things rough on the human relationship scale right now right here. she is a good person but I am not. well, not really. it's just that I don't understand things. like proclamations, reality,

subject matter, excreatia [*sic*], trips to Paris and yellow sub-
marines. it's just that so many things interest so many people and
they don't interest me. it causes a grinding, a gnawing, a wearing
away of the parts. eliminating people is more important than
finding them. the walls are my honeys, the walls are my whores.

how's that for a speech from the pulpit?

Hang onto Michigan, Malone, while I watch them unwind
down that long stretch, the strain of numbers while the geese
paddle senselessly...

ah, boy, the taste of the arrow ain't no mushroom.

[To John Martin]
July 1, 1978

Still more poems..., that particular mind-state holds and
there's nothing I can do about it.

The lack of good fat prose worries me but there have been,
and still are, worse things to worry about, if we must do that.

Working on drawings [* * *]

Women is my proudest and best work. The arrival, that day,
of that book in the mail will be the day the sun bows down to me.
Not too much, I hope.

p.s.—We have a long journey together, Ace. Do you think you
can hold up? Better cut down on the boozeroni...yeh...*

[To John Martin]
July 16, 1978

Yes, John: I've heard it against Black Sparrow from my
"friends" for some time. And I figure you've rejected them. It's
the nature of the writer to believe it's the editor's fault if they

---

*John Martin does not drink alcohol.

aren't published. They never consider that their stuff might simply stink. I don't listen to them much and get rid of them as soon as it's possibly able to be done in a fairly decent manner...To hell with them...(bad grammar above...ah, well...)

But for *our* sakes we ought to have a working method. I sign a contract with you for each book; all I want is what is in that contract, nothing extra. So the semi-yearly or yearly statement takes care of that. Nobody likes to work in the dark. And your idea of continuing to pay me in spite of what occurs, we don't need. Just what is due. If the sales fall off, let the checks fall off. And if you die or sell Black Sparrow, then whoever takes over and continues to sell my books should pay me my just accord as per contract. I don't ask any more than any other writer, nor do I ask less. If this is understood then we have no worries. My job is writing, yours is editing and publishing. Let's keep the air clear and neither of us will go down the tube, together or separately.

I await *Women* unlike I've ever awaited any other book. As I wrote it I could feel it happening—that certain carving into the page with certain words in a way that you feel the power and the magic and the luck. I don't think you've ever taken a gamble like this, nor have I. We've rolled for the works here, knowing damn well about the rancor and bitterness and good old simple white hatred this thing would cause, and in a way while writing it I even now and then gave them a little flick here and there so that they could scream and bitch just some more. We'll hang together —you from the right branch, me from the left. O.K? Let's get the son of a bitch out. I meet people in the marketplace and liquor stores, they keep asking me, "When's *Women* coming out?" This is our big baby, John...I congratulate you on your courage... some of those literary tea cup ladies and boys just ain't gonna like you very much now. Me? I'm used to it. And please don't think I'm against you. You were there when nobody else was. I don't forget.

Linda isn't against you either. She hears the bad mouths. We know where that comes from...She sends regards. [* * *]

[To Carl Weissner]
July 16, 1978

[* * *] On page 25 of the German photo trip ... of course, it isn't going to be what anybody expected, for my mouth is in my ears and my eyes are in my asshole and my asshole is in my mouth. o, boy. anyhow. then I am interrupted by the poem and the racetrack and the bottle. only to say, no excuses—everything as it always was.

Linda has not really gotten to eating again since Germany. I watched her. I knew she was starting too fast like a child broken into a candy storehouse, she'd have to pay. I've got this crazy food thing. I've starved so many years, got raised in the depression. I just can't stand to see the stuff thrown against the ceiling. I was very glad that you were about to clean up people's mental excesses toward food when their bellies couldn't follow up. And with food that *expensive* ... you were a brave man and you did the brave thing. I don't give a damn *who's* paying for a thing, I don't like to see it beat to Death with a stick.

Jack Micheline by a couple of nights ago. He talked and drank and read me his poems and showed me his drawings, then slept on the couch and puked all over the place, missing the huge wastebasket I had placed right where his head was supposed to be. [* * *]

It's been a long journey and a clean, hard, decent fight. I'll always remember you, baby, in your white tennis shoes and your good quietness and your good laugh, and your honor and your knowledgeability. You've got it. You'll keep it. You drive a good car and a good life.

[To A. D. Winans]
July 27, 1978

[* * *] bad night last night, right, no left arm tightened up, hurt like mad, from thumb to elbow. no sleep, no great thoughts. they just send you pain now and then and it sits on you. most people say mental pain is the worst but at least you can fight your way out of that; the other way you depend on outside sources

and they may be wrong. I thought in terms of stroke but today the doc said it was nerve-ending fuck-up generated by the spine. now that's not so bad. except I drank 3 bottles of wine and it didn't ease a thing. enough.

the German trip, yes. I only wanted to do one reading to help the cause: mine. read in Hamburg. there don't seem to be so many haters over there. they seem to be trying to ingest the poem and get what there is. they listen quite carefully and seem to laugh when it seems the place to do so. the German girls are quiet in a beautiful way. and the men have a quiet reserve. it was, it created a feeling of no-con and a sensible generosity. [* * *]

The photographer who recorded Bukowski and Linda Lee Beighle's trip to Germany was Michael Montfort. These photos were subsequently published with text by Bukowski as Shakespeare Never Did This *(1979, 1995).*

[To Carl Weissner]
August 1, 1978

[* * *] Still on page 30 on the travel book; the photos rather staid—don't tell Michael I said this—they need a drink or a goose in the ass. anyhow, I might save the thing? so putting off getting into it I wrote 12 poems this week, most of them 3 or 4 pages long and about half of them pretty fair. If I ever go to France there'll be no photographer along and nobody is going to plan me a little picture tour. I know people mean well, they want me on a boat or looking at a castle. I think slowly. next time it's my turn. I felt as if I were tied with ropes and drugged most of the German trip. in France if I wanna sit at a fucking table and drink for 3 days I'll do so. unless a man's nature is allowed to reach the surface it's no good being anywhere. well, enough of that bitching. [* * *]

Barbet Schroeder was later to direct Barfly. *The documentary here referred to is* General Idi Amin Dada: Self Portrait *(1974).*

[To Carl Weissner]
August 24, 1978

[* * *] Barbet Schroeder, the French film maker, by the other night. We drank, of course. I don't know if you're familiar. He's done *More, Koko* and a documentary on the African dictator, the crazy and original one. Sends so many bodies down the river the crocodiles can't eat them all and it fucks up the power supply and the lights go out. He wants to do one of my long short stories, a 90 minute work. I don't know if I have anything that might fit that length. [* * *]

Saggitaire phoned. Want me to come to Paris. I said, "o.k., write details." So it's probably Paris around Sept. 16 or 17 for 5 or 6 days. They will get air fare and hotel, including Linda. They speak of meeting the press on the 18th and going on the # one t.v. station on the 22. Should do. [* * *]

My tax accountant over the other night. He said that I was antagonistic. He wants to talk about his soul and tell me how intelligent he is. I don't want to make a life time friendship, I just want him to tell me how to save money. That's what I'm paying him for. I think I'm getting guidance from a bum. It fits my theory that most people can't do anything near what they claim they can do. [* * *]

[To Carl Weissner]
November 3, 1978

Has Mikey burned down east Germany yet? And you tell Voltrout, Linda's love and mine to her for her hospitality and her understanding, her gentleness. And like I said over the phone, thanks to you for getting part of the hotel bill; now we know why it was so small, and thanks even though you shouldn't have, you bastard. And thanks for driving us for hours and days and suffering with us and drinking with us and living through air-line fuck-ups with us. Now your suffering due to us is over for a while. [* * *]

I was dissatisfied with the first 50 pages I wrote on the first German trip and I'm now writing it all over again, up to page 40. It's looser this time with more madness. I was guided too much by the photographs the first time. I've got to write my thing and just hope the photos fit... *Women* still at the printer's in Ann Arbor, Michigan. This is the slowest book getting off the blocks. The lag is maddening. *I finished the novel in August 1977.* [* * *]

Hope Ginsberg isn't screwing up your brain cells too much. With that guy it's one line at a time, then forget that line and go to the next, which will have nothing to do with the line which preceded it or the one to follow...

Bukowski and Linda Lee Beighle moved to their new house in San Pedro in November 1978.

[To Carl Weissner]
November 11, 1978

[* * *] I am still fighting the little horrors and fuck-ups of moving but am levelling out now and trying to work my way toward the typer, the only normal place for this abnormal fleshpot.

Women still not out...

This is one fine town; it lacks some violence and madness but I have enough of that to compensate, and the harbor is fine and the god damned boats, the fresh fish each day, the wine at night, and still can get to the racetracks. Linda downstairs reading a book on organic gardening. the dream is to grow vegetables out front in an attempt to beat the mortgage rap. many new things and it's about time...

Butch the cat has cost me over one hundred bucks trying to get his head patched after a cat fight. he tore off the 3rd bandage tonight. got to take him back to the clip-joint vet place tomorrow... [* * *]

[To John Martin]
November 18, 1978

The new check looked damn good; I think with that and with my hustle on the side we might pull it off, for a while anyhow, and meanwhile it's an outrageous experience. Now that I look back I don't think I should have taken such a big bite of pie but the 2 trips to Europe this year left me a bit more confused than usual. If it bites into the tax load to a decent extent then it'll be worth it; better into real estate than into govt. And I can always pull out and get something back. And we lucked it getting it at 10 percent just a month or so ago and now mortgage rates are 11 percent and rising. Maybe it's all good luck. It's sure a long way from that $1.25 shack in Atlanta, reaching and waving at that broken electric cord, playing with suicide, freezing, starving, no out. The gods are giving me plenty of variety and I guess they aren't through with me yet. The test is always there and it will always be there, yes, yes.

o.k., back to the travelogue. [* * *]

[To Carl Weissner]
November 28, 1978

[* * *] Went in today and hit them with 2 mortgage payments instead of one. I hope to get a year ahead on payments so when lean times come I will have time to make certain moves. Meanwhile, the downstairs bedroom is a good place for drunken guests. Myself, I fell down the other night against the edge of the fireplace, really crushed my side in, much blood and it took me a good hour or so to get up the stairway to my bed. I am still in shit poor shape, hard to sleep with the pain and so forth ... the travelogue thing proceeds, should soon be finished.

Got proofs from *Hustler* on my story "Break-In." I discovered an error, I had a 32 magnum in there and there isn't any such thing so I phoned the copy editor and told him to change it to 38 magnum and while talking to him I learned something: Larry Flynt ain't just kidding about his religious stance. The copy editor told me that my story had several "god damns" in it and that Larry wouldn't allow God to be used like that in his mag so my people instead of saying "god damn" would have to end up saying "damn." Also 20 other lines deleted. [* * *]

Oh, thanks for the rundown on the Big Book, I like to know what's happening so my mind is clear for the old piano. payments are all in order; I realize John shouldn't get payment for *Notes* but since he only takes a 20 percent cut out of U.S. sales I told him it would be all right. People like Ferlinghetti, for instance, take 50 percent plus the agent's fees.

We would really like to see your family over here while we have this house and the big yard in front, big hedge to hide us from the street and neighbors who just say hello, and Mike would LOVE the FIREPLACE!!! and Voltrout and Linda could go bathing at Cabrillo beach while you and I worried about survival of the written word and ourselves. But I know you'd need some angle to get over here, a grant, something, and maybe you could only come alone which would be fine but not as good as with the good Voltrout and the jumping fireman Mikey. [* * *]

[To Carl Weissner]
December 6, 1978

[* * *] The typing is worse than usual, real cold tonight, will hit 29 degrees, which is cold for Calif. Linda screamed over the phone that the walnut tree was going to die and I should cover it with a sheet and tie it and I went up this rickety-ass ladder with sheet on pitchfork, I swung in the wind, the bastard was too tall for me, let it die, me swaying in this sky, thinking, all I need now is a broken hip or leg; I've just mended from falling into the fireplace. was never crazy for walnuts anyhow. So that's why my fingers are cold, just got in from out there …

Had some luck the other night, going through old contracts, came across this one I signed with Ferlinghetti on *Erections* in Jan. 1971. And I saw where I had made him cross out the 50-50 deal on foreign rights and write in: "25% publisher, 75% author" … And, of course, I had forgotten all about that, so I jumped to the machine and wrote Nancy Peters about it and she says, o.k., sorry, we'll straighten it, we owe you $4,500 from last year, we're broke, but don't worry we'll get it to you … So, there's a break, I must been thinking in 1971. On the *Notes* contract it reads 50/50 though. But on *Erections* it's going to be a big help through the French, Italian, German, Swedish sales of that book. so, some luck is coming and I'll take it all … [* * *]

●

•1979•

January 2, 1979

Hello Lou:

I lost your card letter, finally found it.

No, I hadn't heard you had a heart attack; you keep taking those pills.

Marina Louise is now 14 years old; she's a tall gentle girl.

I'm living with a good woman, Linda Lee, and have moved out of east Hollywood, at last ... Got into this home in San Pedro because my tax accountant talked me into it. But I may have bitten off more than I can handle—mortgage payments simply hellishly high. Big old house, large front yard, there's a balcony outside this room that overlooks the harbor, a working harbor with ships coming and going; fresh fish every day, 2 cats, a lemon tree, a tangerine tree, fig tree, other trees. I find that I am still able to type here, just finished a travelogue of my last trip to Europe. Went to Europe twice this year, got drunk and vile on national French television. Much luck with my work in Germany, France. Also work translated into Italian, Swedish, Spanish and Denmark dickering for some work or other. But it's a recent windfall and may not last. I'll really miss this old big house if I have to resell. And it's about time I had luck with a good woman. Linda Lee is a good match for me. If Jon were alive he'd really get his kicks out of seeing me live in this place after all those small rooms and courts. After all, it was you and Jon who really got me started. Remember those days? The presses?

257

Breaking in shipment ... the flood ... fire ... attack ... moving from city to city. I often talk about you two. those crazy editor-publishers, starving to bring out these beautiful and immortal printing jobs ... books that people now look at in wonderment ... remember our nights of drinking? with the roaches climbing the walls? pages of Bukowski stacked in the bathtub and sky-high around the walls? It was a crazy and magic time, and the good old *Outsider* too ... never quite a magazine like that ... I no longer hear from William Corrington, he wrote a novel about the Civil war and went to Hollywood, and that was it. I hear he is now studying politics and wants to be Governor of Louisiana. I've written 3 novels now, one just out called *Women*. Also a few books of short stories and quite a few books of poems. I want to go out writing, though, and now with this mortgage on my back I will damned well have to. There's no stopping for me anyhow, it's ingrained....

I know that New Orleans is bad for your emphysema but I think it's the place for you spiritually. When I think of you and Jon, I think New Orleans. I'm glad you're working at an art shop on Bourbon street. You are a New Orleans institution, a grand lady. There should be a place there for you always, Gypsy Lou Webb. Remember standing in the cold trying to hawk those paintings on the sidewalk? They ought to write songs about you. Please try to feel as good as possible. I guess you know old Henry Miller is still alive? His son wrote me a while (Larry) and told me that I was the world's greatest writer. I told him to look over his shoulder and he'd find him. (He lives with Henry.)

So we're still fighting from this seaport town, still trying to get the world down. I still drink too much. Recently fell down against the side of the fireplace, drunk, then smashed the coffee table. Linda Lee put cat medicine on my side. This cat Butch got messed up in a cat fight, cost us $200 to put him back together. Then the front wheels fell off of my 67 Volks. but as *you* know, there's always trouble. We go on for a while ... Sorry I waited so long in answering ... have been searching for your letter for days. It was damned good to hear from you. may the gods and the luck be with you ...

258

[To Carl Weissner]
January 2, 1979

got your telegram, much thanks, and a lucky and good new year to you and Mikey and Valtrout... Are you going to translate the novel (*Women*)? if so, maybe I better xerox the sections Martin cut out, maybe you'd like to use them, I don't know. I feel maybe the novel got a little long for John M. so some of the *Women* bit the dust. let me know. of course we hope Lutz takes the travelogue. I have submitted it to City Lights here, maybe Lutz should know this? I talked Martin into it, although he wanted to do it. [* * *]

Barbet is here and we are trying to get into the screenplay but it seems like all we do is get into the wine. [* * *]

shit, this sure sounds like a business letter but sometimes they have to be written. o.k., now going down to listen to *The Honeymooners* on TV...

[To Carl Weissner]
February 20, 1979

[* * *] Trimmed ⅕ of fig tree today, looking up into sky, branches falling on head... began to see white and green lights... took a breather... went into house and smoked ten beedies... About half-finished with screenplay with Barbet Schroeder to direct and film. He likes it better as I go on. He says, "The beginning is quite depressive..." So now a few laughs have come along... somehow... but it's called *Barfly*, about that period in my life when I just sat on a bar stool for years. Parts of that just can't be too god damned happy...

On the Frankfurt thing, sure yes, of course... Linda loves to travel... We're hoping for the Park Hotel again, but if we have to hang out in Frankfurt, o.k. [* * *]

259

[To Gerald Locklin]
March 15, 1979

[* * *] On *Women,* a little tragedy there. Prefer you keep it fairly quiet. Like you know, I tell John Martin to go ahead and correct my grammar but this time he went too far. I should have read the proofs more carefully but am lazy. But when the book came out I read it. Shit, man. I guess he thinks I can't write. he threw shit in. Like I like to say, "he said," "she said." that's enough for me. But he threw stuff in, like "he retorted," "he said cheerfully," "I shrugged," "she seemed to be sore." Shit, it goes on and on... There's even one place where a woman had on a green dress and he put her into a blue dress. At least he didn't change her sexual organs. Think of playing with Faulkner like that? Anyhow, I climbed him pretty hard for it and so the 2nd edition will read on a back page somewhere: "second edition, revised." [* * *]

[To Carl Weissner]
March 24, 1979

I haven't heard from the Italians so I suppose the trip is off. I think they must have had the idea I was queer enough to leak promotional blood for free.

Thanks for word on *Fuck Machine.* I'll kind of slip it off on City Lights so it will scare them into knowing I have my ear to the ground. Montfort is having some trouble with Ferlinghetti. He went up there with his photographs and Ferling. refused to see him that day because he had gotten drunk with Yevtushenko the night before. Further scam is Yev. was upset and screamed because there was no mirror in his dressing room. Also he demanded mention in a newspaper column that he was chasing women. Me, I think a man is wiser running from women than chasing them. Anyhow, I don't know if the scam is true or not on Yev. but anyhow M.M. is back with his photos and no contract. Maybe we'll go someplace else or maybe we'll forget it. Lutz might be enough for us. Paranoia everywhere. I've had people scream at me that I'm not treating M. Montfort right on the

260

book. I don't know what the hell they're talking about. I'm offering him half, and I know that the book would sell without the photos but that the photos would not sell without the prose, so I don't see how I'm particularly laying anybody open.

I am re-writing the screenplay, taking out the bad first parts. No problems with Barbet, yet. I've agreed with his criticisms except in a couple of places where he didn't quite understand what I was doing.

The January tour sounds all right, ugg, all those *egos*, if that doesn't develop into something sick I'll not only be surprised I'll be reborn. It's all right with me if we don't have to sleep on the bus together, the whole ego gang. I mean, there's got to be a hotel room each night. If that's understood, o.k. But why in January?

Linda and I send luck and love to the Mannheim gang.

Oh, I have 3 *new* tires on my car, first time in my life. And I bought a new German cross (medal) for my windshield, real thing, $30 from the Alpine Village, a German tourist place up the freeway 5 minutes. You ought to see this one shop. An old gal sits there among this memorabilia: helmets, guns, medals, bayonets. Eva Braun's brooch and bracelet are there (documented) and can be had for 5,000 dollars. Linda wants it ...

[To John Martin]
April 1, 1979

The screenplay is taking longer than I expected but I should soon be back to normal. A few poems enclosed. Did some more last night which are better and will send along soon.

You said you were going to send the new proofs of the 2nd edition of *Women* a couple of weeks back. Nothing has arrived.

Also, somebody told me they were at a university in Tucson and they saw much Bukowski material. Is this the univ. with our archives? I've heard nothing from them. At first it was going to be 10 grand every two years, then it got down to 4 grand for the bunch, and now I hear nothing. Do you think it unkindly of me to ask?

[* * *] I've been drinking too much lately and have made plans to cut it down somewhat. Also there have been some rough

seas on the home front here. Everything seems to get in the way
of the writing but maybe it creates it too. The seas seem to be
smooth now. Back to the movie. Fante is now writing something
called *How to Write a Screenplay*. He's one wonderful person.

[To Carl Weissner]
April 23, 1979

[* * *] I did it. I finally finished the screenplay. Took me 3
months. So far I am calling it *The Rats of Thirst*. It's a short sec-
tion of my life when I sat around on bar stools, starving and
crazed. Now I am just crazed. The screenplay is fairly violent but
accurate and it might even be humorous, though in writing it I
never intended it to be any one of these things. I don't know
what I intended it to be. Anyhow, I'm now back on the good old
poem again. Sent a few to the French mag *Nomades*. It is easier
to write poems while drunk and I like the easy way. Drank 4 bot-
tles of German white Saturday night after a good day at the race
track. Linda is fine. Everything is all right around here, I mean as
much as it can get all right. I might slide back into the short story
again—the short story has always been a good friend of mine.
The next novel, I feel, is still two or three years off—I mean
before I start writing it.

I dig in the old garden a bit now and then. The neighbors
like it when they see me doing that. A man working in his garden
is not a dangerous man (they think). They've heard some wild
screaming nights over here when I've gone mad on wine and run
about the house naked, up and down the stairs, falling, cursing
and all that. They prefer me in the garden. [* * *]

[To John Martin]
April 24, 1979

Here are some poems.
I've heard from two sources that Sagittaire is going to fold. I

262

wonder how this will affect royalties? My guess is that they are certainly selling books and as long as they sell them they ought to pay up. According to Garnier: "Looks like Hachette, the biggies who sponsor the Sagittarious endeavor, got fed up with the publishers' 'bad moves'. Looks like they paid too much money to get your books! At least that's part of the problem. They had to shed some twenty grand, or so they say, to secure your remaining opus. And now Hachette says they can't tolerate this, it's got to stop."

I have no way of knowing how much you are selling book rights for but if you are asking too much it could be bad for me. As you know, I've agreed to let you jump from 10 percent to 20 percent because you do a hell of a lot of work free for me, archives and many things I don't know about. I don't mind this extra 10 percent, it's as if you were my American agent, and friend. Linda wanted me to limit you to 10 percent but I said, no. A few of these writers who you *don't* publish come around and speak bitterly of you but I know damn well they'd say you were great, one of the greatest if you published their work. Meanwhile Linda listens and becomes confused.

I want my head clear so I can write. In a sense it is easier writing in a small room and talking to the mice and drinking cheap beer. What comes to the top comes there undisturbed. Now there is really more pressure but I'm going to beat that bastard too: Mr. Pressure. I get all these letters from people who claim I have saved their lives; little do they realize I am still trying to save my own. Yes, I'm drinking, and rambling. Take it easy.

[To Carl Weissner]
April 27, 1979

[* * *] On *Shakespeare Never Did This*, Michael Montfort is trying to squeeze Ferlinghetti out of his usual 8 percent but I don't know if anything has been done yet. Is it possible to give Ferlinghetti the English speaking rights instead of just the American? The book will sell twice as much this way. [* * *]

I think I told you I finished the screenplay. Barbet is out sniffing around for money. All he needs is a half million or a million, haha. I think it's a lively work and if it ever comes to being produced it will be entertaining but maybe offensive to certain types who can't understand laughter through violence. [* * *]

[To John Martin]
May 7, 1979

Well, I hope everybody's feeling better and that we can get on with the game.

I understand that now there's a paper strike going on. I went out and bought 6 packs of 200 pgs of typer paper. How's that for a 6-pack? So that ought to last me a month or two ... but how are you going to print books? The little darlings will think that you don't like them ...

[To John Martin]
May 8, 1979

Here's a copy of *Barfly*, the screenplay. As you know, I did quite a bit of barstool duty between the ages of 25 and 35. This screenplay takes in 4 or 5 nights or days (or maybe more) from that time. Right now Barbet is off to Europe looking for various sources of money to get it into motion and unto film. He claims he can do it for a half million. I have an idea he will get the money and that he will direct the film and get it done. he seems to know how to do such things.

Anyhow, the screenplay is available for book production. There are no restrictions in the contract on this and Barbet says he has no objections, and there is no money to be paid to him, although, of course, credits must be given.

So read it when you get time and if you like it and want to publish it, fine. Of course, I understand that you are overloaded on Bukowski, but I always want you to have first look. If, for any reasons, you don't want to, or can't, do it, please return as I only have 3 copies of the play. I'll try City Lights. Financially it has really helped to have 2 U.S. publishers, especially in the

264

European market. I think rather than let *Barfly* lay fallow, I should get it out. Yes, I suppose there are dangers of overexposure but then I think I write too much for one publisher to keep up with me, and from a different viewpoint it might not be fair to plow half of it under. Or so I'd like to think.

So lemme know whatcha think...

[To Carl Weissner]
May 21, 1979, drinking zinfandel, 1975,
via Louis M. Martini, St. Helena, Napa County...

Thanks for yours. Well, *The Rats of Thirst* has been changed back to the original title, *Barfly*. Barbet says this more fits the motion picture world, and he knows more about that than I do. Of course, I am more literary and prefer *The Rats* but since Barbet is on the run for money he has enough troubles without me fighting him about it. I got ten thousand dollars for writing the damn thing and there's more to come when and if it gets into shooting and then the 5%, and so I am sitting here (as you know) a long ways from the days of starvation but there still remains enough madness and confusion to carry me through. I was born a misfit and remain so. Simple acts of life that most men can carry off without a thought can and do befuddle me. Luckily I have gotten paid for being an ass, and only the angels can bring one that. [* * *]

Martin has some guy Fonzi (?) offering a great movie contract for some of the Sparrow books...the contract is so good it's almost frightening. It seems a long time back since I was freezing in that $1.25 a week paper shack in Atlanta, starving and waving at an overhanging electric light cord (shredded) with my hand, seeing how close I could come...I might be back there yet.

Shit, look, I just bought a new 1979 BMW, sunroof and all the bits, $16,000 cash. The tax accountant says I can get a 52% tax write-off, which means instead of giving the 16 grand to Sam I only give him 8 and I got me a new car. No, it doesn't *quite* work that way, but almost. The idea is to keep yourself down from the upper tax brackets one way or another and if you put all the money in the bank and don't come up with tax write-offs the damn govt. just walks in and takes almost all of it, and so they force you to spend, they force you into a different life style, and I guess that can harm the writing but if I'm a good enough writer I can overcome that; if I'm not a good enough writer then I'm going to get what I've got coming to me. o.k.

I guess the d.a. [Los Angeles District Attorney] is worried about the pocketbook because it reaches more people at a smaller price, and it's nice to be accused of "obscenity" and "advocating violence." it puts me in the same camp as a lot of immortals. not that I am concerned with being immortal, only that there were some good word-throwers among them.

for you, I imagine translating can really be hell because one thing it does is keep your energy from getting at and doing your own work but it also keeps you out of the factories and/or teaching literature at some fucking university with the girls in the front rows flashing their thighs at you for grades. and what is really important, I think about the ways you can *improve* on these writers (including me) by putting them into German; part of your personality does enter and that's a creative act, my friend.

thanks for letting me know all the things, and as always luck and love to Voltrout and Mike, and to you too, from Linda Lee and me. Christ, we've just found a small tree and it's bearing apples! and the roses are pounding into the sky, it's dangerous and beautiful, and there's no gasoline in California and we wait in two hour long lines in our cars listening to rock music, drinking beer, getting angry and shooting and knifing each other. this Rome is falling, tottering, insipid. I don't care; if anybody's got it coming, we have.

[To John Martin]
May 31, 1979

I got the 2nd printing of *Women* today. Looks fine, thanks. People keep commenting on what a good job Barbara did on the cover. [* * *]

Well, the apricot tree is full and there's even a little apple tree going at it, and the horses are going well, and Linda and I are not fighting.

[To John Martin]
June 10, 1979

I know you have the movie on your mind right now. That's fine. But, meanwhile, here's more poems, good or bad.

I know you do a lot of work on the side to protect my ass, to see that I don't get burned, and I want you to know that I'm aware of that and grateful for that.

Don't worry, I'll never be as rich as you are; you are running an industry; I am a member of this particular asylum, you know.

[To John Martin]
June 18, 1979

We'll just have to forget about "the image." I never hide anything.

The car is a 1979 black BMW, sun roof and all. 320I. (52% tax write-off.) [* * *]

[To Carl Weissner]
July 14, 1979

Actually, I am glad the Jan. tour has been called off. When I think of freezing my bunghole and reading 5 times in one week I don't miss it. If I were alone I would never have said "yes" to it. Linda is so crazy for travel I was doing it for her. And you know the first rule: never do anything for anybody else. So I'm glad it's called off. [* * *]

I seem to be writing only poems now, ten to twenty a week,

they seem to be all right, the *New York Quarterly* and *Wormwood* taking some and not returning the rest—yet. The *Quarterly* is going to publish a "craft interview" with Bukowski in issue #27, I think. I tell 'em my craft is to get drunk and write, mostly after the racetrack. I more or less tell them to jam it, but they don't seem to mind. I think the editor is partial to crazies. o.k. [* * *]

A couple of movie deals swinging in the wind. If one of them goes through I'll have to see my tax man and figure out how to spend it so the U.S. tax man doesn't get most of it. Like I get 52% off on the old (1979) black BMW. Now I may have to get the house painted and put in a jacuzzi. First, let's see. You know, writing is a strange thing: IT CAN STOP. So I'm always precautionary, figuring out how I can pull it out if the roof falls in. I can see myself in a tiny room sucking on a beercan and staring [?starting] all over again. It would make a good story. As always, there's no rest in my mind, no matter what kind of life it is. The cemetery is the best bet on the board; all we do is stall that number off as long as we can. I'd like to hang around a bit longer, I still love the sound of this typer, the drink to my left, the cigarette to the right, the radio sending me music that is centuries old.

The horses have been lucky lately. Only a week left and the track closes. Don't know what I'll do then. Probably sleep all day. Sometimes I get this urge to go to bed for a week and stay there. I used to do it. It's great. When you get up you are powerful as a polar bear and everything looks great and different. It lasts about 2 days. Then it's back to shit in the streets and in the heart and in the stratosphere.

Linda sends love to all and wants to know if there is anything we can mail you folks from good old Southern California? An oil well? The Queen Mary?

[To John Martin]
August 2, 1979

[* * *] Behind on a lot of standard paper work here; have to get it done; it ain't poetic but if you don't do it, they send in the troops. I am fighting against computer errors from the Authorities

right now. It's amazing: you write them back a factual truth and the machine is off-feed and it spits it all out and says, no, no, no. And that's all they go by. Almost every day, besides some demented fan mail, I get some sort of letter claiming that I owe something for something that I never purchased, like 3 greyhounds and a washing machine propelled by wild goldfish....

Weissner's translations were published as Western Avenue: Gedichte aus über 20 Jahren 1955–1977 *by Zweitausendeins, Frankfurt.*

[To Carl Weissner]
August 2, 1979

yes, all the people who see *Western Ave.* marvel at it, and I know the translation is epic and gutsy. see ya ended with Bogart, you romantic. good. quite. I know you ought to win the war of awards, but "ought to" and politics are different things.

on the Italian thing, I just looked at the list of 21 American poets and knew it was a puke situation—little flamboyant sweeties who love to croon into the mike. the vanity of these types is only exceeded by their lack of talent.

over here, still going upstairs with the wine and typing out poems almost every night. the disease appears to be permanent. After *Women, Shakespeare,* and *Barfly,* I just fall back onto and into the poem like a champagne bath. on *Barfly,* Schroeder appears to be reeling in a backer and also is considering using this fellow Woods who was the only compelling force in a film which failed for me: *The Onion Field.* The schedule is that we get drunk with him and attempt to make him over into a Chinaski. no easy thing. the fellow talks very fast, seems desperate enough but not tired enough. we could re-do him a bit. I think that *Barfly,* properly done, should shake some asses in the theater seats. I don't trust Hollywood, of course, but this thing ain't exactly Hollywood ... meanwhile, some of the Italians came by (Di Fonzi and crew) and we got drunk with them, and they ain't

269

hardly Hollywood either, so I'm not dead yet. but so far there's been more talk than money. [* * *]

[To John Martin]
August 18, 1979

This is 60 buck portable so in case I ever go to Europe I'll have something to escape to besides the bottle. But it just doesn't have the soul of the old ... Olympia, which is still being fixed. Delay, of course. Yes, nobody can do anything ... poets can't write poetry, cabbies can't drive, so on ... Got car out of garage ... 2 day wait ... drove one block, had to take it back in again ... The people are bothered with *nerves,* they don't want to do what they are doing but they don't want to starve either so they just *pretend* to be doing something, but they can only back off from it because it's just rote and dizziness, they want the money without the effort. The thing has even spread into professional sports. The artistry has gone out of everything; it's all being done on a very dull and low level. The tax man fucks up, the waitress fucks up, the cop shoots the wrong guy ... on and on it goes. I don't mind so much what they do, humanity has hardly been one of my loves, but when what they do gets in the way of my existence, when I have to take hours and days to straighten out *their* errors and malfunctions, *then* what *I* am trying to do becomes affected and I begin to fail somewhat because they fail entirely, and we are all stuck in the same bog. o.k.

I hear through the vine that Galiano has already shot *Rape Rape,* that he is getting Polanski (Roman the child-fucker) ready to direct another ... meanwhile, no monies, not even option money. contract signed for $44,000. sometimes I feel like getting an m.g. and walking into an office and gunning these bastards down, and within my nature I am perfectly capable of doing that. Nothing miffs me like lying and cheating and outright stealing, plus indifference and silence about matters ...

[* * *] In the future the money won't be like this because now (if it comes) it comes off of a mass of work already published and they have just about caught up with us. [* * *]

[To John Martin]
September 7, 1979

Yes, the world's at war and they don't know it. You're right. And it can get irritating at times when they scratch the back of their necks and get ready to pick the best bowling ball. Not that a person shouldn't enjoy himself when his house is burning down, it's only what they select for enjoyment that (which) puzzles me. So? Well, it's like Schopenhauer basically said in a certain place: I certainly seem to suffer like a son of a bitch most of the time, living among them and this, but, for it all, I have one thing that I am glad for and that is that I am not them....

I've walked up the railroad tracks and I'm still walking up them. The essence doesn't change. There are still things to be handled; there will always be things to be handled. Nobody ever gets caught up and finished on what there is to do. And even if you do, for a moment, feel a central peace, there is always somebody walking behind you with a switchblade. The philosophers of the centuries have probably said the same thing but in, and with, such an involuted and private and dead language that they themselves were part of the failure they were speaking of.

Women are strange, they are positive: they want to build swimming pools while you wonder who the hell and how the hell the water bill is going to be paid? They are thinking about next Saturday night while you are thinking about 3 years from now, *if* you are here. Somebody has to be the wolf, somebody has to be the hunting dog, somebody has to drill the 3 and 2 pitch between first and second. When you slow down a step, the good times are over. Good times? There were never good times. There were bad times and times not as bad. People like to talk about the Brotherhood of Man. Two types: those who have nothing and would like a Brotherhood because they *think* that would bring them something; and those who have everything (materially) and speak of the Brotherhood of Man as *now* because they think it's working for them at the moment.

As far as relaxing goes in the midstream of the dangerous tempo, I've done it. I got drunk for ten years without doing anything. Anybody can be a slob but to be a deliberate slob takes some doing, well, at least a minor inventiveness.

There is something about these now, they simply don't have the hardness and/or the honor of those who grew up in the 30's.

271

Even their body movements, their speech is putty-soft and irreverent to the Fact. And the Fact is what occurs when you face something head-on. I once spoke of the Absence of the Hero, that was sad enough. I now speak of the absence of a human among humans, one face in a crowd of no-faces. Now it's feces and a flavescent flatulence. Nobody scares me anymore; a cop pulls me over, gets off his bike, he has a valentine ass and an english toffee face; no matter if he pulls his gun and blasts my brains out, he can't even do it with style and aplomb, he's just a mechanism, a test-tube baby, doing his thing to protect a neurotic wife playing with cheap coke in a housing development in Dijo Valley.

Sometimes there's a small chance, you can see it for a moment in the face of a waitress in a cheap cafe, an old waitress, beaten, nowhere to go, there is some truth in that face, which is more than there is in the truth of the face of your landlord or your president. Of course, she can't speak to you and you can't speak to her. Words would mutilate, words have too long been used the wrong way. You put in your order and wait. Sometimes you see it in the face of a boxer, a prize fighter, sometimes in the face of an old newsboy. But you don't see it too often, and you see it less and less.

So, this isn't really a letter and it isn't really a poem; it's good not to fit the form, always. The two bottles of wine have been good, and sleep is good too, lately I've gone toward sleep like I've gone towards drunkenness. Here's the last glass. Let me pick it up, drink it. It's gone. I light the last cigarette, and once again I think of my boy John Dillinger. Now look, you see, I'm going to piss and then to sleep it off....

your boy, Henry

[To John Martin]
September 17, 1979

Yes, it goes on and on....
I was in a health food store with Linda the other day and there were 3 or 4 lines snaking around and the clerks at the

counter were chatting limply with the customers at hand and the customers at hand were chatting limply with the clerks, and even those others waiting didn't sense that time was being mutilated, that silliness and ineptness were dripping from the walls. There was no fire or motion anywhere. And it just wasn't a physical stagnation, you could sense their wilted cottonball spirits... zeroes giving off horrifying death-rays.

I told Linda, "I'll bet John Martin and I would have these lines worked down and away in no time at all."

"Sure you would," she said, "but you see, people just aren't like that nowadays."

oh, my god.... [* * *]

[To Carl Weissner]
September 17, 1979

The *ecce homo* book by George Grosz was an astonishing birthday gift. You certainly know my taste. Some of this man's work reminds me of my own short stories. It is some book and one that can be looked at over and over again. But, Carl, you needn't remember my birthday, you are doing too many things at once, take it easy. [* * *]

Smog and heat have descended; this area usually all right, fairly smog-free but the Santa Ana winds blew it in from the inner city and we've had it for two days... Linda downstairs looking at an anti-war movie, *Coming Home*. I don't bother with those. I don't think any artist is being daring and original when they state that War is Bad. That takes as much courage as hitting grandma behind the neck with a two-by-four. [* * *]

[To Gerald Locklin]
September 19, 1979

[* * *] I am honored that you are laying the *Piano* on some of your students for a week. The idea, of course, might be to let

them know that writing needn't be hard work; the hard work is getting out of bed in the morning or at noon; the hard work is looking at people's faces in long supermarket lines; the hard work is working for somebody else who is making money using your life's hours and years. The typing comes easy, especially with the chilled wine in the thermos to the left of the machine. [* * *]

[To Hank Malone]
October 15, 1979

So you're still in Highland Park with Sharon—she seemed a good one, might do you well to stick around. I've been with one almost 3 years, basically good sort, although some of her ideas on the Hereafter and her particular god seem to me to be pretty assy, her other qualities seem to overcome most of that. She's the "Sara" of the novel *Women*. Linda Lee, actually. [* * *]

No, I didn't vomit on national tv in France. I just got stinking drunk, said a few things and walked off, pulled my knife on a security guard. Actually it was good luck. All of the newspapers in France gave it a good write-up except one. It went over good with the people of the streets. Went to Nice next day, was sitting getting drunk with Linda Lee at outside table and 6 French waiters waved, then walked up in a line, stood and bowed. I write better of the incident in a book due out in November via City Lights, *Shakespeare Never Did This*, all about the European trip. Actually, it's two European trips jammed into one with photos. I think it might be lively writing.

Finished a screenplay called *Barfly* for Barbet Schroeder and he claims he's going to do it, although at the moment he's only pulled in $200,000 for production and it takes maybe 5 times that but he's good at that sort of thing. Meanwhile, *Women* and *Factotum* have a good chance to become movies. Di Fonzi of Italy says he is going to produce it here in America (them) and he seems to mean it. So it's contract time and lawyers, all that shit. I drink with strange people now, including James Woods of *Holocaust* and *The Onion Field*. He wants to be the Chinaski of *Barfly* and I think he's a good actor ... Meanwhile, I still write 15 poems a week. I've got this room upstairs overlooking the harbor and I drink 2 or 3 bottles of wine and tap it out. *NYQ* just accepted 12 poems. So I'm not finished yet...

Just back from Vancouver. Read to 680 at Viking Inn, standing room only. Drank before reading and 4 bottles of red wine during. Got back to hotel, fell and cracked my head open real damn good on the heater. Probably my best poem of the night. [* * *]

[To John Martin]
October 25, 1979

It takes about two weeks to get over one of those readings. I don't understand how the poets can go on reading, some of them giving two or three readings a month...Yes, I know how they can do it: vanity. And also, lack of energy: when they read they sound as if they were lisping into teacups.

Back at the track, trying to forget all that nonsense. I play the horses like the average man plays chess or maybe like an extra average man plays chess. I know all the traps, bad plays, panic plays. I've only had time to attend the meet 6 days, won 5, lost one day. I bet moderately. I've averaged about $90 profit a day. I suppose if I were a desperate man playing for the rent and the baby food I would lose. But going to the track, making my bets, following my knowledge, this teaches me *movement.* A cutting through the fog. I can understand why Hemingway went to the bullfights. There is death at the track too and there is life and sometimes victory. All the women I have known have been incensed with my horseplaying. They think it is very foolish and when they attend the races with me they become angry because I usually win and they usually lose. The problem is that they don't put any effort into the game, they are listless and distracted. And it's strange that most of them believe in some kind of God. That doesn't take any effort either. At the track one must overcome a 15 percent take.

Well, it's been about 20 years since my first book, *Flower, Fist and Bestial Wail* was published when I was 40. I think it's been a good twenty years of creation and I think it's still coming.

275

And even if it should stop now, I'd feel particularly lucky. And I was lucky when the Sparrow came by and you printed my stuff when it wasn't particularly *literary*, you know what I mean. I'm sure you've heard plenty about it from some quarters. So it's been a good show. Let them rage, let them weep, let them bitch. o.k.

Poems enclosed.

[To Carl Weissner]
November 9, 1979

[* * *] Back from Canadian reading. Took Linda. Have video tapes of the thing in color, runs about two hours. Saw it a couple nights back. Not bad. Much fighting with the audience. New poems. Dirty stuff and the other kind. Drank before the reading and 3 bottles of red wine during but read the poems out. Dumb party afterwards. I fell down several times while dancing. They got me on the elevator back at the hotel and I kept hollering for another bottle. Poor Linda. Afterwards in hotel room, kept falling. Finally fell against the radiator and cracked a 6 inch gash in skull. Blood everywhere. Hell of a trip. [* * *] Nice Canadian people who set up reading, though. Not poet types at all. All in all, a good show.

Thanks for sending rundowns on monies. Have rec. all. All is well. Mortgage half paid for. I figure if I get this place paid I can make a stand here after the talent diminishes and they start closing in. It's a great place, Carl. I wish your gang were here in that downstairs bedroom. You'd all like the harbor, and the people. San Pedro and Mannheim are my two favorite places. [* * *]

[To A. D. Winans]
December 29, 1979

I don't see how you've stood the little mag game as long as you have, but no, I can't read, I don't know which is worse,

276

that Frisco gang or the so-called New York School. [* * *]

It's not true, as per rumor, that I have purchased a sports car; it's a 1979 BMW and now it is in my poems instead of the 69 Volks. About buying a house, it's not that easy; I've got a mortgage around my neck. Both investments were made to help avoid some of the tax bite out of European royalties. Here in America, if you don't lay the money off, they take it. I offer no excuses for buying a car or living in a house. Although some may take this as a sign that I am losing my soul, most of these same have been saying for years that I am losing, have lost, my soul. If these would pay as much heed to their typewriters as they did to my soul (or lack of) they might (?) get some work done. [* * *]

[To John Martin]
December 29, 1979

There won't be any poems for a little while. It won't mean I've died. Barbet laying some more money on me and I'm going to re-work *Barfly* a bit. It shouldn't take too long.

We had one large producer willing to make *Barfly* into a major motion picture. Only one catch—he wanted to use Chris Christoferson [*sic*] as Chinaski, and in the part where Chinaski comes back to the room and lays in the dark listing to classical music, he wants Chris Chris to break out his guitar and start singing. We told him, no.

1980. It's been a long war. We're rushing in fresh troops. Enemy still everywhere.

Happy new 365,

your boy, Henry

•

Index of Principal Names

280

CHARLES BUKOWSKI is one of America's best-known contemporary writers of poetry and prose and, many would claim, its most influential and imitated poet. He was born in Andernach, Germany to an American soldier father and a German mother in 1920, and brought to the United States at the age of three. He was raised in Los Angeles and lived there for fifty years. He published his first story in 1944 when he was twenty-four and began writing poetry at the age of thirty-five. He died in San Pedro, California on March 9, 1994 at the age of seventy-three, shortly after completing his last novel, *Pulp* (1994).

During his lifetime he published more than forty-five books of poetry and prose, including the novels *Post Office* (1971), *Factotum* (1975), *Women* (1978), *Ham on Rye* (1982), and *Hollywood* (1989). His most recent books are the posthumous editions of *Bone Palace Ballet: New Poems* (1997); *The Captain Is Out to Lunch and the Sailors Have Taken Over the Ship* (1998) which is illustrated by Robert Crumb; *Reach for the Sun: Selected Letters 1978–1994* (1999); and *What Matters Most Is How Well You Walk Through the Fire* (1999).

All of his books have now been published in translation in over a dozen languages and his worldwide popularity remains undiminished. In the years to come Black Sparrow will publish additional volumes of previously uncollected poetry and letters.

SEAMUS COONEY was born in Ireland and educated there and in the United States. He now teaches English literature at Western Michigan University in Kalamazoo.